Angus McLean

Lindigo, the White Woman

Or, the highland girl's captivity among the Australian blacks

Angus McLean

Lindigo, the White Woman
Or, the highland girl's captivity among the Australian blacks

ISBN/EAN: 9783337315542

Printed in Europe, USA, Canada, Australia, Japan

Cover: Foto ©Andreas Hilbeck / pixelio.de

More available books at **www.hansebooks.com**

LINDIGO,

E WHITE WOMAN;

THE HIGHLAND GIRL'S CAPTIVITY AMONG THE AUSTRALIAN BLACKS.

By ANGUS McLEAN.

Melbourne:

H. T. DWIGHT,

NEAR PARLIAMENT HOUSES.

MDCCCLXVI.

MELBOURNE:

WALKER, MAY AND CO., PRINTERS,
99 BOURKE STREET WEST.

LINDIGO.

CHAPTER I.

AN AWKWARD INTRODUCTION.

"PLAGUE tho fish,—not another cast shall I make,—
better feast my eyes on this grand scenery." These
were the words which escaped from the lips of an unsuccessful angler, on the river Linn, in the western Highlands, one calm summer morning. Then tossing his rod
on the bank, he stepped up towards the end of the old
wooden bridge which spanned that noble stream, where
it discharges itself in the head of Loch Linn.

The young sportsman thus unceremoniously presented
to the reader, was apparently a stranger in those parts,
judging by his garb, and the visible admiration he
manifested in beholding the surrounding prospect. His
handsome figure and noble bearing proved him at once
to be some young scion of the English aristocracy.

The magnificent scenery which presented itself to his
view was truly sufficient to enrapture the mind, and
calculated to revert youthful and excited thoughts like
his to many romantic tales and scenes associated with
the Highlands, often read of, but never before now experienced in their true effect.

The winding Linn, which meandered slowly through
the glen, glittered over its pebbly bed, and exhausted its
sparkling waters in the head of the estuary, lay at his
feet. The hills and mountains, rising gradually on both
sides like waves, cast their frowning shadows on the
bosom of Loch Linn. On the south side rose Ben Mòr,
towering above the rest, and as if looking over with
contempt on its insignificant rival Ben Veg, which held
its station on the north side; both appearing like
gigantic sentinels watching over the peaceful scenery
below.

Loch Linn lay in sweet repose, disturbed only by an occasional splash from the silvery trout and salmon, manifesting their impatience to ascend the tempting stream by leaping in the air, and falling back again into their limpid element.

The numerous islets which studded the distance swarmed with seafowls, sending up their chorus to welcome the morning sun, in conjunction with the feathery warblers which inhabited the plantations on both sides.

About a mile from the bridge, on each side of Loch Linn, were situated two elegant mansions, whose dazzling windows, white walls, gables, and blue slated roofs, stood in bold relief amidst the dark green foliage of the orchard trees around them.

Extending further along the margin of the estuary, lay extensive meadows and fields of corn, enclosed by secure hedges, proving the comfort and affluence of their respective owners.

Both farms were laid out on the same plan, and as if each proprietor strove to excel his neighbour in improving and developing to the utmost extent the resources of his extensive property.

Large herds of sheep and cattle were browsing over the meadows and sides of the hills and glens, with their young gambolling by their side,—and enjoying their delicious morsels of green herbage, moistened by the morning dew. The milch cows giving vent to their impatience in supplying their young with their liquid burdens, by an unceasing lowing, whose melodious echo resounded through hills and dales, added to the sweet ditties of the dairy maids, all contributing to entrance the soul of the stranger, and fancying himself transported to some fairy land.

While his mind was thus intoxicated with the effects of such charming novelties, and as if to complete the scene, his eye caught sight of a female form emerging from among the labyrinth of shrubs and bushes which fringed the borders of the gravel walk leading from the mansion on the north side, and apparently coming towards the bridge where he stood.

Anxious to have a nearer view of the sylph-like figure

which tripped along, now and then bending to pluck a choice flower from each side, and fearing his presence might prevent her approach, he hid himself behind a hazel bush by the end of the bridge. Thus, in perfect security from being observed by any person coming nigh, he awaited with a beating heart, creating many lovely images in his own mind to correspond with the Highland maiden now fast approaching, and who, as he anticipated, on coming to the bridge halted within a few paces of his ambush. But what must have been his surprise and admiration in beholding in her a far lovelier and more beautiful creature than his wildest imagination could form, and rivalling the heroine of Loch Katrine—"The Lady of the Lake"—of which his own peculiar situation, and the similarity of both cases, reminded him. The following lines of the famous Scottish poet, which were so applicable to the fairy form before him, flew to his memory :—

> "And ne'er before did Grecian chisel trace
> A nymph, a Naiad, or a Grace,
> Of finer form or lovelier face ;
> What though the sun with ardent frown
> Had slightly tinged her cheek with brown ;
> The sportive toil, which short and light,
> Had dyed her glowing hues so bright ;
> Served too in hastier swell to show,
> Short glimpses of a breast of snow ;
> What though no rule of courtly grace
> To measured mood had trained her pace ;
> A foot more light, a step more true,
> Ne'er from the heath-flower dashed the dew ;
> E'en the slight hairbell raised its head,
> Elastic from her fairy tread ;
> What though upon her speech there hung
> The accents of the mountain tongue,
> Those silver sounds so soft, so dear,
> The listener held his breath to hear."

There, indeed, stood the counterpart of Ellen Douglas, although seemingly not so ripe in years.

For a few moments she remained in the same position, so still that no visible motion of her finely modelled form was perceptible save the heaving of her snow-white bosom which was partially uncovered.

She was clothed in a plain dress of Mackay tartan, with plaid and bonnet of the same material. Her unrivalled fair neck and shoulders were bare, contrasting admirably with her rich brown hair, which fell in natural ringlets round them.

Her rosy cheeks were slightly tinged with brown, giving her a more healthy and interesting appearance. Her large liquid black eyes were shaded with long lashes of the same hue under arched pencilled brows. Her smiling cherry lips were parted, disclosing the most exquisite set of ivory teeth.

Her tiny feet and ankles were encased in white stockings and slippers, which were partly exposed by her holding her skirt from the dew in one hand, while in the other she held a bouquet of flowers.

Gazing intently towards Ben Mòr, from which direction she apparently expected some one, and, not observing the object of her search, she heaved a deep sigh, and, to the stranger's astonishment, murmured audibly in pure English—"Whatever is detaining him?"

The enraptured stranger stood transfixed in his hiding-place, and afraid to breathe lest the beating of his heart should frighten away from his gaze the beautiful creature who now made a move round the bush where he stood, towards the bank of the river where his rod and basket lay, and which she had not noticed until almost treading upon them. On making the discovery she gave a startled scream, and gazed cautiously around, when the stranger made himself visible, and in set terms apologized for not making his appearance before.

The young maid seemed terrified and confused, and made no reply, but began to retrace her steps; when, in so doing, she had to pass close by the stranger to regain the path. Seeing all chance of detaining or engaging her attention vanish, a desperate and inconsiderate resolution seized him, which on maturer consideration he might condemn. Instantly, picking up the flowers which she had dropped in her affright, he held them towards her with a bland smile—remarking—"Unless I am to be honoured by retaining such a beautiful token from so charming a donor, I beg leave to return them." The coy maiden being too confused to return an answer to this gallantry, held out her hand to receive her flowers, when the unprincipled stranger, taking advantage of the opportunity, seized her hand,

and suddenly pulled her towards him, then encircling her tapering waist with his other arm, attempted to embrace her.

She shrieked loudly for help, and struggled hard to release herself, but all in vain. That moment her quick ears caught the sounds of well-known strides bounding over the bridge, when she cried imploringly—" Charlie, dear, save me!" The words had hardly escaped her lips, when the stranger was laid his whole length on the sward, and a youthful Highlander held her insensible form in his arms.

This third person who arrived so opportunely on the scene, was a young man nearly of the same height as the stranger, but although apparently younger, had the advantage in symmetry of form. His eagle eyes and fine open countenance showed great courage and daring. His well-developed limbs, dressed in the Highland garb of Royal Stuart tartan, proved great bodily strength and activity. A handsome fowling-piece, and a brace of ptarmigans lay on the ground by his side, over which stood a couple of well-bred pointers.

When the discomfited stranger regained his feet, and perceived the young couple so fondly locked in each others arms, his rage and mortification burst forth in the following words :—" Were it not for that damsel in your arms, I would teach you a lesson which you would not easily forget," and casting his eyes on the game, he added—" who has given you permission to shoot on this estate?" " You cared but little a few minutes ago what insult you would commit on this innocent maiden, and as for my shooting on this estate, it is no business of yours," replied the Highlander defiantly. " We will see," added the stranger, with a malignant look, and seeing no use of retaliating at present, he picked up his rod and basket, muttering future revenge.

While the young Highlander is restoring his inanimate charge into consciousness, we shall endeavour to enlighten the reader on the several characters who played such a conspicuous part in the above drama; but in order to bring forth more fully the events and circumstances which led to such awkward consequences, we must take him back a short period prior to the commencement of our tale.

About that time, several Highland chiefs, or lairds, became greatly embarrassed, through passing the most of their time in the English metropolis, striving to cope in style and grandeur with the more wealthy noblemen of that kingdom; when they ought to have been living moderately on their estates, attending to their improvement, and studying the comfort of their tenants, on whom they depended for their income. The consequence, therefore, may be anticipated; through heavy mortgages which they were unable to liquidate, the estates were sold to some wealthier purchasers, and, in many instances, to English proprietors. Such had been the case in the instance of the estate on which the above scene took place. Its former proprietor had, of late years, taken up his abode in London, where he contracted enormous debts, and had been compelled to sell his valuable estate, which became the property of the Earl of Saxton, who made the purchase for his son and heir, Lord Lundy, then in his nineteenth year, and the first person presented to the reader; and, who, on coming into possession, started at once to the Highlands with a large circle of friends, to pass the season in shooting and other amusements. So precipitate were their movements, that no one on the estate was aware of their arrival at the castle, or even conscious that the property had changed proprietors.

Kinlocklinn was, at that time, inhabited by two of the wealthiest and most comfortable tenants on the whole estate. The one Mr. Stuart, who lived in the mansion on the south side, and father of Charlie, the young Highlander above referred to, and the other, Mr. McKay, who lived on the north side, and father of Isabella, (or Bella, as she was called), and the heroine of this tale.

Mr. Stuart was one of those noble specimens of ancient Highland gentlemen who are now so rarely met with. His unbounded hospitality and generosity, made him an object of universal veneration and esteem among all classes of society.

He could trace his lineage from the Royal House of

his name, whom his ancestors had always upheld until
the last struggle of Charles Edward, when they lost
their rights to Kinlochlinn, which they held for gene-
rations, but since held by them under tenure.

Mr. Stuart was also a distant relation to the unfortunate late laird, whom he served as agent or factor, in consideration of which he held his extensive farm rent free.

Passionately fond of his only son Charles, now
eighteen, he spared no means or pains in giving him
all the advantages which the best college education
could afford; and also furnishing him with all necessaries
becoming a thorough gentleman and sportsman ; and
never before was the liberality of an indulgent and
affectionate parent towards a dutiful son more amply
rewarded.

Naturally quick and brave, blended with a most
honourable and amiable disposition, and possessing great
strength and agility according to his years, Charlie
Stuart was considered the most successful and accomplished sportsman in his part of the country.   Whether
on mountain or moor, fishing in a stream or lake, his
steady and quick eye made him a leader of all parties.
Being a great favourite of the late laird's, he had full
liberty to shoot and fish on the estate.

He was also an excellent horseman, his parent furnished him with the best hunter that could be procured,
and he was capable of managing the wildest horse with
ease.

Mr. Stuart had been a widower ever since his son's
birth.   His wife had been a very amiable person, and a
near relation of Mr. McKay's.   Her loss was greatly felt
by all her acquaintances, especially by her excellent
husband, who could never think of replacing her by
marrying another.

Mr. McKay was also a very excellent man, possessing
a great share of common sense, and more experienced in
worldly affairs than his neighbour, having passed part of
his early life in India, where he had a rich brother, and
where he accumulated what was considered in the Highlands a fair competency.   He married after his arrival
from abroad a lady of the McDonalds, with whose

brother he became acquainted in the Company's service in India. They had only two children. George, a companion of Charlie Stuart's, and who was then at Oxford through the liberality of his wealthy Indian uncle.

The other child was our heroine, Bella, now in her fifteenth year; her mother died when she was ten. Bella was considered from her infancy one of the sweetest and most affectionate creatures in existence, and gained the love and admiration of all who knew her, possessing every charming quality, added to a rare and extraordinary grace and beauty. Always in the company of George, her brother, and Charlie Stuart from her childhood, and when any innocent disagreement took place between herself and George, Charlie always took her part. No wonder, therefore, she loved him better than her brother. Charlie being naturally warm-hearted and kind, having no brother or sister of his own, concentrated all his affections on this tender flower, whose meek temper coincided so faithfully with his own; consequently the attachment became mutual, and even when grown up there was no alteration in their affections. It almost puzzled themselves how to account for such partiality, for when George left for London, and Charlie for Edinburgh University, Bella could not comprehend how she missed the latter's company more than her own brother's, who had gone to another kingdom. Charlie, on the other hand, wondered how little he cared for the company of the fashionable Edinburgh ladies, when away from his old playmate, Bella McKay. The only conclusion he came to, was that she was an older acquaintance, and called after his own mother. Thus argued these children of nature, never dreaming that something more than friendship was budding in their young hearts, which they themselves were yet ignorant of.

Both families thus stood on the most intimate footing, and regularly visited each other, the only point of dispute between the senior members of the family being a difference in political principles, particularly as to the monarchy; while Mr. Stuart still strenuously advocated the claims of his namesakes, the Stuarts, to the Crown, Mr. McKay supported the House of Hanover, and so strongly had this loyalty taken possession of their hearts, that the one named his son after Charles Edward, while the other named his after King George.

This cross-fencing, however, always ended in a drawn battle, and never in the least interfered with the harmony which existed between the families.

CHAP. II.

THE FAIRIES SPIRITING AWAY THE VENISON.

WE left Charlie Stuart with the fainting form of Bella McKay in his arms, after being insulted by Lord Lundy at the bridge of Linn. The innocent maid, having never before been approached with such improper freedom, particularly by a stranger, became so much alarmed and terrified, and had exerted her powers to such a degree to release herself, that she fell off in a swoon in the arms of her deliverer.

Poor Charlie, never before being placed in such a situation, and ignorant of the proper restoratives for such an emergency, was under the impression that his dear playfellow had for ever bade adieu to this life. He therefore burst forth into an agony of despair, and as if to call her back into life again, gave vent to many endearing lamentations and epithets.

In the midst of this passionate gust, Bella at length awoke as out of a heavy sleep, but was yet too feeble to move or articulate a word. Slowly opening her eyes, and gazing abstractedly in the fond and anxious countenance which bent over her, and as if relapsing into her former insensibility, she closed them again.

"Bella, dear, live for me!" moaned her supporter, pressing his burning lips to hers as if to breathe life into them again. The fond pressure revived her instantly, and his last words sounded lovingly in her ear, which at once reminded her of the position she was placed in. Gazing around, she noticed her bosom exposed by a rent in her dress caused in the struggle, and which her supporter was now covering over with her plaid. Conscious

shame came to her aid even in the arms of her dear
friend, and with some embarrassment she faintly murmured, " I am well now." Noticing her confusion,
Charlie helped her to rise. After being placed on her
feet again, she gazed cautiously around, and inquired,
" Is he gone?" On being satisfied on this point, Charlie
offered to accompany her part of the way home, to which
she agreed, and took his proffered arm, being still too
weak to walk unsupported.

On their way along, in discussing the delicate subject,
it was arranged between them that, as no serious harm
had taken place, they would keep the whole a perfect
secret even from Mr. McKay, her father; having no
doubt but the stranger must be one of those bold Englishmen who usually visit the Highlands in the shooting
season, and had taken up his abode at the Castle.

Relieving Charlie of her arm, Bella proposed to travel
alone home, being within a short distance of the house,
fearing her father might suspect something seeing
Charlie in her company. Her companion consented reluctantly to this proposition ; and, bidding each other a
silent adieu, their eyes met in a long and affectionate
gaze, which sent the warm blood over their handsome
faces, infusing pleasant and strange sensations through
their young hearts which before this moment they were
strangers to, and which gave new life to their souls.

Charlie had hardly left when her father, with an
anxious countenance, came to meet her, chiding her for
keeping breakfast so late ; no one, not even Mary Grant,
knowing what had become of her.

Bella apologised with embarrassment, remarking that
she had been tempted, through the fineness of the morning to extend her walk to the bridge, where she had accidentally met Charlie Stuart, who had been shooting
ptarmigan in Ben Mor, and, knowing her partiality to
the birds, he presented her with a brace, which she now
exhibited to her father.

The daughter being a poor adept at dissembling, the
practical eye of the parent detected some unconscious
confusion in the manner of his usually unreserved child,
especially when mentioning the name of Charlie Stuart,

who before this she spoke of without the least embarrassment.

Another mystery which attracted his attention was the disarrangement of her hair and dress, particularly the before-mentioned rent in the bosom of her dress, which she endeavoured to hide by wrapping her plaid around her even in such warm weather. However, as she had not mentioned or made any remarks which might throw any light on the cause of his suspicions, and knowing her timidity and purity, he only replied, "Charlie is, indeed, always kind to you, and you ought to be very thankful to him." "Indeed he is, papa; my own brother George could not be more so," added his innocent daughter with such earnestness and enthusiasm which banished at once certain suspicions which for a moment took possession of him, and condemnatory to the unimpeachable character of his young neighbour. He, however, hinted to her never again to ramble about without her maid, for fear of causing the like anxiety.

Bella was glad when they arrived at the house, and quickly slipped up stairs to change her dress and arrange her hair, and in a few minutes she appeared at the breakfast table as if nothing had happened.

"Well Charlie, my boy; back already from Ben Mòr; and, as I live, the best shot in the country coming home empty handed! why I must really make a notch in the gate-post." Such had been the greeting which Charlie received from his father on approaching the house this morning, and which a little confused the young man, on his first time coming home, as his father had remarked, without game.

"I have been indeed almost unsuccessful father, the only game which fell to my lot was a brace of ptarmigan."

"Better than any my son, they are becoming a rarety these days, although I have seen them plentiful enough in Ben Mòr, let me have a look at the poor birds for the sake of old times."

"I am sorry that I am unable to satisfy your curiosity," replied Charlie, colouring, "As I was passing by the bridge, I happened to meet Bella McKay taking a walk, and as she seemed interested in my game, I presented them to her."

"Quite right, my boy," replied the father, whose quick eye detected the confusion and blushing countenance of his son, when mentioning their fair neighbour's name, and longing for the union of both families in a closer tie than friendship. "Bella is indeed a treasure, and happy the young man who will possess such a prize for his wife. By-the-bye Charlie, don't you see a great change in her since you left for the University? Why, she will soon eclipse your fine Edinburgh ladies."

Charlie was not sorry to see an interruption to this panegyric, which, indeed, tallied with his own feelings, for Donald Munroe, his servant, whom he sent early to the post-office, made his appearance with a package of letters.

Mr. Stuart's exuberance was sadly damped, however, by the news which the mail brought that morning, and the disappointment it conveyed to the excellent man weighed ever afterwards heavily on his mind. This was the downfall of his friend and chief, the proprietor, whom he so much revered, and whom he never dreamed would be succeeded by an Englishman. The blow which he sustained, was, indeed, severe. His son's best prospects were for ever annihilated, and a noble clan of ancient standing were now deprived of their head. What a stroke to his hopes and expectations! Many a time he belied his far-sighted neighbour, Mr. McKay's, prophecy—that their laird would bring himself to beggary. It was now but too true!

Charlie shared in his parent's disappointment, not solely for his own sake, having youth and vigour on his side; but knowing his father's nourished hopes regarding Charlie's own future prospects, and also his ancient clanish principles, and the total extinction of a long line of chieftains.

Among Charlie's correspondence was one epistle which partly dispelled the gloom his father's news had produced, and which brought smiles again to his countenance. The character of the writer may be better judged by inserting his communication, which ran as follows:—

"GLENGARRY,—MY DEAR PRINCE CHARLIE—Here I am safe and sound, having arrived last night, and determined to be beforehand with you in our correspondence, as I know you have hardly breathed your mountain air as yet.

Not wishing to bother you regarding the parental reception of their hopeful son and heir, I shall pass at once to the more interesting subject, namely, my sporting qualifications. Suffice it that I started early this morning with my Gillean, and made a successful stalking by bringing to earth five boomers, (your humble servant placing three to his credit,) which were got home in good time, skinned, and above all, distributed among the cotters, a point which I am very particular in executing on my annual visit among them.

"Your sober, steady-going fellows would think, of course, their day's sport over, but such is not my motto. To style it scientifically, I only considered this a preliminary arrangement for my future proceedings.

"Aware that great feasting would succeed my liberal supply of venison among the cotters, which would attract all their attention, leaving me a favourable field for the prosecution of my plans. I accordingly set to work with my little tiger *Gunna Smile*—Popgun—a little brat of a foundling, who never, I believe, had any parents except fairies, and who had been reared up in our house. This little imp, whom I trained myself, being the veritable mortal fit for my purpose.

"I therefore opened my siege by reconnoitering Mairi Thormaid's dwelling, a sort of half-witch or walking chronicle, whose only profession is to gull the superstitious neighbours with fairy tales, and other terrible anecdotes, in return for which they supply her larder for the year.

"As no notice would be taken of Popgun by his going in or out among the boothies, I sent him to Mairi Thormaid's to report progress, and he soon came back with the favourable intelligence that Mary was in the middle of one of her fairy tales, which she was relating with her usual solemnity to two old crones of her own stamp ; and, better than all, that a pot of venison was boiling over the fire, very likely for a feast.

"Furnishing myself in this instance with a hook and line, I ordered Popgun to re-enter the domicile, and under the pretence of warming himself at the fire, to look out for the hook, which I was to lower from the roof, and when an opportunity presented itself to fasten it in the venison, then make his exit unperceived.

"I was not long in gaining the low roof, and as there was no chimney, save a hole for the smoke, or farleus, I lowered my hook under the cover of the smoke, and Popgun was not long finding a chance to hook and make his exit, when I began to haul gradually.

"The effect may be anticipated. Mary had worked herself and listeners to the highest pitch of superstition, relating the powers of the fairies, when some commotion in the pot attracted their attention, and seeing the venison leaving its boiling element and ascending slowly towards the roof, the paralized crones gave one united scream, and in attempting to spring up from their low seats, held by each others skirts, tumbled over the stools on the floor in their hurry. Amidst this screeching and confusion I made my escape safely.

"The next on my list was attacking Alastair Gealtair—Alexr. the coward—nick-named so by his aversion to fire-arms or their reports. It was said of him when young and joining the militia, that he fell as if dead on the first platoon, and ever since he cannot bear a shot fired near him.

"On reconnoitering his boothy, I peeped through an aperture in the window, which was partly filled up with old clothes, and beheld to my satisfaction old Alastair directly opposite, and in the act of discussing a steaming dish of venison. His brawny sun-burnt chest, as usual bare, and his better-half taking her seat at the end of the table. I supplied, or armed myself in this instance with an old blunderbuss, selected from the Governor's ancient armoury, and loaded with powder and a fresh piece of deer's liver. Resting my ordnance in the aperture, I took a deliberate aim at the exposed and expansive target, the freckled and carbuncled chest before me, and blazed away. You may guess the effect. The old Gealtair fell back with a terrible groan, exclaiming in Gaelic—'*Trocair air manam!*'—Mercy on my soul! When the smoke had cleared away a little, I beheld him lying on his back, on the bed where he had been sitting, as if dead, the liver spattered over his bare chest, and the old wife lamenting over him, wringing her hands and exclaiming—'*Tha fuil a chri mach!*' His heart's blood is out! Knowing well that the neighbours would soon be attracted to the scene of battle through her wailing, and that the old fellow was scatheless, save the fright, I withdrew my forces, and beat a hasty retreat to my garrison, where I am now penning my exploits, and which, you must confess, were brilliant, particularly my last sortie. Give us an account of your proceedings, and I shall report progress, in return. Yours truly, JOHN MacDONELL,
                                   Alias Iain Lom."

The author of this strange production was a young man of the MacDonells, of Glengarry, and a fellow collegian of Charlie's. Although their dispositions differed very much, a close friendship sprung up between them at the University. John, although the most mischievous young Highland gentleman that ever breathed, was a good-hearted fellow at the bottom. His extraordinary inventive mind, and his expertness in personating others, in disguising his person and voice, astonished every one.

He was never easy but when playing some mischievous trick on some unfortunate dupe, and his witticism and satire gained for him the sobriquet of *Iain Lom*, the name of an ancient bard. However, as some of his pranks will come before the reader at intervals through this tale we shall not comment further on his character.

CHAPTER III.

STOPPING UP THE WEST.

WE must now follow Lord Lundy after his chastisement at the hands of Charlie Stuart. Ruffled in his temper, and galling under his first punishment in life, he retraced his steps to the river bank, where he was soon met by another gentleman of maturer appearance. This was his lordship's cousin, the Honourable Captain Somerville of the Guards, who had accompanied his lordship on a leave of absence during the shooting season to the Highlands.

"Well, my noble cousin, any luck this morning? Look here I have been very successful," exclaimed the captain, displaying some fine trout to the sullen gaze of the discomfitted cousin, "as I live, your noble countenance looks more disappointed than if all the beauties of our court had cut you, for the sake of the caprice of a few trout." "Indeed, captain, you are mistaken, my disappointment does not proceed from the caprice of trout, nor yet a court lady, but rather a simple mountain maid, and although I may run the risk of your bantering through my romantic and unsuccessful freak, I cannot keep it from you, never having been so annoyed before."

His lordship here stated the whole circumstance. How the scenery, and the singular beauty of the Highland maid, had made such an impression on his mind. How his own rash and inconsiderate conduct (for which he was now sorry) in endeavouring to detain her, had brought upon him the humbling rebuke of the Highlander, or most likely her brother: and how that he would now give his whole fortune to recall his conduct and be established in the romantic beauty's good graces.

As his lordship anticipated, the gallant captain enjoyed the affair amazingly, and considered it a capital joke, but on seeing the seriousness of his lordship, and the apparent impression the whole event had exercised on him, he desisted, for fear of displeasing. He, however, used all his tact to banish the deep impression which the extraordinary beauty of the Highland maid had

B

made on the heart of his noble cousin, but without avail. His lordship was resolved on making amends, and, if possible, at all risks, to gain her affections. Many suggestions were accordingly proposed by both on their way back to the castle, for its consummation, but the following one, which was proposed by the experienced and gallant captain, was resolved on shortly after their arrival at the castle, after having consulted a servant regarding the present inhabitants of Kinlochlinn.

This servant informed them that the occupant of the farm and mansion on the north side, was a comfortable tenant named McKay, who had one son, eighteen years old, and a daughter, Isabella, fifteen, and very beautiful. The farm and mansion on the south side was occupied by Mr. Stuart, the factor of the estate, who had one son, eighteen years old, and now at Edinburgh University.

It must be remarked that this servant was not aware that Charlie Stuart had arrived the day before on his annual visit to his home at the vacation, and also forgot to mention that George McKay was in England; thus relieving his lordship of all apprehension that the young Highlander who had chastised him was the young maid's lover; he, therefore, with his cousin, had no doubt but the rash young man must be her brother; consequently, the captain's plan of proceedings was as follows:—First, in case the young couple might have told their father; and in order to bring about a reconciliation, that his lordship should invite him to the castle, and receive him favourably; then, in order to pave the way towards his daughter's affections, to offer him the agency or factorship of the estate in place of Mr. Stuart. Secondly, that his lordship should give a grand entertainment to all the tenantry on the estate at an early day, when all athletic games and feats pleasing to the Highlanders should be introduced, with suitable prizes to be contested for. And, in addition to these, other prizes for which gentlemen would contend, such as a steeplechase and a rifle match. In these last, the gallant captain argued that his lordship would signalize himself, (being one of the most accomplished in England), that his name would be raised in the estimation of all present, particularly the fair sex, and the coy Miss McKay above all. The whole to conclude with a grand ball, when all the beauty and youth on the estate would attend.

This grand and elaborate programme put forth by the honorable and gallant captain, found favour in his lordship's eyes, although they were principally suggested or framed to satisfy the appetite of the proposer, who, himself, was a great celebrity in these sports and amusements; especially where the fair ones were concerned.

According to the above arrangements, John Brown, his lordship's valet, was dispatched next day to Kinlochlinn, with a note to Mr. McKay.

As this messenger will figure on several occasions through our tale, we will give the reader a glimpse of his character.

Mr. Brown was a thorough cockney, and passionately fond of fine clothes and airs, and above all to make a *impression on virgins* (as he termed them). When not in his noble master's presence, he affected more airs than that distinguished personage, and was often mistaken for him by strangers, a circumstance which greatly flattered the valet's vanity. Being now for the first time among the *ignorant Eelanders*, he resolved on creating a sensation among them, or, in his own words, *astonish the natives*, and captivate the hearts of the *lassies*. While he is, however, riding towards his destination, we shall introduce another couple, who will be useful to our tale hereafter.

The first of these is Donald Munroe, Charlie Stuart's body servant and foster-brother. His father, old Munroe, had been a piper in Mr. Stuart's family, until his son grew up, and was initiated in that accomplishment. Donald was only six months older than Charlie, and a very active and good-looking young man.

Having very little to do, especially when his young master was in college, Donald passed most of his time in shooting, fishing, and looking after the game and forests with his father, and occasionally playing pibroch.

Being of a very lively and amusing disposition, he took great pleasure in inventing tales and fabricating innocent anecdotes, to gull the most simple and ignorant among the small cotters on the Lochlinn estate.

Among the most conspicuous of his victims and dupes were some half-dozen small cotters, living in a wild and unfrequented point, or *rue*, at the south entrance of Lochlinn. This solitary spot was rendered almost inaccessible by land, by a barrier of cliffs which separated it from the main, and through facing the Atlantic was liable to strong westerly gales, from which it derived the singular name in Gaelic of Ton-ghaoi (or Windy-Bottom). The inhabitants of this sequestered point were, as already mentioned, owing to their seldom mixing or associating with the outer world, yet ignorant of many enlightened and modern facts regarding the construction of the globe and firmament. In short, they believed the earth to be a flat or plain surface, bordered or capped over with the firmament, which was composed of some clear substance, through which the sun, moon, and stars travelled.

The winter before the opening of our tale having been unusually wet and stormy, Donald Munroo had little to occupy him, he therefore bethought himself of visiting Ton Ghaoi for Otter-hunting, and also to give these simple people a taste of his pibroch, of which they were passionately fond.

On leaving, his father commissioned him to tell the Ton Ghaoi people that the factor's (Mr. Stuart's) boats were in need of repair for conveying seaweed for manure in the spring; they required oakum for that purpose, and as these people were always supplied with that article from pieces of cable cast on their wild coast from wrecks, that he (the factor) would thank them for sending him some.

On arriving among these simple people, Donald gave them a hearty taste of his music (all having gathered round him in the house he lodged at for the night), and danced to their hearts' content to the sound of his lively reels.

After this the piper was besieged and pressed on to open his budget of news concerning the outer world, and above all what were the opinions of the people in general regarding the unprecedented and fearful wet winter they were visited by this season.

The mischievous piper seeing the eagerness and thirst of the ignorant and innocent people for some interesting news, began with the following fabrication, which he related with the greatest *sang froid* to his gaping audience:—

"That reminds me of my message to you all, as I suppose you have not heard of the great news of the world. An act of parliament has been passed lately which requires that every person in the three kingdoms shall procure all the oakum they possibly can before a certain day, and the whole is to be shipped off towards the west, The reason of this is, that last summer being so dry the west firmament became cracked, causing a great leakage, which if not stopped up and caulked will produce another flood, and drown every person on the face of the earth. Every individual therefore on this estate, is commanded by the factor to send as much oakum as possible to his place before a fortnight, and anyone not complying with these orders is to be turned off the estate first Whitsuntide."

Precisely that day fortnight, as Mr. Stuart and old Munro were taking their rounds about the farm, they espied an unusual fleet of boats sailing up Lochlinn ; and, on landing near the factor's house, their cargoes of bags were discharged. In order to ascertain the nature of the cargo, and who the new comers were, both walked to the beach and accosted the *Ton Ghaoi* people, who at once explained their business.

Mr. Stuart turned round with a smile to old Munro for an explanation, and that individual immediately predicted his mischievous son's tricks, which he whispered to Mr. Stuart, and fearing if the people were to know what dupes they had been made, that they would revenge themselves the first opportunity, he therefore prayed that Mr. Stuart would leave them still in ignorance.

The worthy factor told these simple men, that as the weather had cleared up, the act, or order, would most likely be countermanded. He, however, accepted of the oakum (which would last for years), and treated the donors to a copious supply of *uisgebea*, which fully compensated them for their trouble.

Such were the young piper's tricks, which, however, placed him pretty high in the estimation of all the young people, particularly the fair portion of them ; but notwithstanding all their winning looks and coquettish allurements to entrap the handsome piper's heart, none of them were able to accomplish that object, for this special reason that it was already an inextricable captive to the charms of Mary Grant's sparkling black eyes.

Mary was the only child and daughter of Donald Grant (Mr. McKay's grieve or overseer) and Bella McKay's waiting maid. Being only a year older than her young mistress, and a brunette, Mary was considered the smartest and prettiest lassie in that part. Always attending on her young mistress, and having many advantages in dress (of which she was passionately fond), and many other feminine accomplishments, Mary became an " object" of attraction to all the young men in the neighbourhood ; but, although she bestowed on all of them a wink and smile, her heart was invulnerable, being safe in the possession of Donald Munroe.

It had been universally admitted that Donald played his best reels and strathspeys at balls and weddings, whenever Mary graced the floor, to whose well-played music she did full justice, and beat excellent time with her lively pretty feet, which she exhibited by wearing a smart short dress. Mary also, on her part, rewarded her lover by favouring him with the cap in the cushion dance, and the smack that followed always created smiles and significant winks among the young assemblage. Donald Munro and Mary Grant, thus avowed lovers, formed many little schemes and plans to forward their own wishes, and also an attachment which they believed to exist between their young master and mistress, Charlie Stuart and Bella McKay. Whether they judged these young couple by their own feelings, we know not ; one thing, however, we know, that by bringing them often together, they themselves would have more opportunities of enjoying each other's company, as they constantly attended on them. Still, we must not charge

hem with selfishness, or being bent only on promoting
heir own courtship, for they eagerly wished for the
ncouragement of the other young couple's, which would
lso be a good cloak for their own.

Among other plans which were suggested, and which
hey proposed to put into execution whenever Charlie
tuart arrived on his annual visit, was to telegraph that
yful event, that Donald on the same evening, while play-
ig his *round* of pibroch on the lawn before Mr. Stuart's
iansion, would include that popular air, " Prince
'harlie's Salute," or, as it is better known in Gaelic by
io name of " *Isabail nic aoi*"—(Isabella Mackay)—a
amo given to that prince when the air was first com-
osed, and which ran in the following parable :—

GAELIC.	ANGLICE.
Isabail nic aoi,	Isabella Mackay,
'M bun a chro laoi	'Tending the kye
'Munadh na fri,	'Mong mountains high,
Gun duinue mar ri,	With nobody nigh,
Si na haonaran, &c.	So lonesomely, &c.

Thus, as will be seen, the pibroch was applicable to
ich of the young couple, Charlie having long been nick-
imed Prince Charlie, and Bella's name also being in-
uded in the air.

True to his promise, on Charlie's arrival Donald gave
nt to the favourite air in his masterly style, sending the
rilling strains through hill and glen, and over the
reno waters of Lochlinn.

Bella, who was ignorant of the plan, or that her young
ighbour had arrived, was sitting in her room, and her
aid, Mary Grant, bustling about the apartment, chat-
ring away as usual some local gossip, but hearing the
und of the distant pibroch, in a pause in her own con-
rsation, through the open window, advancing quickly
e leant out, and listened attentively for a few seconds,
hen instantly recognising the favourite air, she bounded
ck in transports of joy, gave a couple of turns on the
or, clapping her hands, and exclaiming, " He's come!
e's come !"

Bella stared with astonishment at this unaccountable
nduct of her maid, and thought she was taking leave of
r senses, and on inquiring the cause of her hilarity, and

whom she meant having come, Mary answered, " Oh!
the Prince! I mean Mr. Charlie, to be sure!"

Bella blushed unconsciously, and wished to know what
proof she had of such a fact, when Mary a little embar-
rassedly narrated the plan Donald and herself had invented
in order to communicate the agreeable intelligence.

Her young mistress coloured more deeply on hearing
her own name coupled with Charlie's in the air, and on
learning that both of them were the subject of Donald
and Mary's gossip (by the maid's own confession) she
was therefore resolved for the future to be more reserved
in Charlie's company, and never again to manifest the
same joy and happiness on meeting him before Mary or
Donald. Vain reasoning. Little did she know how her
very looks and pretended indifference betrayed more
fully the state of her mind to the more practised eye of
her maid; and this evening, in listening to the music, that
she more than formerly extolled the beautiful pibroch,
and Donald's excellence in giving it more justice than
any other piper; but above all, the bright hue of her
cheeks, and the brilliant light of her eyes, when noticing
some object opposite in Charlie's room, with something
like a spyglass levelled at her.

Mary was indeed correct in her conjectures, for Charlie
paid his visit to Mr. McKay that evening as usual on his
arrival from the University.

What conversation had taken place between himself
and Bella on that occasion we know not; however, this
much came to our knowledge, that when Charlie had
taken his leave of Mr. McKay, Bella met him (I suppose
accidentally) in the lobby, and that the young student
promised to shoot a brace of ptarimgan in Ben Mòr next
morning, provided the young lady met him at the bridge
of Linn to receive the same. Hence the unfortunate
recountre, detailed in the first chapter, which was mainly
attributable to Mary Grant's prying black eyes, and prevented her modest young mistress trusting her, as usual,
in her company, particularly as she expected to meet a
certain young gentleman with game. We also suspect
that the same reasons sent Donald Munro to the post-
office on that morning instead of accompanying his young
master as formerly to Ben Mòr.

CHAPTER IV.

THE FIRST LETTER.

We left Mr. Brown proceeding on his way towards Mr. McKay's residence with his lordship's note. Mounted on a spirited horse, and dressed in his best livery, with his mind meditating on the sensation his appearance would create on the ignorant people he was going to visit. Approaching Mr. McKay's house in a swinging canter, the first person he encountered after springing out of his saddle with a cavalier air, was Mary Grant, who had been wondering what stylish gentleman was coming.

Brown, who was instantly struck with the pretty Highland lassie, brought all his fascinating powers to bear in order to take her tender heart by storm. Approaching her with a theatrical air, he presented Mr. McKay's note, at the same time placing his left hand on his heart, making a low bow, and addressing her in the following strain:—

"*H*adorable *H*angel, pardon my presumption in presenting you with a billet which his lodship has done me the *h*onour to convey to Mr. M*a*ky, the gentleman of this *H*establishment."

Never before having been addressed in such high-flown language, moreover by such a handsome and well-dressed gentleman, Mary tripped away gaily on her mission, delivered the note to Mr. McKay, who, on perusing it, sent her back immediately to conduct the bearer to a room, where he was to be treated to eatables and drink.

On executing her commission, Mary was again besieged with a repetition of Mr. Brown's encomiums on her charms, which raised her vanity to the highest pitch, and sent her up-stairs (she hardly knew whether on her head or heels) to her young mistress' room; and which, on entering, she startled its fair occupant with the following effusion :—

"Darling Miss Bella! such a charming gentleman below with a letter to the master from some lord at the castle. You never heard such fine words as he said to me and such beautiful English. He called me his *h*adorable *h*angel, and many other fine things; and such splendid clothes, with a gold band round his hat! If

Donald Munro had heard all the things he said to me; I am sure he would be jealous." Thus Mary went on in breathless excitement, casting stolen glances at herself in the mirror, to the amusement of her young mistress. The note from the castle, however, changed Bella's risibility to anxiety and fear, dreading that it might have some relation to the affair at the bridge of Linn.

Her speculation was soon interrupted by her father ringing for her, and with seeming happiness informed her that an English lord had purchased the estate, was now at the castle, and demanded his (Mr. McKay's) presence there.

Bella heard this news with terrible misgivings, which her looks betrayed to her astonished parent, and which did not tally with his own pleasant mood.

Mr. McKay met with a flattering and most hospitable reception at the castle from Lord Lundy and his gallant cousin, which he acknowledged with becoming politeness, and was greatly honoured by the many favours which the young nobleman had bestowed upon him, particularly the agency or the factorship of the estate.

He was quite charmed with the sense and judgment his lordship manifested in his future plans, particularly giving a bonfire and entertainment to the tenantry, which, he remarked, would restore harmony and good feeling between landlord and tenant, and remove any prejudices which the Highlanders would naturally entertain against a stranger, and an Englishman, or any clanish leanings towards their former unhappy laird.

Lord Lundy was glad that Mr. McKay approved of his arrangements, and left the management of the whole to him, with power not to spare any expense or trouble in bringing forth the gathering in the most elaborate and grand style, and after a few more remarks on different subjects, Mr. McKay took his leave, highly pleased with his visit and future prospects.

Great were the preparations at the castle during that week, and largely were the events of the approaching bonfire or fête discussed by all the tenants on the estate. Male and female, old and young, joined in the universal excitement. Yet there were three who used to be the leading stars and centre of attraction on such occasions, resolved not to attend the grand fête, or took but little interest in its attractions, although they withheld as yet their antipathy to the occasion. These three were the two Stuarts and our heroine, Bella.

Mr. McKay was puzzled at the conduct of his daughter, and her indifference to the coming event, when on every other lively occasion she invariably manifested great delight. One evening he rallied her, and set forth in glowing terms the fashionable attractions and amusements she would meet with at the castle; and above all, dancing, as formerly, with her old partner Charlie Stuart, whom he declared was grown a fine young man.

Bella blushed deeply on hearing her young neighbour's praise from the lips of her parent, but instantly remarked seriously, that she would far prefer remaining at home; and as for Charlie Stuart, she did not think he would attend either.

This unconscious betrayal of her feelings and opinion still more surprised her parent, who was unable to unravel the mystery.

Being now Mr. Stuart's successor in the factorship, and sole manager of the coming fête, and also the person entrusted for issuing invitations, he therefore thought proper to visit his neighbour personally, in order to remove any unpleasant effects which his appointment might create, or any prejudices which Mr. Stuart might entertain against the new proprietor.

On making his visit, Mr. McKay set forth in glowing terms Lord Lundy's many wise and excellent qualities, which, he had no doubt, would greatly benefit the estate and the tenantry at large, and concluded by giving Mr. Stuart and his son a pressing invitation to the grand banquet which his Lordship's bountiful liberality offered them all.

Mr. Stuart excused himself by saying "that he was growing too old to care about such entertainments, especially when the rightful proprietor was not to be the host, but with regard to Charlie, that he could go, of course, if he chose." His son at once interrupted him by remarking, "that he had no idea of attending, whether his parent did so or not."

Mr. McKay was greatly disappointed and amazed at young people in these days, how little they cared about such amusements, and added "that his own daughter manifested the same indifference about going, and which he feared would be the case, having depended on Mr. Stuart bringing her in his carriage on that day, as he himself would be early at the Castle conducting the arrangements, and not wishing to bring his daughter that early."

Mr. Stuart and his son sought each others looks, when the older remarked, "that he would certainly consent, for Bella's sake," which admission greatly pleased their neighbour, who left in far better spirits than he expected, at the satisfactory termination of his mission.

That evening Bella McKay, as was her wont lately, sat at the window of her room, with an elbow resting on the sill, and her delicate white hand supporting her transparent brow, with her eyes fixed on some object opposite. A great change had taken place within a few days in the looks and manner of the charming girl.

The rosy, laughing young creature, whose buoyant spirits were the theme of everyone, was now changed into the pale and thoughtful woman. Mary Grant's lively chatter was unable to rouse her pensive young mistress, or divert her thoughts from the one object which haunted her mind. Charlie Stuart's despairing and endearing words—"Bella, dear, live for me!"—were still ringing in her ears.

Strong, indeed, must be the feelings, she thought, which prompted her former shy and modest playfellow to give utterance to such expressions. She wondered at her own blindness in not discovering before now his many noble qualities, and handsome and manly person. Her father's remarks concerning him—"That he was grown to be the handsomest young man in the country" —opened her eyes, and revealed all his superior qualities, and instilled through her pleasant and delightful sensations, which gave her new life.

The object of her gaze and reverie was no less affected with the malady which had taken possession of herself. Ever since that eventful morning, his gun, fishing-rod, and boat, were neglected. His station was taken up—particularly at eventide, when Donald Munro played on the lawn—in his room, with the window raised up, and a telescope in his hand, levelled at a certain object in a window opposite. His father attributed his son's change and dejection to his own cause, namely, the downfall of their chief and laird. This, although it partly added to his depression for his parent's sake, was not sufficient to create such a sudden revolution in his lively spirits.

Bella McKay's feeble and despairing cry, "Charlie, dear, save me!" sounded still in his ears. Her beautiful form, when she lay helpless in his arms, haunted his thoughts. She was no longer the lively little child of former years, but a beautiful budding flower, which wanted all his care and attention to protect from the wanton advances of the bold libertine.

While Bella, as before-mentioned, was ruminating and calling to her mind many pleasant hours passed in the company of her young neighbour, Mary Grant tripped into the room, and, after closing the door carefully after her, pulled a small billetdoux from her bosom, laying her left hand on her heart, in that attitude which Brown enacted towards herself, and making a low reverence, said—"A love-letter, my dear madam!"

Bella coloured unconsciously on recognising the handwriting, although this had been the first addressed to herself; she therefore with trembling fingers broke the seal, and read as follows :—" MY DEAR BELLA,—I have not had an opportunity of a private interview with you, to ascertain whether it is your intention to grace the coming fête at the castle. From some hints, however, which dropped from your papa to-day, I inferred that you have objections, which, although he is unable to comprehend, I can easily divine. I also hold the same objections, knowing, of course, that our *common enemy* is included in Lord Lundy's retinue. However, to lull all suspicions, I consider it more advisable for you to submit to your father's wishes, and my attendance accordingly I consider imperative. It has been arranged that my father will drive you in his carriage, so that we shall call for you on our way. Let me know your intentions by Donald, who, by the bye, is glad to have an opportunity of having a chat with Mary.—Yours sincerely, C. EWD. STUART."

Bella lingered for some time re-perusing and repeating each sentence, and overjoyed at the interest the writer had taken in her behalf by resolving to accompany her at the risk of the consequences which might follow. At last the impatient maid, who fidgetted by her side, longing for another chat with her lover, reminded her young mistress that Donald was waiting for an answer. Instantly procuring writing materials, she penned the following reply: "MY DEAR CHARLIE,— Many thanks for your kind interest in my behalf. I shall be indeed guided by your advice, having such a sincere friend to protect me in a place where I have the greatest antipathy to enter, and which will be solely to please papa.—Yours sincerely, BELLA McKAY."

This billet was joyfully carried by Mary in her bosom, casting a mischievous look at her blushing young mistress when closing the door after her; but the tormenting little maid did not wait for a rebuke, if such was in store for her, for the quick patting of her small feet down stairs left Bella, in great relief, to commune once more with her own pleasant thoughts, and which we shall not disturb, or pry too closely into, but follow her maid. On delivering the note privately to her lover, a long chat ensued, in which the coming bonfire was the principal subject. Mary concluded by giving Donald a detail of the compliments passed by Mr. Brown on her own beauty, his fascinating manners, and, above all, the attention she expected to receive from him at the bonfire, which would raise the jealousy of all the other young girls. The thoughtless Mary, so full of her own pleasant anticipations, never dreamt that she was kindling a raging jealousy in the bosom of her true lover, which he partly manifested at parting, by not bestowing upon her his accustomed kiss, which greatly surprised the young maid.

CHAPTER V.

THE BONFIRE.

THE wished-for day at length arrived on which the bonfire was to be held at the castle, and many a cheerful countenance might be seen making its way towards the the scene of attraction. Mr. Stuart, according to promise, called at Mr. M'Kay's, driving his old family carriage. Bella, who was ready some time, hailed his arrival with a beaming countenance, but which was suddenly, however, changed into disappointment on seeing him unaccompanied by his son. Mr. Stuart instantly interpreting her looks and hesitation, exclaimed encouragingly, "Step in, my dear; I fear we shall lose some of the sport. Charlie will soon overtake us on that unruly animal 'Black Prince,' which no other person can ride but himself. I really think he preferred driving to-day for a wonder, as he tried several times to coax Munro to mount the hunter, but Donald thinks more of his limbs than trust them to such a fiery animal."

This intelligence brought back the cheerfulness to the beautiful countenance of our heroine, which made her spring up into the carriage, and taking her seat beside her respected and agreeable neighbour, who enlivened their drive by many pleasant and interesting remarks.

They had not proceeded more than half their journey when Mary Grant (who was sitting with the driver, old Munro) screamed out, " Gracious! He'll leap over us!" Bella, who was constantly casting stolen glances on both sides of the road, looked out to see what was the matter, and exclaimed with admiration. " Oh! look, Mr. Stuart, what a noble sight! How splendid he looks! How admirably he curbs him!"

Mr. Stuart followed her gaze, and beheld, indeed, a most exciting sight—his son curbing the infuriated Black Prince, who, on seeing the carriage and horses before him, endeavoured to gallop off at full speed, only for the bold and excellent horsemanship of his rider, who brought him at last to the side of the carriage, quite humbled, tossing his proud head and glossy black mane, and champing his silver bit, as if asking forgiveness of the beaming countenance which greeted himself and master.

On arriving at the Castle all the guests had already arrived; and Mr. Stuart led his young charge towards the grand entrance, where Lord Lundy, surrounded by his friends, was receiving the company.

Mr. McKay being master of the ceremonies, introduced his neighbour in due form; afterwards his daughter, who, on perceiving his lordship advancing graciously with an extended hand towards her, suddenly shrunk back, to the amazement of all the spectators, withholding her hand, and casting on him a disdainful look, making a cold bow, and then turned round, leaning on her neighbour's arm.

His lordship bit his lip in disappointed vexation; and, in order to divert the spectators' attention, turned round to Mr. McKay, who had not observed the strange conduct of his daughter, he being engaged with some other object.

"Really, Mr. McKay, you are very absent," exclaimed his lordship, forcing a smile; "you forgot to introduce your son, whom I presume is yonder young gentleman," pointing to Charlie, who had entered, and witnessed the whole.

"I really must beg your lordship's pardon," replied Mr. McKay; "but I am sorry to say that I have not the honor of being this gentleman's father. Allow me to present my neighbour's son, Charles Edward Stuart—a name greatly venerated amongst us Highlanders." On hearing these words his lordship turned deadly pale, and stopped short, Charlie at the same time eying him with a scornful look; and both, bowing stiffly, turned on their heels and mixed with the company.

This strange conduct puzzled the spectators; and some attributed his lordship's visible coolness towards Charlie to his loyalty to the present Sovereign, and hostility to the base Pretender or any one bearing his name.

The gay assembly were now invited to the balcony to witness the games and sports contested on the lawn before the Castle. It would be superfluous to enumerate here each and every feat, with the several prizes; suffice it, that the majority fell to Donald Munro, to the gratification of many present, especially Mary Grant, who, regardless of Mr. Brown whispering compliments to her charms, waved her white pocket-handkerchief at each successful feat of her lover.

A most interesting match was now commenced, in which the gentry only took part. The prize was a splendid rifle to be presented to the best shot at 200 yards. The competitors fired in succession according to their lots, but none penetrated the mark, which was a small bull's eye in the centre of a target composed of a deal board. The Honorable Captain Somerville hit the edge. When his lordship's turn came he penetrated the very centre, thus leaving no chance to Charlie Stuart, who was the last on the list. A look of disappointment was visible in every Highland face on seeing themselves beat by an Englishman, and their only hope in Charlie Stuart (who was admitted to be the best shot among them) was now annihilated.

However, the latter, who shared in their disappointment, fell on an expedient to save the honour of his country, and which astonished the spectators as to its novelty. This was by placing a wafer in the hole which his Lordship's bullet had pierced through the target; then taking his stand at the distance, instead of taking a rest like his predecessors, fired off his arm, the ball carrying away the wafer, without touching the wood.

The applause which followed this feat was most deafening. Hats, bonnets, and caps were hurled into the air, and the surrounding plantation echoed back the exclamations. However, the prize was not yet won; the umpires decided this a tie, and both competitors had to fire again, using the wafer, and firing off their arms.

Charlie's turn now came first, when he repeated his former shot, without touching the wood, Lord Lundy's ball carrying a portion off, he consequently lost.

The next sport was a stag hunt. A large red deer was let loose in the park, and all the best hounds were unleashed after him.

This was an animated and most interesting scene: to see the noble forester hotly pursued by his speedy and wiry pursuers. The first that showed in front were a

C

couple of English thoroughbred greyhounds, the property
of Lord Lundy ; at a short distance behind them followed a large grey Highland staghound, the property of
Charlie Stuart, followed by a number of inferior dogs.
This order was kept the first round of the park, without
gaining on the stag, who was unable to find an opening
in the high wall.

Bran—which was the name of Charlie's hound—was
unable to reach his more light and speedy competitors
on level ground, especially in a short distance ; however,
on the second round his powers of endurance began to
tell, and he soon closed on the leading couple.

The excitement now became intense ; the three dogs
were abreast, and taking the same bounds, when " *Bran
gu brath !*"—Bran for ever!—could be heard in every
tree and high position around the castle, where every
individual had taken a station. It soon became manifest that Bran was the superior animal, as he gained
on the stag in every stride, which, on seeing himself
hard pressed, faced the high wall, and cleared it at a
bound.   Bran, on coming up, followed his example, to
the surprise and admiration of the majority of the spectators, and in a short time overtook his game, which he
despatched in a moment. The other dogs were unable to
clear the park wall, and were consequently led away.

Donald Munro led Bran to the castle to receive his
reward, which consisted of a splendid garland, of great
value, which was to be suspended round his neck by
one of the fair occupants of the balcony.

Mr. McKay, on exhibiting the glittering trophy,
invited one of the ladies to volunteer to execute
the pleasant commission, when the Hon. Miss Somerville, the Captain's sister, descended the grand stair-
case, and took the garland ; on approaching the noble
hound he manifested his displeasure at the freedom of
the fair stranger by giving a low growl, which made the
fair lady retreat at once, and give up the attempt; on
perceiving this, Bella McKay tripped down the stairs,
smiling and blushing, took the garland from the honourable lady, and placed it on the hound's neck, which soon
changed his former sulkiness into pleasure at the caress-
ing, delicate hand, which stroked his rough coat.

This ceremony, which greatly pleased the majority of the assembly, particularly the owner of the hound, had made a far different impression on the noble host, who saw two of his schemes miscarry. However, as the principal and more praiseworthy feat was yet to come on, in which his own superiority would be displayed, he withheld his disappointment.

This was the last and most exciting event—the steeple-chase, the winner of which was to receive a beautiful milk-white lady's pony, fully caparisoned, and which he was to present to the fair lady of his choice, among the beauties of the assembly.

The equestrians were mounted, and soon took their station before the castle; but, on looking over the list of entries, Charlie Stuart was missing; and it was not until the last sound of the horn that he made his appearance.

It has been already stated, that Charlie was an excellent horseman, and his indulgent parent purchased for him the best bred hunter that could be found in the country; not that the Highland hills were adapted for such costly cattle to hunt over, or travel, but only for the name and honour of possessing such an animal.

This horse—"Black Prince," was a very powerful animal, and having very little work to perform, became very fiery, spirited, and almost unmanageable. Having a long rest while his owner was away at the University, he showed more restlessness on this occasion than formerly, especially before the grand display which the castle presented.

On mounting at the stables, Charlie was unable to bring his charger to the start, which was under the balcony that the equestrians might receive the congratulations of its fair occupants; but if the truth must be told, it was rather that the principal competitors would be able to display their handsome persons on their beautiful thoroughbred hunters. Charlie finding persuasion unavailing, and time up, applied whip and spur to his headstrong charger, who seeing any more opposition vain, bounded off to the castle as if he was going to charge the cavalcade. The brilliant assembly of ladies gave a scream of affright on seeing "Black Prince" with his rider approaching with such a threatening attitude; but the skilful equestrian curbed his fiery animal in time, brought him submissively into his place in the ranks pawing the ground, and tossing his glossy black mane, as if looking with contempt on his companions.

Many exclamations might be heard from all parts, particularly from the balcony, such as—"How grand! What a splendid animal! How beautifully he curbs him!" &c.

Lord Lundy and his cousin, the gallant Captain, who were two of the best horsemen in England, and mounted on magnificent thoroughbred hunters, were thunderstruck at the sight of Black Prince and his rider, never for a moment expecting to meet such a promising mount in the wild Highlands. A shade of disappointment passed over their countenances, and the Captain, drawing close to his cousin, whispered in his ear, "I fear, my noble cousin, the day means to go against us, and that this match will share the fate of the others."

"It seems like it, Captain; but mind, if I fail, you must uphold our honor."

"I will do my best, my Lord; but who would expect to meet such horseflesh among these mountains?—and if I mistake not, a good horseman, too. See how well he is at home: an excellent seat, by George!"

"Don't you think the animal is rather heavy for such work; surely our thoroughbred cattle ought to show the way over these leaps, particularly the last rasper; there's nothing like blood, Captain!" The latter answered by a dubious shake of the head.

The start now took place, and the whole cavalcade made for the first of the leaps, which were all composed of stone walls, Lord Lundy and his cousin clearing it beautiful, Charlie afterwards, and the others bringing up the rear. In this order they kept for some time, the English horses proving superior in speed and taking the leaps at the same time, while Black Prince followed at some distance, hard held, but clearing the leaps at least a foot higher than the others. The hard pace now began to tell upon the leading pair, when Charlie giving his horse more rein, soon closed, and the three took the second leap from home together.

The excitement at this moment became intense, but his Lordship's horse began to drop behind, while the other two were neck and neck coming to the last leap, which was a foot higher than the rest.

Both horses were in the air at the same time, when the Captain's horse struck heavy, fell on his head, breaking his neck, pitching his rider some yards before him on his shoulder, and Charlie came in a winner amidst deafening cheers.

Lord Lundy's horse refused the last leap, and was not persevered with.

At the final struggle, when the two leading horses were coming to the last leap, Bella McKay, who was leaning on Mr. Stuart's arm, became excited and alarmed that some accident would happen, her eyes became dim, and seeing a horse and rider coming to earth, she gave a faint scream and fell insensible in her supporter's arms.

On recovering, she asked feebly "Is he safe? Is Charlie hurt?" Her kind friend assured her that it was not Charlie but the Captain who had fallen; but not seriously hurt, although his noble horse was past recovery.

The blushing girl, who thus unconsciously betrayed herself to her neighbour, stammered out some unintelligible thanks that no one was hurt.

When order was restored, a groom appeared leading the beautiful pony, and Mr. McKay, in presenting it to Charlie, expressed himself as follows:—" I have great pleasure in presenting this handsome and valuable prize to my young and promising neighbour, which he has so gallantly won against such noble competitors, and trust at the same time that he will adhere to the rules of the games by presenting it to the lady of his choice, among the beauty and brilliancy of our fair assembly."

The young man received his prize, and modestly raised his eyes to the balcony, where a great deal of whispering and blushing was going on, each wishing to be the fortunate recipient of such a valuable gift from so handsome and accomplished a donor.

Charlie mustered sufficient courage to address himself in the following words:—" Not deigning to flatter myself with the vain idea that my gift, however valuable,

could be acceptable to the humblest among such beauty
and attraction; yet I dare hope that there is one
among them who, in this instance, will excuse my presumption. I shall, therefore, call on my young and
beautiful neighbour, Miss McKay, to accept from the
hands of her old playfellow this token of his regard."

The lovely young girl thus called upon tripped down
the stairs with smiles and blushes, and, with becoming
modesty, held out her hand to receive the present,
and on taking hold of the bridle, raised her eyes
for a moment, when hers and Charlie's met, which sent
the crimson over their handsome faces, and increased
the whisperings among the spectators, and the burning
jealousy of Lord Lundy. He now saw all his plans for
raising himself in the estimation of Bella McKay, and
his vain anticipations frustrated. The very means he
adopted, at great expense and trouble, to signalise his
achievements, proved the very weapons of his own dis-
comfiture, and the stepping-stones for exalting his rival.

Not wishing to expose his mortification and disappointment, the *fete* was carried on with as much hilarity
as if he were the successful candidate, and his liberality
and hospitality were in no degree lessened.

The assembly were now invited to partake of the
grand banquet. That for the gentry was laid out in the
great hall of the castle, and that for the commoners on
the lawn, between the castle and *Loch-nan-eal*, a beautiful
lake, formed by nature, and bordered by plantations.
Eatables and drinkables of every description were pro-
fusely supplied to all classes, which raised their spirits
to the highest pitch for the dancing that followed.

Piles of combustible materials were lit at dusk on the
margin of the lake, around which groups of merry
dancers were formed into reels stepping out and revolv-
ing to the tune of several bagpipes, whose thrilling
strains echoed through woods and hills.

The castle hall was brilliantly illuminated, where the
higher class held their grand ball, and where equal
enthusiasm prevailed.

Although there was no lack of amusement and enjoyment, and all classes of society seemed to be in the

height of happiness, yet there was one couple—who, on all former occasions, distinguished themselves for animation and delight—were far from being affected with the universal hilarity.

These were Charlie Stuart and Bella McKay, who, by a preconcerted plan of Lord Lundy and his gallant cousin, were kept separate during the evening.

It was arranged by these two, that his Lordship should engage Bella for all the dances during the evening, and should any unforeseen etiquette, which, in his position as host, made his absence for any time imperative, the captain was to take his place, and engage the young lady in question; thus separating the young lovers (as they now had ample proof) for this time, and also besiege the young lady's heart, that she might become reconciled, and look more favourably towards his Lordship. So successful had this plan proved, that the lovers, who, at all former balls, were partners in every dance, could not on this occasion exchange a single word, or give vent to their new-born passion, save by a few stolen glances from different sides of the hall. My young readers, who have experienced the first effects of dawning love, can better judge their feelings.

Too modest and inexperienced to make any advances in the presence of so many spectators who were witnesses to the incidents of the day in which they themselves figured so conspicuously, and conscious that the majority of the brilliant assembly were watching their every movement.

Bella submitted to this unavoidable and compulsory separation with a heavy heart through etiquette and dread of parental displeasure. But how much more miserably Charlie passed that evening, suffering under the first pangs of jealousy, attributing Bella's estrangement to the fickleness of her sex, or sharing in the ambition common to them by being flattered, and appreciating the homage and attention paid them by superior and more wealthy suitors, never doubting but this was voluntary conduct on her part.

What added more to his misery was the whispering of the dashing and gallant Captain in her ear, and her

visible confusion when he himself met her gaze, with
suspicious looks from the Captain.   Unable any longer
to withstand such a sight he strolled out on the balcony
to cool his heated brain.

We must here state that Charlie's charges against his
fair neighbour were unfounded in this instance, although
appearances went very far to confirm these suspicions.

Many attempts were made by Lord Lundy during
that evening to overcome the coy maid's prejudices
against him, and ingratiate himself in her estimation.
He eloquently pleaded his cause, and begged that she
would forget his rash and thoughtless conduct towards
her at the Bridge of Linn, which he would now give
worlds to recall.   All these flattering protestations were
unavailing; although Bella forgave him, she could never
forget, or return the attachment which he professed
towards her.

The Honorable Captain lent his powerful aid as me-
diator, but Bella cut him short by informing him in ex-
plicit terms that she could never listen to the addresses
of any man breathing, however exalted, who would act
such a dishonorable part, or conduct himself in such a
manner towards any unprotected female, and therefore
wished to bury the subject for ever, otherwise she would
be compelled to shun the company of any person who
would introduce the subject.

The Captain, not wishing to be deprived of such
pleasant company, and seeing any further pleading fruit-
less, dropped the subject, and turned the conversation
towards the channel which he well knew the current of
his fair companions thoughts ran, namely, in extolling
Charlie Stuart's manly and accomplished qualities. The
blushing cheeks, the downcast looks, and the stolen
glances at the object of his enconiums, plainly told the
experienced officer how her young heart was engaged;
and little did Charlie think, at that moment, that those
glances, which he so unjustly interpreted, were the dumb
symbols of overflowing love towards himself.

When the young man issued from the hall, tormented
by conflicting feelings, he encountered his servant
Donald, who, apparently, had partaken of a share of his

own malady, stepping moodily the whole length of the balcony.

"How is it, Donald," asked his master, "that you are not among the gaiety yonder at the lake."

"Not to give you an ill answer, Mr. Charlie, I care but little for their enjoyment, for I think one half of them are going daft, particularly the girls; there is that Mary Grant, with her head stuffed with high notions crammed into it by that *flunkey* Brown, and too proud to give a poor countryman a look, and if these glass doors tell the truth, I think her young mistress is infected with the same distemper."

This was a home thrust to his master, who could not deny its truth; but the following conclusion to Donald's grievance brought a smile to his countenance: —"I wish I had an opportunity to cure them of that notion."

"How could you cure them?" inquired his master, curious to know his servant's remedy for curing High-land girls' love for Englishmen.

"Bless you it is the easiest thing in the world; just if these spindle-shanked Englishmen were coaxed to wear our Highland dress for one night, not a single Highland girl would ever look at them afterwards.

Light as his young master made of Donald's cure, the latter proved its efficacy, as will be seen hereafter.

Their conversation was now interrupted by the appearance of Mr. McKay, who was in search of Donald to play the "Reel of Tulloch" on his pipes, as the English gentry were very anxious to see that interesting dance.

Mr. McKay pressed Charlie to join in it, and both re-entered the ball-room, when her father approached Bella, inviting her to dance with her old partner Charlie Stuart, as his Lordship, who was sitting by her side, did not like to dance the reel, being ignorant of it.

With what alacrity and visible joy the young girl sprang to her partner's side at this intimation. A bird released from its captivity could not show more happi-ness than the charming girl when clinging to her lover's arm on their way to the end of the hall, to take their places. What a revolution came over the motions and looks of the interesting couple, as they glided through the intricate reel, drinking love from each other's beaming looks, as if unconscious of the existence of any other person in that large hall.

Bursts of admiration were heard from all parts of the room, such as, "How charming they look! What a match! How gracefully they move!"

The objects of these remarks were truly deserving of such compliments; both dressed in full suit of Highland costume, Bella in her favourite silk McKay tartan, and Charlie in his Royal Stuart.

With what jealous looks Lord Lundy watched the happy pair! What a sudden transformation came over the listless and disinterested partner of his dances during the evening! How happy he would feel were the least of her sparkling looks or sweet smiles bestowed upon himself!

When the music had ceased, and the couples were taking their seats, Charlie was going to conduct his fair partner to her former seat beside Lord Lundy, Bella clung to him nervously, and whispered in his ear, " Not there I beseech you, let us seek the fresh air." With a heart bounding with joy, Charlie wheeled round on his heel at this intimation, leading his willing charge to the balcony.

On arriving at the other end, Bella drew a long breath as if relieved of a heavy weight, on escaping from her tiresome company, and exclaimed, " Oh, what a relief."

"It is indeed, very oppressive in there," replied Charlie, misinterpreting her.

" 'Tis not the closeness of the hall I mean, but in getting out of the tiresome company with which I have been persecuted all the evening," added Bella.

"Indeed," replied her companion, as if doubting her words; " I thought the company was very agreeable to you, the Captain's in particular."

Bella raised her eyes to him mournfully, on hearing, for the first time in her life, the reproachful tone of his voice, and, in quivering accents, said: " I thought you would be the last on earth to insinuate, or harbour the belief, that I could ever enjoy the company of one, or friend of a person who conducted himself so ungentlemanly towards me, when he believed me unprotected. The Captain is certainly more bearable and charitable towards my feelings, and you should know how he praised your conduct, and all your achievements this day." The truth now dawned on her repentant hearer. Twas not his own cause the Captain was pleading that evening, which caused Bella's blushes, and the stolen glances she threw at himself. He, therefore, with an impulse, not peculiar to him, drew the blushing girl towards him, and pressed her momentarily to his heart, replying vehemently—" Pardon my folly, dear Bella, I was only annoyed and disappointed at being separated from my old partner this evening; I shall never after this moment, harbour such stupid suspicions." A moistened eye and a fond pressure of the hand was the only acknowledgment to this outburst of feelings, and the happy lovers turned their gaze towards the novel and romantic scene before them. The happiness which this hour imparted to their young souls was an era in their life, and was indellibly imprinted on their minds, through the many vicissitudes and misfortunes of their after life, as yet a stranger to their buoyant spirits.

It was, indeed, a scene calculated to nourish a budding and ardent love. The beautiful *Loch-nan-eal* lay in still repose like a mirror, reflecting back the fantastic shadows of the dancers round the fires, which shot incessantly over its unruffled face, like so many sprites or goblins. The plantain trees stood solemnly like so many gigantic spectators, echoing back the merry peals of the enthusiastic revellers, who wheeled and stepped in many groups to the thrilling strains of the Highland pipes.

What a crowd of delightful and happy sensations filled the hearts of the young lovers, as they stood silently contemplating the enchanting prospect; their minds were too full, and their modesty yet too powerful to allow them to give utterance to their feelings. But those deep sighs and stolen looks in each other's eyes, told more than the most eloquent language could impart.

Yet, there hung around them some unfathomable cloud which they could not dispel. Was it a presentiment,

or some invisible power which threatened to separate
their young hearts at this early union? Alas! the
mysterious veil could not yet be removed. It might be
as well that their present happiness should not be
clouded by the misfortunes which were in store for them.

Daylight soon warned them that their absence might
be noticed, and which also put an end to the great festi-
val or bonfire, and the happy assembly turned their way
towards their respective homes, where the celebrated
gathering became one of their fireside *sgsulachdare*, or
winter tales, for years after.

CHAPTER VI.

THE PROPOSAL.

No incident of any import took place since the bonfire at the castle, nor had the principal characters on
that occasion met for some time, until one day Mr.
McKay sent for Charlie Stuart, intimating that his
daughter wished to ride the pony which he had presented to her, and therefore besought him to accompany
her in her ride, lest any accident might happen her,
or the little animal proving untractable.

We need not mention how happy the young man felt
on the occasion, or how gladly he accepted the invitation which would give him another opportunity of conversing, or holding an uninterrupted *teté-a-teté* with his
fair neighbour. Mounting his charger, Black Prince, he
rode light-heartedly to his neighbour's house, where he
found Bella already robed in her becoming riding-habit,
and a man holding the beautiful pony saddled.

With a bounding heart he sprung from the saddle
and assisted Bella into hers, then remounted again, and
the pair slowly cantered out of the gate, their eyes
brightened with animation at the prospect of a pleasant
ride, and each other's company.

Mr. McKay, who saw them starting, followed them
with his eyes until they disappeared among the hedges,
and murmured with a sigh, "Poor children, how happy! It
would be a pity to part them,"—then re-entered his house.

Meanwhile the equestrians directed their steeds towards their old and favourite haunts, among the many interesting indulations which bordered the shores of Lochlinn.

After visiting each favourite spot associated with so many endearing reminiscences of their childhood, they checked their steeds, and brought them to a slow pace. Moving at a steady walk, they both dropped their reins on the manes of their horses, and fell into a state of musing.

The docile animals, who now kept the same step, were apparently like their riders, on intimate terms with each other, and instinctively disposed to favour the lovers' wishes by keeping close together.

Not a sound was heard to disturb the free current of their thoughts, save the measured tread of their horses' feet, and a few notes from the feathery warblers, who seemed to lower their key on this occasion lest they should disturb the universal silence.

At length, after an escaped sigh, which was echoed from one to the other, Bella remarked—" Do you know, Charlie, that something tells me that this will be the last time we shall visit these dear spots together, at least for a time."

"Strange! I was just under the influence of the same presentiment when you spoke, but I hope it is all imagination," answered her companion.

" I hope so; however, I cannot shake it off, and I view these familiar scenes now, as if I were bidding them farewell," added the pensive girl.

They now conversed for a while, but unable to dispel the strange impression despite their efforts, when they shaped their course towards home.

On riding leisurely through clumps of underwood, and entering a narrow lane, a roebuck sprang a few yards before them, when the sharp ring of a rifle came from behind a bush, and the buck, which was pierced by the ball, sprung back in his death struggle against Bella's pony, and frightening it to such a degree, that he almost threw his fair rider—then gallopped off at full speed towards the shore.

Bella, who dropped the curb rein in this sudden start, could not check the terrified animal in his speedy career, and she had hardly nerve enough to hold her seat.

Charlie, on seeing the flying steed making for some precipices which bounded the shore, made off after him; but considering that his pursuit directly after would only increase the pony's fright and speed, he resolved on making a detour, and prevent any catastrophe. It, therefore, took all Black Prince's speed and efforts to gain the goal when the pony was within a few strides of it. With uncommon presence of mind and magnificent horsemanship, Charlie strained his horse between the pony and the cliff, swerved him half round, flung one arm round the form of Bella—who was in the act of falling off—and with the other hand brought Black Prince to a dead halt, thus saving horse and rider.

Alighting in an instant, with his fair burden, who fainted in his arms, he soon, however, brought her to, and galloping after the pony, which was now quite humbled after his severe race, brought him back, and both resumed their journey once more.

Proceeding a short distance, they beheld Lord Lundy, the originator of the would-be disaster, and who had been a witness to the flight of the pony. Not wishing to encounter the object of, their hatred, they changed their course, and arrived at Mr. McKay's by another route.

Mr. McKay met them at the gate, and something in Bella's looks, and the disarrangement in her dress and hair, attracted his attention, but the young couple unfortunately resorted to the same expedient they had used on another occasion (the memorable event at the Bridge of Linn), namely, to keep the whole to themselves. Their reason on the present occasion being that if Mr. McKay came to know that the pony had ran off in such a manner, he might think that he would be apt to do so again; consequently, he would not allow her to ride afterwards, which would deprive them of another pleasant recreation.

Fatal resolve; better for them that they had told all, which would have saved them many days of misfortune and trouble.

Alighting from their steeds, Mr. McKay anxiously
inquired whether the pony proved untractable, or whether
Bella had met with any accident. The young people
were a little confused, but Charlie answered, evasively,
"Not at all, Mr. McKay, see how docile he looks,"
which, indeed, was true, as the little animal was now
quite submissive.

Bella slipped into her room in the interim, to escape
her father's scrutiny and interrogating. Charlie, also,
on the same grounds, mounted his horse, bade his neighbour good evening, and rode off hurriedly home.

Lord Lundy, after suffering a repetition of his former
jealousy, on seeing the lovers again so familiarly enjoying each other's company, and his rival, Charlie Stuart,
once more distinguish himself by his gallantry and devotion in saving Bella's life, which his own unguarded and
accidental shot had imperilled.

To see Bella once more in Charlie Stuart's arms when
they alighted from their horses, was bitter gall to his
heart, and he made a solemn vow internally that, as he
could entertain no hope of separating them, or gaining
possession of her by fair means, he would do so by *foul*.

Many desperate and dishonorable expedients are resorted to, even among the highest classes of society, by
persons suffering under the unfortunate passion of
jealousy; and it will be seen that the high-born and
noble Lord Lundy was no exception to this rule.
Baffled in all his attempts to attract the simple and
plain Highland maid, who made such a deep and ever-
lasting impression on his heart, which had withstood
all the allurements and fascination of the beauty of the
English court.

Under the impression that the young couple had not
perceived him, and were ignorant of the author of the
misch.... (although, to do his Lordship justice, he was not
aware of their vicinity when he fired the shot, and on
perceiving the mistake he followed them in alarm, lest
any accident should take place), he had just appeared
in sight when Charlie, at the critical moment, gallantly
forced his horse between the pony and the precipice, and
saved Bella from a violent death. It was then on seeing

her safe, and so fondly in the arms of his rival, that his former jealousy returned with redoubled inveteracy, and it was under such conflicting emotions that he did not call at Mr. McKay's to apologise and inquire after Bella's health. He, however, sent for Mr. McKay, one day afterwards, to sound him, in order to ascertain whether he became acquainted with the affair, and also the 'unfortunate meeting at the Bridge of Linn on his first arrival. If Mr. McKay was ignorant of these affairs (which he thought possible) he had matured a plan, after considerable pains and study, which he thought would turn that gentleman against Charlie Stuart, and forward his own wishes.

When Mr. McKay waited on his Lordship at the castle in conformity with the summons, that nobleman received him with unusual cordiality and marked attention; and after touching on several subjects, his Lordship opened his negotiations in the following words :—

" I have sent for you, Mr. McKay, in order to ascertain certain delicate facts which I have been for some time 'loath to touch upon, but as they concern us both, I consider myself justified in introducing them on the present occasion. However, as I feel rather puzzled how to begin, I hope you will excuse my asking you several questions first, to which, I hope, you will give candid answers."

" Certainly, my Lord, I shall be most happy to give you all the information in my power on any subject which may interest your Lordship," replied Mr. McKay, a little surprised.

" In the first place, I want to know whether you were aware that your daughter and your young neighbour, Charles Stuart, were riding out together some days back, and whether they mentioned anything that took place, or had seen me on that day."

" I am aware that they had been riding certainly, as it was at my own suggestion they went, but as for mentioning seeing your Lordship, or that any thing had taken place, they never breathed a syllable about it; and now, since you have mentioned it, I noticed something unusual in their manner, and particularly in my daughter, as she kept her room that evening; but you make me very anxious, my Lord, I beg of you to explain yourself more fully."

" Pardon me, Mr. McKay, I must tax your patience a little longer; and now oblige me by telling, whether the young couple told you that they saw me at the bridge of Linn one morning when I first arrived here, or whether you observed anything particular about your daughter at that time."

" Never, my Lord, she has not mentioned a word about seeing you, but I remember one morning about that time, her having walked alone as far as the bridge, and that she mentioned having met young Stuart there, after coming home from the hills where he had been shooting, and gave her a brace of ptarmigan; and I must also confess that something unusual in her manner and dress attracted my attention."

" Poor innocent child, I thought so. I knew that she was too modest to mention such a delicate affair, or to involve her misguided young neighbour. You need not look so alarmed, Mr. McKay, nothing serious has taken place as *yet*, but you must promise me that you will never mention, or hint to either, by word or look, what I am going to tell, and on this condition I will make you acquainted with the affair."

Mr. McKay made the promise, and his Lordship proceeded to tell him that he (his Lordship) and the Captain, the morning, after their arrival, went to fish on the river Linn, above the bridge, that the Captain went upstream, while he himself went towards the bridge, when he was attracted by the screams of a female; that when he approached the spot he beheld Charlie Stuart endeavouring to take improper liberties with Bella, both of whom he recognised at the bonfire. That, on making his appearance, the young man desisted, but followed her a little distance towards her home, likely to make up for his delinquencies; and that his Lordship, taking them for some humble people, never troubled himself about them, and had almost forgotten the affair, until the other day when he saw them riding as he was out shooting; they dismounted, on the plea of tightening the saddle-girths, when young Stuart repeated his former advances, and only for his Lordship himself firing off his rifle, would have committed an insult on her person.

Mr. McKay was overwhelmed and shocked at this abominable revelation, and only for the position of his Lordship, would not have believed that his young neighbour (whom every person thought so highly of, and he himself knew from his infancy to be an honourable and unimpeachable young man) would ever be guilty of such conduct. All this he told his Lordship, but the crafty nobleman smiled at Mr. McKay's inexperience of young men now-a-days, particularly when mixing with other libertines in colleges, although their former habits might have been well enough.

" Now," added his Lordship, " having seen the heroic conduct of your daughter on two occasions, resisting the advances of a familiar and old acquaintance, and, above all, her generous nature in not exposing him, as he deserved: these qualities, added to a rare beauty and modesty, such as I never met with, even in our higher English circles, have so captivated my heart since I first beheld her, that I now lay my hand and fortune, with your approbation, at her feet."

" Really, my Lord, I am so overwhelmed with all that you have told me, that I am at a loss how to speak, much less how to answer your extraordinary proposal. I hope, however, on maturer consideration, that you will see the folly of such an idea; the great difference of position, which your noble house would never overlook; and, further, that you are still a minor, which would bring down upon you and I (were I ambitious enough to accept your flattering proposal) the displeasure of your noble parent, and may disinherit you. You will, therefore, I hope, banish all these unreasonable notions from your mind, and before you attain your majority you may depend upon it they will all be obliterated from your memory."

" Never, Mr. McKay, I am quite confident ages would not consume the ardent attachment that has taken root in my heart towards your beautiful daughter. It is not a passing romantic fancy of youthful folly, but a burning, and strong passion, which I am certain will increase with my years. However, on considering the sense and propriety of your arguments, I will promise to curb my passion, and make the sacrifice of delaying my nuptials until I become of age (although trying to my feelings), when I shall be at liberty to marry the chosen of my heart. I have also prepared for your objections, and to meet them will suggest a plan which I hope will receive your approval, and which is this—I understand you have a wealthy brother, a merchant in London, who has often sent for your daughter, for the purpose of finishing her education, and introducing her to society. You will, therefore, send her there, or accompany her yourself, and start with us to-morrow (as myself and friends intend leaving), the Captain and I having received pressing despatches to that effect. I am confident, if you approve of my proposition, and if your daughter is introduced among high society, which I shall feel great pleasure in doing, and present her to my own relations—I am sure they will appreciate her worth. Another reason which influenced me to suggest this proposition, and in which I know you will concur, that she will be removed from the immediate neighbourhood of that young libertine, who has dared to insult her, and who may repeat his base improprieties, if not sent to a place and among society becoming her, and which he dare not approach."

Whatever hesitation and objection Mr. McKay held towards his Lordship's suggestions, the last appeal dispelled them, and decided his determination. His young neighbour's hypocritical conduct (as he now considered it) became more detestable in his eyes, and the use he made of the confidence and friendship placed in him, instead of being a protector to his daughter, becoming himself the aggressor, and assailing her virtue. Under these indignant emotions he replied—

"Your last observation, my Lord, has decided my mind, and the outrageous conduct of the young man whom I always considered my dearest friend and a pattern to all young men, and whom I some day thought of entrusting with the happiness of my child. If, therefore, as you imagine that my daughter will meet with the reception you anticipate from your relations, and if your own feelings towards her should not change in the interval, I shall be most highly honoured by your addressing her when the term of your minority expires; with this proviso, however (which, pardon me, I do not think likely), that she herself will have no objection, for I would never press her against her will, were the suitor the Prince of Wales."

The last words brought the colour to his Lordship's face; however, he smothered any little disappointment which the remark created, and pressed the speaker's hand with great earnestness and thankfulness.

When Mr. M'Kay was taking his leave, after all the arrangements for their departure next morning were settled, his Lordship gave him instructions to serve a notice on Charlie Stuart, to the effect that the privilege he heretofore held from the former proprietor for shooting and fishing on the estate was now suspended.

CHAPTER VII.

HOW TO CURE HIGHLAND GIRLS' LOVE FOR ENGLISHMEN.

THE progress which Mr. John Brown, Lord Lundy's valet, made on the susceptible heart of Mary Grant greatly flattered that young man, and alarmed her true and devoted lover, Donald Munro. In order, therefore, to reconquer the fair citadel, the piper resolved on bringing all his ingenuity and forces to bear for the consummation of that object. However, no feasible artifice appeared to him, save the one which the reader has already heard, and which he hinted to his young master the evening of the bonfire. The favourable opportunity for prosecuting his wished-for plan at length arrived.

John Brown, on the other hand, satisfied in his own own mind that his impression on the heart of the pretty, lively Highland girl was quite successful, all he now wished for was an occasional chance of paying her his respects and enjoying her pleasant company; and in order to accomplish that object, he thought it proper to cultivate Donald Munro's friendship and companionship through whom he expected to be introduced among Mr. M'Kay's servants, and into his establishment. In gaining thus the confidence of Munro, on whose ignorance, as he thought, he could play by making a tool of him, he would find access to Mary Grant. The wily piper, who was not to be caught with chaff, soon perceived the drift of the *flunkey;* however, feigning ignorance and simplicity as to his object, Munro manifested great willingness in forwarding Brown's addresses.

One day on meeting each other, among other topics discussed between them, Brown hinted that he heard of a *brews,* or an illicit whiskey distillery, being carried on among the hills, somewhere near hand.

This was the very thing which Munro wished for, and answered that he himself was among the few who were privy to the situation of the *brews,* and, as a favour, would conduct Brown (who apparently felt very curious to see it) to the secret retreat; and, to make their visit more acceptable to the smugglers, he would bring his pipes, to which they were very partial. Brown was in ecstacies at the proposition, and the pair started off.

The valet often during the journey secretly wished that he had not undertaken the journey, which was, of course, prosecuted on foot, and which threatened every moment the destruction of his gaudy livery. However, not wishing to show the white feather, or that Donald should have anything discreditable to tell Mary against himself, he strove to follow his agile guide, who sprung from one obstacle to the other, like a native mountain deer.

The travellers at length came in sight of the mysterious retreat, which was situated below them in a dell or chasm between two rocks, which served as a natural wall, over which was erected a roof formed of rough timber, and covered over with turf or *scraths.* A cascade of running water flowed by the end of the building, from which a long wooden trough conducted a constant supply of water to the worm. Clouds of dark smoke which issued from the building, hung round the dell, giving it a terrible and forbidding appearance to the eye of the affrighted cockney, who viewed the scene with awe and misgivings, and brought to his mind tales of robbers and banditti, and their wild haunts. Munro read at a glance the state of his companion's feelings, and saw that his courage began to fail him. Seeing that his own plans might miscarry were Brown to beat a retreat, he propped up the latter's pluck with the following encouraging words—" This looks rather a wild and unpromising place to the eye of a stranger, but if you once visit it, and become acquainted with the jolly fellows who inhabit it, you will be much pleased, and also contribute to the many novelties you have met with in the Highlands, which your London acquaintances will, I am sure, be happy to hear when you return."

These words had the desired effect; Brown's courage and love for novelty at once returned, and he intimated his willingness to descend the dell at once. Donald now proposed a plan which would add to their stock of amusement on coming so far, after their toil and trouble. This was that, on nearing the brews, Brown should enter alone, while Donald would hide in some cover convenient, and being a stranger and his singular livery, he would be taken by the smugglers for a gauger, which would cause a panic among them, and a hasty retreat of the smugglers, but which would be explained afterwards by Donald himself who would recall the fugitives.

Brown at once entered into the spirit of the *lark*, as he termed it, and both commenced the intricate descent.

According to arrangements, Donald ensconsed himself behind a tuft of heather contiguous, and Brown advanced towards the abode with an effort and forced consequence; plucking up his fast sinking courage, he entered and stood horror struck in the entrance.

As Munro predicted, the smugglers had already deserted, for the brews was untenanted by any human being. The valet gazed around the wild and novel habitation. A row of large vats containing some bubbling liquid stood against the rock or natural wall; a large boiler over a fire occupied one end of the building, and another of a different construction occupied the other. This last boiler or pot had a head on, from which proceeded the worm which coiled itself down into an upright cask like a large serpent, and over which a constant supply of water from the before-mentioned trough flowed. But what attracted the awe-struck and terrified stranger, and almost made him beat a hasty retreat, was an enormous black buck goat which stood in the middle of the floor with his terrible horns, long beard, and staring grey eyes, as if to contest his entrance.

Brown's knees trembled under him on gazing at the animal, which he expected every moment would make a spring at him and toss him on his horns. While thus debating in his own mind whether to retreat or call out to Munro, and as if to finish his career in this life, a sack from behind was slipped over his head and body, and a strong cord, which ran through its mouth, tightened with a jerk round his legs, upsetting him in an instant, leaving him powerless on the floor at the mercy of the smugglers, who now stood over him, debating in Gaelic how to dispose of the supervisor, as they imagined him.

Whenever the unfortunate prisoner was able to clear his breathing organs from the dust and finely cracked malt which fell from the sack, he roared out lustily for Munro, expecting every moment to be pitched into one of the large boilers, or over a precipice.

It must be here mentioned that, as Munro anticipated, when the smugglers, who were three stout young fellows, perceived Brown in his strange clothes approaching, they took him, not for a guager, but a supervisor, or head excise officer. They instantly retreated to the other end of the brews, taking the sack, which was made for such an emergency; and as Brown hesitated in the entrance, surveying the interior, particularly the pot buck, one of them slipped the sack over his head and body as already mentioned.

The question now was how to dispose of him, and as neither of them could understand a word of English, much less the strange noise which issued from the sack (as Brown's dialect was not the most intelligible at the best of times), they interpreted the word Munro (that name being pronounced in Gaelic *Rouch*) for *mo shron*,

or my nose; as if the prisoner complained of the mal-
treatment of his nasal organ; to which they answered,
" *Ciod as mo viru do shron, na do thou*" (what care we for
your nose or nether end), and applying their toes un-
mercifully to that delicate part at the same time.

The unfortunate prisoner now roared out—" Am no
'xiseman, 'am his *Lod*ship's *walct* !" when the last words
were interpreted by them for, *Na loisg a whaleid*—
" Don't burn the wallet"—imagining that he appeared
like a wallet while in the sack, and dreading they might
throw him into the fire.

This was answered by "*Cha loisgsinse a whaleid aeh bog-
aidh sinse i*" (We shan't burn the wallet; but we'll soak her.)

This last interpretation brought a fit of laughter from
Munro, who was peeping through a hole at the amusing
scene, and which betrayed his ambush. He soon came
to the unlucky valet's rescue, and saved him from a
thorough ducking, which his gaolers were on the eve of
putting into execution.

On being liberated from his uncomfortable imprison-
ment, Brown gave vent to a storm of abuse and threats
of informing against the smugglers, which, if they
understood, would have inevitably tempted them to put
in force the unpleasant process of ducking him, notwithstanding Munro's intervention. This fact the latter hinted
to the enraged valet, which, for his own safety, silenced
him at once, and order was soon restored between the
belligerents, through the able mediation of the piper.

A copious supply of the different drinkables which
the brews contained was served round, soon changing
the offensive propensities of the parties into that of
cordiality and good fellowship; and to crown the amnesty
and hilarity, Munro played several lively airs on his
pipes, to which the smugglers danced with right good-
will, and pressed Brown to join, in order to make up a
reel of four, the gloomy dell resounding with their merry
exclamations.

Whether it was owing to his heavy potations of drinks
before now strange to him, or that some charm was connected with his wild and novel situation, we cannot say,
the valet never felt himself so elated or prone to uncon-

trolled hilarity. The perspiration streamed down his face with the excitement, and his proficiency in the Highland fling, (under the able tuition of the younger smuggler, or sack inventor, who professed great regard for Brown and who, bye the bye, was a very mischievous person) became every moment more apparent.

Feigning great regard to Brown (entirely for practising his fun on him) the young smuggler, on the plea of wiping the perspiration off the valet's face with his fingers, which were previously drawn round the bottom part of the large copper boiler, where a coating of black had accumulated from the smoke of the peat fire ; and never had an actor, when preparing a character in a burlesque or tragedy, delineated such expansive eyebrows, mustachoes curling up the cheeks, imperials down the chin, and a perpendicular stroke down the length of the nose, as the mischievous smuggler had traced on the handsome and clean-shaven face of Mr. Brown, who now more resembled an Italian bandit than Lord Lundy's valet, butler, and body-servant.

After the dancing, the company proposed a song, and several Gaelic verses were sung by each of the smugglers, who, in their turn, called on Mr. Brown.

A small keg was placed on end at one side of the brews for the accommodation of that gentleman, while the rest ranged themselves immediately opposite, where they were soon treated to a variety of his vocal abilities, and his relish for singing and *wetting his whistle* became more and more apparent as he proceeded, which highly delighted his audience, although the majority of them were ignorant of the meaning of every word that issued from his lips, and we must confess, it would defy better versed people in the English language to make it out, as his tongue had apparently became much thicker; the letter R being entirely banished from his vocabulary, and the V and W having exchanged places.

The singer also had a habit of closing his eyes, to give more pathos to his poetical effusions, and this was accompanied by inclinations of the body forward at the end of each verse.

His mixed potations now began to show themselves,

and Morpheus threatened to close his vocal career, when his voice lowered from its former high key to that of a low cadence resembling the lullaby of a sleepy mother to her restless babe at midnight.

If the smugglers were amused at the comic character before them, there was one tenant of the brows who did not look on the painted face of the singer with the same satisfied air. This was the pet goat.

Stepping up quietly, and taking his position immediately before the sleepy Brown, and taking every inclination of his head for a challenge to himself, the buck now returned each of these salutations by bringing his horns within an inch of the singer's forehead. At length a heavier and lower lurch forward succeeded, when the enraged buck (whose temper was raised to its highest pitch) raised himself on his hind legs in that attitude of antagonism peculiar to them when fighting, and coming down with his formidable horns on the unfortunate valet's head, sent him sprawling on the ground roaring out "am mudered! am mudered!"

The laughing spectators raised up the fallen hero, and found that no serious damage had been done to his cranium (his hat having fortunately broken the force of the assailant's blow), the only visible marks being two bumps on his forehead. This was, however, sufficient warning for the valet to leave a place where he would be liable to receive a repetition of such unwelcome visitations, and a motion for departure was made by himself and Munro. It was not without a great deal of argument that he could be convinced of his real antagonist, or that it was the buck instead of one of the party that had committed the assault.

After quaffing another *cuach* as a *deoch-an-dorais* the pedestrians again commenced their journey homewards. They had not, however, gone far when the shades of evening closed around them, adding to Brown's difficulties, and not only leaving his handsome livery in a sorry plight, but his valuable carcase also, and but for his previous potations and the encouraging effects of the *uisgebea* within him, he would several times have lain down till morning where he fell. Another inducement which cheered him in his perilous and difficult progress, was that Munro intimated that the nearest habitation to them was Mr. McKay's, where the pleasure of seeing Mary Grant and enjoying a jolly evening in her charming company would be a balm to Mr. Brown's present feelings and distresses, and fully compensate for the difficulties encountered in their rough journey.

What surprised the valet more than anything else, was that Munro never met with a single fall, and appeared to travel as steady as in daylight on the king's highway. He therefore concluded that Highlanders could see in the dark like cats or dogs.

On their route (which was a short cut) lay a peat moss where turf was being procured, and unluckily they came across a long but narrow pit, brimfull of water, which stretched across their path. Munro intimated that its breadth was but trifling, and took a short running leap, clearing it at a bound, invited Brown to follow his example. Whether the valet's visionary organs were at fault, or whether he was unable to accomplish the feat, we cannot say, but on taking the leap he fell short a foot and disappeared like a solan goose when diving for fish in the sea. Munro, however, notwithstanding his immoderate fit of merriment, caught the immersed Brown by the hair, and dragged him on *terra firma*, where he stood trembling, jumping and gasping, doubting his own existence.

Mr. McKay's house was at length gained, and Munro conducted his dripping companion to one of the servant's rooms, where he furnished him with a hot cup of toddy and a suit of Highland garb as a change for his wet livery, and which the piper declared would make a complete conquest on the heart of Mary Grant, who was very partial to the costume. This fact the duped valet had evidence of before, and the effects of the last tumbler, which had already the effect of softening his heart towards the fair sex in general, and Mary Grant in particular, he subjected himself to the ordeal of being kilted and *sporraned* by the able hands of Munro; they then adjourned to the servants' hall, where the occupants were ready to receive them to join in a merry reel-

The entrance of Brown, and the ridiculous figure he made in his novel garb, caused a taxation on their gravity which they were hardly able to hide. The unfitting costume, which was apparently made for a far stouter person, hung round his spare frame in a most clumsy manner, reminding them of a *fuathaiche* (a cross-stick, with old clothes on) placed in a field to scare crows. The hose were folded round his spare shanks, and strapped round with the garters as if bandaged by a surgeon after sustaining a fracture.

Brown advanced towards Mary Grant grinning, with his still painted countenance, notwithstanding his sousing, and in a theatrical attitude and low bow, engaged her for a reel, thinking himself quite proficient, after the young smuggler's tuition.

The company's merriment now received an addition through the pranks of a young herd boy, who stuck, unperceived, a bladder full of wind on the valet's back when dancing, and which kept continually bobbing at every movement.

Brown's idea of Highland-fling was to cross his legs as. often as possible and wheel suddenly round. On one of these occasions he had unfortunately crossed them too far, when they did not obey quick enough to time, and his equilibrium being at fault after the toddy, he came down on the broad of his back on the hard flags, bursting the bladder under him, causing a terrific explosion, which shook the very building, followed by his roaring, "'Am shot! 'am shot!" which was as loud as the concussion. On being once more placed on his feet, and convinced that a mine had not sprung under him, his agitation was subdued by the party forming themselves into a half-circle round the fire to finish their evening amusement by singing, Donald Munro at the same time bringing to light a couple of bottles of whiskey, which he had carried from the brews, and which never tasted water. These were converted into strong hot toddy, in a large jug, which went rapidly round, the singers moistening their musical organs, and which diffused lively sensations through their frames. The effect on Mr. Brown was apparent by his gallant attentions to the female portion of the company, more especially Mary Grant, who already manifested extraordinary symptoms of the cure of her love for the Englishman, through the efficacy of Munro's dose. However, to make it more complete, the piper hinted to her that she was not to spurn the valet's advances this evening, in order to carry on the sport. Thus Mary Grant was obliged to succumb, and bear more of the Englishman's now unwelcome attentions.

There was another female among Mr. McKay's domestics who, however, cordially accepted Mr. Brown's gallantry and advances. This was an old maid of some sixty years, of very eccentric notions and disposition. Her name was Mary, also; and to distinguish her from Mary Grant, she was generally called Mary *Mhor*, or Big Mary—although there was not much difference between them in stature—while the latter was called Mary *Veg*, or Little Mary.

Mary *Mhor* still held many youthful and romantic ideas, which had rather increased than diminished with her years, and felt greatly annoyed at attention being paid, in her presence, to young girls by the men. Thus, on seeing the valet's addresses to Mary *Veg*, her jealousy became almost uncontrollable, and brought to bear all her youthful fascinations (which, according to accounts, she had been gifted with a great share of) to charm the English stranger. A hint to Brown from Mary *Veg* helped to facilitate this wish, and the valet's sight being not of the clearest after the toddy, had not noticed Mary *Mhor's* wrinkles or defects, and also under the impression that the old maid had some influence over the young one, or may be an aunt, he resolved on gaining her good-will by paying great attention to her. If Brown, however, had his optics as clear as usual, and in daylight, we question whether his gallantry towards Mary *Mhor* would be carried on with the same zeal.

Her occupation in Mr. McKay's establishment was that of spinning, and her constant vicinity to the heat of the fire dried up her skin (for flesh she had none) into innumerable wrinkles. The toothache had made also a sad havoc among her teeth, leaving but four solitary tusks to tell the woeful tale. Her hair which was once fair, now turned into dirty grey, but was carefully concealed by a close cap and false brown *dosan* or front locks. She was passionately fond of a strong cup of tea, and people whispered that she would not *refuse* a tumbler of toddy.

It was between this person and Mary Grant that Brown had taken his seat in the singing circle, with an arm round the waist of each, and as the songs and toddy went round, the valet's squeezes or hugs became more often and affectionate, but unfortunately not very clear on which side of him the younger or the elder Mary sat; thus conferring the caresses and whispers which he intended for Mary *Veg* on Mary *Mhor*.

Matters went on in this way for some time, until the lights were getting low, and the servants had slipped away one by one to bed, until the whole, with the exception of the comfortable trio, and Munro, were left in their glory.

Another break-up was also made by Mary Grant, who slipped cautiously away on the plea of replenishing the sinking light; but, instead of doing so, she unluckily extinguished it altogether.

Brown made a sad mistake at this time, being under the impression that the elder Mary was the person who got up, and had put out the light (as he hinted to her) in order to give him an opportunity. He therefore turned all his attention and affection on Mary Grant (as he supposed), drawing her yielding form towards him, and returning his embraces, throwing her arms round his neck.

Mr. Brown was now in the height of happiness; gave vent to an eloquent burst of love for his admired Mary, who acknowledged his vehemence by an affectionate squeeze, and some indistinct whispers in Gaelic, which he called *posers*. Old Mary, with the effects of toddy and love for the handsome Englishman, imagined her youthful days had returned, and was now in the height of happiness, although unable to understand a single word of the passionate whispers uttered in her ear. The word *poser*, however, was quiet sufficient, as she thought it related to marriage or *posadh*; and hearing it several times mentioned by Brown, she had no doubt but he was proposing to her, when she answered suddenly, " *Posaidh mi phosus du* " (Marry, of course I'll marry you).

Donald Munro and Mary Grant, who were quietly listening to this amusing dialect behind them, could hardly contain their merriment, until at last Morpheus closed the scene, and the latter couple withdrew from the room, to chat over their own love, and make up for lost time. Mary confessed her own foolishness in ever thinking of Brown, or listening to his nonsense, and vowed never more to be carried away by the flattery or gaudy dress of an English flunkey.

ı Daylight soon warned Donald that it was time to ;eave, but this time with a double kiss at parting, as a guarantee for future constancy.

It was the custom of Bella M'Kay to rise early in the morning, and take a walk, attended by her maid. The latter now, on Donald's departure, went up to her young mistress' room, and found her already dressed.

Passing the servants' hall on their way out, Mary begged of her mistress to enter it for a few seconds, and that she would behold there a picture which she never before saw rivalled. Conscious that none of the servants were up at that early hour, Bella consented to be led by Mary, curious to see the strange picture; and sure enough there, it sat before her, and only for the duet of snoring which issued from the group, she would hardly have believed her eyes.

John Brown, in his misfitting Highland garb, and still carrying strong impressions of the young smuggler's handiwork on his countenance, holding the sunken-eyed and shrivelled form of Mary *Mhor* in his arms, her skinny, yellow hands affectionately wound round his neck, with her hollow cheek supporting his, and their heads leaning back on their chairs, Mary's toothless gums wide apart; keeping up a chorus of snoring which almost drew the coals from the fire. Bella could no longer gaze on this singular picture, then made her exit to give vent to her merriment, on seeing which, Mary gave vent to hers, being unable to control it any longer, and which awoke Brown.

The first object which caught his eyes was the merry countenance of Mary Grant, whom he imagined in his arms, when he turned round his astonished gaze on the form which hung so affectionately in his embrace. What was his horror on beholding, instead of Mary Grant's black ringlets, old Mary's short grey locks, which were now exposed, her cap and false locks being displaced by his own caresses, and hanging at the back of her head.

He sprung to his feet in a fit of rage and disappointment, pitching Mary *Mhor* on the floor, when she gave vent to yells and shrieks, which soon brought one of the servant men to the scene of disaster, and who soon explained the matter.

This man was also an admirer of Mary Grant's, although a discarded lover, and an inveterate rival of his more successful one, Donald Munro.

Having conducted the enraged Brown to his own room, where he returned him his torn livery, and supplied him with water and towel, and also some information which was not very favourable to Donald Munro.

On looking in the glass, and beholding his own painted countenance, Brown's rage knew no bounds, vowing future revenge against the piper, and which were greatly aggravated by the servant's information.

CHAP. VIII.

JOHN LOM'S FAREWELL TO HIS FATHER'S COTTERS.

Little did Bella McKay know the diplomacy and vile calumnies which were carried on by Lord Lundy at the castle in order to poison her father's mind against her lover, and how successfully that unprincipled nobleman had effected his purpose in gaining his end, so far, to separate herself and Charlie Stuart.

Before her father had returned from this secret council, Bella received the following affectionate and cheering epistle from George, her brother :—

"MY DEAR LITTLE SISTER,—Do you know that I am in the highest pitch of ecstacy on hearing the gallant manner in which my neighbour, Charlie Stuart, has eclipsed, or, in cockney parlance, taken the shine out of our proud English aristocratic sportsmen. I have just seen a letter sent by the Honorable Captain Somerville to a friend of his here, and must give the writer credit for the impartial and candid manner in which he has acknowledged the defeat. In short, I was surprised at the eulogy with which he characterised Charlie's excellence in all gentlemanly sports and personal attractions ; nor does it seem, according to the gallant writer's account, that my little sister has made less progress towards feminine charms, as she is set down as the heroine or *belle* of the occasion ; and, moreover, that she was the cause of such rivalry and competition. You little rogue ; who would imagine that my shy and quiet sister would create such sensation among noblemen who are used to the attractions and brilliancy of an English court.

"What makes me more proud of Charlie's triumphs is, to show these English that our countrymen are not the ignorant set they imagine, for you could not believe how they tease me about our national deficiences ; but now I can prove to them that one of our Highland striplings discomfited their noblest and most accomplished sportsmen. With kind love to father, Mr. Stuart, and, above all, to our hero.—Your affectionate Brother, GEORGE."

The happy and pleasant thoughts which the foregoing statements conveyed to Bella's mind were soon clouded on the return of her father from the castle, with a mixture of authority and sternness in his words and manner towards her he had never before shown. He told her it was his intention to leave next morning for London, with Lord Lundy and his retinue, and directed her to prepare herself, as she was to accompany them. Her heart sank within her on hearing this unexpected and unpleasant intelligence. Her pleasant dreams were at once scattered, and the hope of enjoying more happy hours in Charlie Stuart's company gave place to a dread and horror of being subjected to the annoyance and persecutions of Lord Lundy's addresses, as she had no doubt that he had deceived her father by some gross misrepresentations in his own favor.

Her first resolve was to inform Charlie Stuart of this sudden alteration in, and determination of her father ; but even this hope and comfort was denied her, by her maid, Mary, informing her that Mr. McKay had given strict orders to all the servants that none of them were to leave the premises on any consideration whatever.

This mode of communication having been stopped, she turned her attention to another expedient, which had been resorted to by herself and Charlie in order to communicate any intelligence, as they had of late visited each other less frequently. This was done by using a black board, on which was written with chalk a few words; the board was then placed beneath the uplifted window, and by the aid of an eye-glass the messages could be read. Bella, on this evening, opened her window, and introduced the board, with the words "Come over" written upon it; but, alas! she received no answer to her invitation. The opposite window remained closed, and even Donald Munro failed to play his accustomed round of pibroch on the lawn. Heavy gusts of wind came from the direction of Ben Mor, raising clouds of spray on the head of Lochlinn, as if nature herself was wrath at the prospect of losing the flower of Kinlochlinn.

The despairing girl stood at her post until darkness reminded her of her duty. She then went to serve her father with his usual evening beverage. As misfortune would have it, Charlie Stuart and Donald had gone for a sail that day to the islets of Lochlinn, and before they returned a gale of wind blew out of the loch, which prevented their reaching home before dark. Charlie was greatly disappointed at not having his usual telegraphic communication with Bella. He, however, resolved upon being early at his post the next morning.

When the appointed time arrived he took his station at the window, but was surprised at seeing no signs of response to his inquiries. He commanded Donald to play his pibroch, and, as an additional favor, to play the now popular air, "Prince Charlie Salute;" but, alas! this failed, and, to his amazement, he now saw that the window was covered inside with blinds. A terrible suspicion seized him. Fearing that Bella was indisposed, he sent Donald to ascertain the truth.

Mr. Stuart and his son were at breakfast when Donald returned. Charlie, during the meal, had not taken anything, nor did he even give a correct answer to his father's inquiries.

Donald, on his return, entered the room with a mournful countenance, and handed Mr. Stuart a letter,

who, having perused it with surprise, handed it to
Charlie, saying, "What can you make of that?"
Charlie perused it mechanically, when the following
lines met his anxious gaze.

"Mr. Stuart,—Sir,—Being about leaving for London
with my daughter, in company with Lord Lundy and his
suite, his Lordship has directed me to inform your son,
that the liberty he held from the former proprietor to
shoot and fish on this estate, is now suspended—McKay."

Father and son gazed on each other, each looking for
an explanation in the other's countenance. Charlie had
for some time expected his Lordship's restrictions; but,
how could he account for his neighbour's coolness, and
the unmistakable tone of his note. Leaving without even
a hint to those to whom he had always made known his
intended movements, if only leaving for a short journey.

And Bella? What could he think of her? Was
she also influenced by the same ambition as her
father? Leaving without even a word or note for
him. Yes, he thought, Lord Lundy had accomplished his purpose; the worldly McKay and his
beautiful daughter were allured by the wealth
and grandeur of nobility. What a blow to his
hopes! the only being he loved was now to become the
bride of his most inveterate enemy. His father, who
perceived his changing countenance, read the struggle
which was taking place in his noble heart, remarked
mournfully, "I fear our neighbour has been allured by
the display and grandeur of the wealthy Saxon; I
expected as much when our rightful chief had unfortunately, lost his inheritance! Our name is doomed
to be removed from its former exalted position and
eventually take its place among inferior clans!
Fate is against us, and our dearest friends are daily
deserting us."

His father's touching remarks added to the distress of
his mind; the world was nothing to him now, when his
dear Bella was almost in the power of his hated rival
without the aid of his own protection: but what! if she
had become a passive auxiliary to her father's ambition.
Harassed by these thoughts, he sought an interview

with Donald, whom he thought would be able to throw
some light on this extraordinary flitting, but he had too
many distressing thoughts of his own to be able to attend
to his young master's. Mary Grant was now thrown into
the company of the gay and insinuating Brown, without
his presence to remind her of her vows of constancy;
London's attractions, he thought, would obliterate from
her lively mind the rustic and simple customs of her
Highland home and acquaintances.

The only information Charlie could obtain from the
disconsolate Munro was, that the old housekeeper who
gave him the note had told him that, the day before, her
master, on coming from the Castle, held a private interview with his daughter, and that Bella and Mary Grant
were busy preparing for a journey, and, by their tears,
were evidently loath to leave; and, further, that Mr.
M'Kay had ordered that no person was to leave the
premises until after his departure, which took place at
daylight that morning, leaving the note for Mr. Stuart,
and saying that he should be absent for some time.

Charlie, as a last resource, sent Donald to the Post-
Office to see whether any information could be procured
there; but, alas! the only letters there were a few from his
fellow-collegians, who were returning to the University,
and one from his friend John Lom, which brought a
smile to his countenance; and which, with the reader's
permission, we will insert. It ran thus:—

"DEAR PRINCE CHARLIE,—

"My campaign in the Highlands came to a termination
this evening, and a grand finale it was; the enemy were entirely
routed by a display of Popgun's artillery.

"To come to the point at once, I must inform you that I have
been for some time collecting my forces for my farewell to our
Cotters, in the shape of squibs, crackers, blue lights, &c., combus-
tibles which are quite unknown to those people, and excellent
inventions to represent fairy artillery.

"I duly initiated Popgun into the use of these articles, and to
favor my plans, an occurrence took place this morning of which I
took advantage. This was a mound, or, as it is called, a fairy fort,
which is situated in the middle of a field in front of the Cotters'
boothies, and which no one ever ploughed, or cut hay from, for fear
of retaliation from its dreaded occupants. However, on this occasion
its luxuriant crop tempted one of the Cotters, who deprived it of
its coat with his sickle, to which all the others strongly protested,

dreading that all would suffer from the vengeance of the fairies. Many complaints were made to the Governor of the unluckly offender, which were only smiled at, at the same time trying to dissuade them from their superstitious belief ; however, I always found an opportunity to strengthen them in their own fancy at parting. At dark, I proceeded to the scene of action with Popgun, taking an iron pot, a plaibeau, a kind of torch used sometimes in fishing at night, made of dried hay, besmeared with pitch or tar. This was lit and placed inside the pot, which was set on the mound. Popgun, who was dressed for the occasion in a red cap and a green glazed cotton dress, performed grotesque and strange antics in the gloomy and flickering light which escaped now and then from the pot. Indeed, the whole was produced in so perfect a manner, that, had I not been in the secret, my own faith would probably have been shaken. Having taken my station within hearing of the Cotters, what followed amply rewarded my pains. A commotion soon took place, and each boothy door was crammed with terrified spectators (the majority of whom, *of course*, expected such a visitation) giving vent to innumerable imprecations on the head of the unfortunate trespasser. But the best part was yet to come. When the light became nearly exhausted, Popgun, according to instructions, commenced to use the fireworks, which he let off in beautiful style. The result to me was truly gratifying. Women fainted, children screeched, old and young men prayed and moaned while they removed, as they thought, the dead and wounded to their beds.

"I was soon left alone and in my glory, at liberty to retire to my quarters, where I now sit penning my despatches. Early to-morrow morning, before the Governor becomes possessed of an account of my exploits, I shall have set out for Old Reekie, where I expect to meet you forthwith. " JOHN LOM."

Every avenue which could have afforded Charlie Stuart amusement at his home was now closed ; he therefore determined upon returning to the University, to resume his studies with renewed diligence, and drown his afflicting thoughts in the perusal of law books, a profession which his father wished him to follow, as the army held out no favourable prospects.

Charlie himself would have preferred the army, as his friend John Lom was about joining a regiment on his return to Edinburgh, but he had no influential patron to assist him; whereas one Mr. Forbes, an eminent lawyer, and friend of his father, promised to support him in that profession. He therefore took leave of his father, and his faithful servant, who, on this occasion, manifested more than ordinary sorrow at parting with his young master.

CHAPTER IX.

FIGHTING JACK.

Upon his arrival at Edinburgh, Charlie visited Mr. Forbes (or advocate Forbes, as he was more frequently called), the leading and brightest luminary of the Scottish bar, to present his father's credentials. Mr. Forbes had been a widower for several years, and had been married to a sister of the late Mrs. McKay, Bella's mother. Charlie was warmly received by the advocate, who introduced him to his family, which consisted of three grown-up daughters, of very attractive appearance, particularly the youngest, a co-age of her cousin Bella, and who bore a most remarkable likeness to her, the only difference being that Catherine's hair and eyes were a shade lighter, but in other respects, even to her voice and movements, the resemblance was so great that Charlie thought himself in the company of his lost Bella, while listening to the sweet and musical voice of her cousin.

A confidence sprung up between the young couple, which soon increased to love, on the part of Catherine, who, in her simplicity, interpreted the Highlander's partiality to herself to that passion.

Charlie was a little disappointed when, alluding to Bella in their conversation, to find that she had never mentioned his name when Mr. McKay and herself called on their way to London, although a mutual engagement was made between them to keep up a confidential correspondence.

The unintentional impression which Charlie had made upon the heart of Catherine Forbes may be better understood by her first letter to Bella, of which the following is a copy :—

"MY DEAR COUSIN BELLA—Your welcome letter, informing me of your safe arrival, came duly to hand. I little suspected when we parted, and promised each other to communicate our secrets, that I should so soon have one to confess. Yes ; even in the short time which has elapsed your poor simple cousin has literally lost her heart ; and who do you think has been the involuntarily robber ? No other than your handsome (and as he terms himself) your old playfellow, Charles Edward Stuart—what a lovely name !

"You little prude, how is it that you never mentioned that you had such a charming neighbour ? But what puzzles me still more is, that you have not fallen in love with him long ago; but there is no accounting for you Highland girls ; I really believe your cold climate has some influence on your hearts; and besides, you are so close, and never sing your love to the winds like us simple Lowland lassies.

"I never met with a young gentleman to whom I could compare Mr. Stuart ; so kind and unassuming, and yet so noble and manly in his manners. You may think it vanity on my part, when I tell you that I flatter myself that he pays more attention to your humble servant than he does to my more attractive sisters. We often talk of you, and he confirms what others have stated, that we are so much alike. He is studying for the bar, and papa anticipates that he will distinguish himself. How I love papa when he says so. You will perhaps smile at my nonsense ; but when you are pierced with Cupid's dart, like I am, you will be equally silly. How is it that you hate Lord Lundy so ? Such a fine-looking man, and such a splendid match ; but for all that, I don't think I would exchange C. E. S. for him, providing I was sure of becoming Mrs. C. E. S. Your affectionate cousin,

"CATHERINE FORBES."

As Catherine remarked, Bella was indeed too close, or rather too modest to confess her love ; she considered it too sacred to be expressed by human lips, much less to commit it to paper. But what was the state of her feelings on perusing her innocent and unreserved cousin's letter ? Would that she herself had been so confiding, and revealed the state of her heart, which might have prevented her cousin encouraging a hopeless passion. Hopeless, did she say ? What if Catherine's love was returned ? She was afraid to ask herself the question. Whom could she blame, when she had left without giving a hint of her intended departure ? And what would Charlie think of her leaving in company with him who they both hated ? Oh, that she could now explain all, and leave the blame at her father's door. It was now too late ; the die was cast, and she must be the sufferer. Her fair and unreserved cousin would gain the prize which she herself had thought was safely locked in her own bosom. Yes, it must be so, for Charlie could not but return her ingenuous and charming cousin's love, when his old playfellow did not as much as bid him adieu ! She must now bury her disappointment in the gaities around her, and obliterate, in the brilliant assemblies into which she was now being daily introduced, her hopeless and romantic first love.

Vain reasoning: she little dreamt what a sacrifice that course would cost her. She knew not what a deep root her affections had taken, and which ages of such life could not heal. The following reply to her cousin's letter will give some slight idea of her feelings:—

"MY DEAR CATHERINE,—Your welcome and interesting letter is now before me. It gives me great pleasure to know that you have made me the confidant of your first love, and I must thus early state that the object is well deserving.

"You wonder that I did not mention Mr. Stuart in our conversation, but I can assure you it was not through any want of appreciation of his many qualities that I omitted to mention him ; for, to use your own words I have never, nor do I, expect to meet with any gentleman equal to him in all that is good and noble. I am now surrounded by the most exalted and fashionable gentlemen which England can produce, but I would rather have one moment of that innocent and rural amusement passed in the company of Charlie Stuart, in our Highland home, than pass a lifetime surrounded by the gaities and festivities of London society. But, alas! such happy times I fear will ne'er return. However, I have one consolation, that that happiness which is denied me, is reserved for my more fortunate and charming cousin.

"You are surprised at my indifference to Lord Lundy's addresses. I will just put a question to you which will at once explain the reason. Could you accept any man, however exalted, if you did not feel for him that attachment which you now entertain for Charlie Stuart ? Your affectionate cousin,

"B. M'KAY."

Catherine Forbes was too much taken up with her own love to detect the indirect hints given in the letter, although a sharper and more experienced eye could easily see and understand such sentiments. However, she was 'cute enough to keep all the contents from her supposed lover, Charlie Stuart; not through any jealousy, but rather a shade of selfishness, in order that she might monopolise all his thoughts.

Thus they carried on their correspondence without Bella ever clearing up the cause of her despondency; and Catherine grew more poetical in her praises of Charles, enumerating with wonderful preciseness all his little attentions towards her, which added so much to Bella's dejection that her communications flagged, and eventually entirely ceased.

Bella was strictly true in her remarks on the fashionable and gay company with which she daily mixed; for never had a girl in her station, and at her age, had the same advantageous and brilliant career before them. A doating and wealthy Uncle, without any family upon whom he could bestow his affections; a handsome and affectionate brother, who now held a commission under Captain Somerville, in the Guards, through the influence of Lord Lundy, and who had introduced her and her relations into the highest circles.

Yet, with all these brilliant prospects before her, Bella was not happy; the only pleasure she had was in the solitude of her own chamber,—with her maid, indulging in fond remembrances of the many happy hours passed in the company of Charlie Stuart.

Her father left London after a short stay, leaving his fond, but unhappy, daughter, with her Uncle for the term of two years, at the expiration of which she was to become the bride of Lord Lundy.

Charlie having now become a constant and favourite visitor at the Forbes's, was considered almost a member of the family by all, particularly Catherine, with whom he always held a long conversation. Bella McKay's silence was attributed by the young couple to high notions which she had cultivated through mixing with the aristocracy; and, above all, the prospect of an exalted connection.

Among the visitors at the Forbes's was a Captain Campbell, belonging to one of the Highland regiments at that time stationed at the Castle. The Captain was a specimen of those jolly Highland officers whose only fault, if fault it can be called, was in indulging (particularly over his whisky toddy) in a little bombast, extolling the feats and bravery of his own clan. This harmless bravado was often brought to an amusing termination by our old acquaintance, John Lom, who had lately joined the same regiment, introducing the Battle of Inverlochy, where the Campbells suffered an ignominious defeat at the hands of the McDonalds, and other clans under Montrose. The account, as rendered by the mischievous Ensign, always set the company in roars of

laughter, in which the Captain himself was obliged to
join, after which he became greatly attached to his
young tormentor.   The Captain, who was a bachelor,
paid marked attention to the older Miss Forbes, by
which means he and Charlie became great cronies,
which not a little annoyed John Lom, who had not been
introduced by either to the family.   This dog-in-the-
manger conduct, as John Lom called it, proceeded from
the Captain's fearing the rivalship of the handsome
Ensign if once presented to the Forbes's.

One evening, while the three friends were discussing a tumbler of hot punch, Charlie gave the
officers an amusing account of an old and eccentric
uncle of the Forbes's, whom he once saw at Mr.
McKay's.   This strange person had been a captain in
the Company's service in India, where he had accumulated a large fortune, and where he also obtained the
name of being the greatest duellist and most certain
shot in that part.   His name was John McDonald, and
was known by the sobriquet "Fighting Jack."   Charlie
was told that he had never visited the Forbes's, neither
had the advocate ever seen him; the only time he visited
Scotland was when Charlie saw him at Mr. McKay's,
and, although the speaker was then very young,
"Fighting Jack's" appearance was still fresh in his
memory, and which he minutely described to his hearers.

Captain Campbell was highly delighted with Charlie's
news, and hoped that he might some day meet with this
wealthy relation, and be induced to bestow a slice of his
riches on Miss Forbes, the Captain's intended.

The conversation now turned upon a private ball,
which was to be given next evening, in honor of Miss
Forbes having attained her twentieth birthday.   The
Captain was in ecstacies; being, as he thought, the leading and greatest favorite, that he would hold the highest
position on the occasion, and commenced as usual to
twitt the disappointed Ensign for not being on the same
intimate footing as himself and Charlie.   At this teasing,
John Lom offered to lay a wager that he would go to
the ball uninvited, be more hospitably received than
any one there by the host, kiss the daughters, and get

Captain Campbell in a rage. This bravado was first considered by the Captain and Charlie as mere bounce, produced by disappointment and irratibility; but, on seeing John thoroughly bent upon the wager, the Captain took it up—the one laying his best horse against the other's. These conditions being settled, the party, after partaking of another tumbler, separated, the Captain and Charlie to meet next evening at the ball.

A select assembly congregated at the Advocate's on the appointed evening; Captain Campbell, who appeared in full regimentals, led the dance, with the heroine of the evening: all the party were in the height of enjoyment. In the first pause in the dance, and as the gallant Captain was conducting his partner to her seat, a servant entered the room with a small note for the host, who, upon reading it, sprung up somewhat agitated, and passed the letter to his daughter, saying, "I suppose you will understand who the writer of that is." Miss Forbes showed the note to the Captain, which ran as follows:—

"MY DEAR BROTHER-IN-LAW,—You will be rather surprised at the unexpected arrival of one whom you never saw. I have just arrived, and on inquiry I heard that you are having a little jollification with your friends, which I hope my presence will not interrupt, unless they wish to have a turn up with

"FIGHTING JACK."

Captain Campbell was greatly delighted when he found that the writer was the eccentric Captain John M'Donald, whom Charlie had described the previous evening.

The Advocate and his daughters smiled, and were consulting as to the best mode of receiving their wealthy Uncle, who might possibly improve their circumstances by leaving a portion of his wealth to them, if they should be fortunate enough to make a favorable impression.

They were not allowed much time for their deliberations, for the servant at the door called out "Captain John M'Donald, of the East India Company's Service," when a tall, gaunt, straight old gentleman, with long white hair, green spectacles, or goggles, shaven yellow face, black clothes, and a gold-headed cane, stalked into the room.

Mr Forbes met him, and with a hearty shake of both hands, gave the stranger a warm reception, expressing the great satisfaction he felt in receiving a visit from his gallant and brave brother-in-law. "Ha! so you are glad to see Fighting Jack, are you? But where are my charming nieces, of whom I have heard so much?—I am longing to embrace them."

The subjects of these flattering remarks were standing behind their father, whispering and blushing on hearing the anxiety he felt to embrace them, being not a little embarrassed through having to be embraced before a roomful of guests. However, as there was a great stake in the case, they endeavoured to make a favorable impression on the nabob; and therefore advanced, each in succession, saluting "Fighting Jack" with a kiss.

Mr. Forbes introduced him to several of the company, and was most particular in introducing him to Captain Campbell, who appeared extremely happy in making the Indian officer's acquaintance, for special reasons, and seemed resolved to monopolise his company during the evening.

As Captain Jack seemed careless about dancing, a select few formed themselves into a group around him in another part of the room, for the purpose of having a Gaelic song, which the new-comer proposed and appeared very partial to, there being several of the party conversant with that language, among whom were the advocate and his daughters, Captain Campbell, Charlie, and a few others. A circle was accordingly formed, and handkerchiefs stretched between them in true Highland fashion, in order to keep up the chorus. Captain Jack proposed to give them a favourite song of his own, to commence with, to the great delight of Captain Campbell, who took a seat beside him, with the elder Miss Forbes on the other side.

After a few preliminary coughs, to clear his voice, Captain Jack commenced, in a key which would defy the most powerful and youthful lungs in the company to compete with; but, horror of horrors! what was their consternation, especially the Forbes', on hearing, in Capt. Jack's favourite song. the forbidden and dreaded satire to the Campbells, "The Battle of Inverlochy," composed by that memorable bard, John Lom, in which the signal and ignominious defeat of the Campbells is set forth in language unparalleled. Those of my readers who have heard or read the song can well imagine the consternation which prevailed on hearing the verses sung in the presence of Captain Campbell, who was very touchy on clannish matters, more particularly when they were alluded to in the presence of his intended bride. It was in vain they coughed, and then hinted to the unguarded singer the great mistake he had made; for the louder they coughed the louder Fighting Jack roared out the dreaded satire, abusing the choristers for their want of etiquette in not supporting him in such a popular ballad.

The thunderstricken and enraged Campbell managed to curb his wrath, on pecuniary grounds. He broke out, however, when he heard the words, "*Ma dhith iad cal chuir sibh asd e*," and sprang up, declaring that he would not listen to such language from his own father. An awkward confusion took place, during which Fighting Jack stood up and confronted the enraged Campbell, coolly informing him, that if he was in the least degree annoyed, he, Fighting Jack, would give him ample satisfaction the following morning, at any time and place he chose; then, picking up his hat and cane, he strutted out of the room, leaving the spectators speechless, not knowing how to act.

Captain Campbell held duelling in great dread, and having heard of the invincibility of Fighting Jack in that art, wished he had bore the dreaded satire sooner than be made a target for his adversary's bullets.

The company were not allowed much time to meditate on the best means of restoring peace between the belligerents, when a servant entered with a note to Campbell, which in the present state of his mind he was unable to peruse with becoming steadiness; he therefore handed it to Charlie, who was near him, being almost positive of its contents—feeling certain that it was a challenge from Fighting Jack.

Charlie, at the request of the company, read aloud the following lines :—

"I have been the most hospitably received guest this evening; have kissed the daughters, and got the Captain in a rage, according to the wager. JOHN LOM."

The duped Campbell now vowed vengeance on the devoted head of the mischievous Ensign, who had so successfully won his best horse, and had played such a trick on the host and his daughters.

The Advocate felt annoyed at the part he and his daughters had been compelled so conspicuously to act, but considering the wager, and the account given by several of the company of the character of the perpetrator, he became more pacified in his intentions towards him, ultimately treating the affair as an excellent joke, in which the Captain joined.

Miss Forbes and Catherine felt rather annoyed and ashamed when they considered the freedom to which they had been subjected by the Ensign's tricks. Not so Matilda, the second daughter, who was of a lively temperament, and a great admirer of bold and daring feats performed by young men. Her love of novelty and fun made her coincide with the perpetrator of the trick, who so successfully passed himself off as her own eccentric uncle; and hearing from Charlie the mischievous propensities of his friend, she had a great wish to be introduced to him.

Nor were John's impressions regarding the lively Matilda less favourable, judging from what he told Charlie the next day, when speaking on the subject, and in his own poetical terms replied to Charlie's question as to what he thought of the Misses Forbes:—"For all the stateliness and elegance of Miss Forbes, the bewitching simplicity of your adorable Catherine, give me the lively and witty Matilda; a sort of lurking mischief flashes from her sparkling eyes, which has produced an echo in my heart, that whispers—'John, that's your prize; if you gain possession of her you will be able to surmount any obstacle, however daring.' Yes, Charlie, I surrender myself as her prisoner."

It cannot be a matter of surprise that these inventive and lively minds soon found means, through Charlie's mediation, of making each other's acquaintance, which soon ripened into love, although John had not sufficient courage to encounter the advocate at his own residence, not being positive that he had quite forgiven the trick which had been played upon him.

CHAPTER X.

MADAMOISELLE DUPONT.

CAPTAIN CAMPBELL was not at all sorry that the mischievous Ensign had raised a barrier to his introduction to the family, and thus saved himself any apprehension of being ousted from the affections of Miss Forbes, never dreaming that John's affections were already fixed upon another of the young ladies. Another objection the Captain had to the acquaintance was the dread of being exposed, through the witticisms of John Lom, in the presence of the ladies.

Some days after the ball, the Captain again began to twit the Ensign upon the obstacle he himself had made to his introduction to the family, and set forth in glowing terms the favourable footing he had among them, stating that he had been commissioned to select a French lady to instruct the Misses Forbes in that language, and that he had advertised for one.

The Ensign, who had patiently borne with all the Captain's teazing while listening to his braggadocia, at last proposed, to the Captain's as well as Charlie's surprise, to renew the wager—that he would a second time introduce himself to the company and dupe the Captain again. This was eagerly snapped at by the Captain, in order to recover his favorite charger, for to deceive him a second time was, in his opinion, an impossibility. Thus the three passed the time pleasantly, and Charlie's disappointment was greatly relieved by the pleasant company in which he daily mixed.

A case of considerable importance came before the courts of law at this time, in which Advocate Forbes was engaged, which occupied a great deal of time for several days. This was a favourable opportunity for the

Captain and Charlie to spend some pleasant hours in the company of the daughters, and of which they took advantage.

On one of these evenings a servant entered the room where the happy company were conversing, with the intelligence that a French lady, giving the name of Madamoiselle Dupont, wished to have an interview with her. "Ha!" exclaimed the Captain, "that is in answer to my advertisement; for mercy's sake, Miss Forbes, admit *Parlez-vous*." This was the sum total of his knowledge of French, and never having been in the company of the ladies of the neighboring kingdom, he was most anxious that she should be introduced. The servant was instructed by Miss Forbes to show the lady in, when the company were soon treated to a sight which was far from their ideas of the appearance of a French lady.

A tall, shapeless lady dressed in black silk, a shawl and bonnet, with a long pale visage adorned with a pair of spectacles, and encircled by a thickly bordered cap, stood before them. On entering she made a low curtsey, and commenced speaking in broken English with great volubility, stating her proficiency in the instruction of her native language, mentioning many families in which she had held the appointment of governess.

Miss Forbes was quite at a loss how to answer this uncouth-looking person, but said that as Mr. Forbes was engaged that evening, she would thank her to call again.

The gallant Captain, not wishing to let the opportunity slip of drawing *Parlez-vous* out, engaged her in conversation, entering into a lively chat for the amusement of the company. A hint from Matilda, inviting her into another room to remove her bonnet and shawl, put a stop to their conversation. In the absence of the stranger and Matilda, Miss Forbes seated herself at the piano, and played several favourite strathspeys of the Captain's, on hearing which he could not resist giving a few turns by himself. While engaged in the lively exercise of dancing his favourite Highland fling, he was joined by Madll. Dupont as partner, who suddenly shot into the room and imitated every step and turn. The figure the two presented at this moment, was highly comical. The Captain, in order to carry on the sport, wheeled round with great velocity, vociferating "Well done, *Parlez-vous!* Another turn! On you go!" &c., &c.

The Frenchwoman, who was not to be outdone, wheeled at every turn of the Captain's, holding her hands over head, cracking her fingers, and whisked one leg across the other, which caused a flapping sound from her silk dress. Miss Forbes' back being towards the dancers, she did not observe the unfeminine exhibition which Madll. Dupont made of herself.

Charlie and Catherine took refuge outside the door to give vent to their merriment, the latter being somewhat shocked at the scene. Not so Matilda, for she appeared to enjoy the fun amazingly. Miss Forbes at last looked over her shoulder, which instantly put an end to the music and dancing, her gravity not being proof against such an amusing scene, when the Captain, in streams of perspiration, and quite out of breath, staggered with his partner to the sofa, where they took a seat in good humor, and held a confidential chat for some time.

On expressing her wish to depart, Captain Campbell prevailed upon her to give him her address, promising to call upon her, engaging at the same time not to read it until she had left; upon which she slipped her card into his hand and wished them good evening, but before quitting the house spent another few minutes with Matilda when getting her bonnet and shawl. When she was clear off, the Captain flung himself on the sofa, and gave vent to his pent-up merriment; but thinking of the card, he took it from his pocket, and read the following to the company:—

"Ensign John McDonald, Royal Highlanders,
Edinburgh Castle."

Charlie Stuart had now passed two years at the University since his return from the Highlands, and during that time he had made wonderful progress in his studies, so much so that he was admitted as an advocate, the first at his age attaining that high position. This was owing to his close application to the study of his profession, his quickness in mastering any subject he set

D

his mind upon, and, through the patronage of his friend Mr. Forbes, who took great interest in his advancement.

During this long interval he never visited his home, and seldom ever hearing the name of his never-to-be-forgotten Bella mentioned. The following article in a London paper destroyed all his hopes of again seeing her, but as the wife of another :—" On dit.—Marriage in high life. It is currently reported in high circles that Lord Lundy, upon his attaining his majority, which will be in a short time, will lead to the altar the beautiful Miss McKay ; or, as she is commonly called, the 'Highland Beauty,' and that the happy pair will then visit the Highlands, and pass the season there."

Bella McKay was no less surprised on reading a similar article in an Edinburgh paper, regarding her former lover, Charlie Stuart, shortly after his admission to the Scotch bar, and which destroyed her last hopes of happiness on earth. The article in question was as follows :—" A case of considerable interest came before our High Court of Justiciary, and which is fully inserted in another column, in which two of our young advocates figured, one as counsel for the pursuer, and the other as defender in his own case. What gives it more interest is that both are reported to be rivals to the hand of a beautiful daughter of a leading member of the bar, and, according to accounts, the issue of the case will decide the claim to the fair prize. We must, therefore, congratulate the young advocate, who so ably and successfully carried the day, not only for the valuable and well-earned laurels, but also in exposing the profligacy of the defender, whose expulsion from the respectable profession by the Lord Chief Justice was a just retribution. We trust that all lovers of honour will join us in complimenting the successful advocate, who made such a brilliant *debut* on his entrance into public life. We have also heard from good authority that he will shortly present his lady love at the shrine of Hymen, and afterwards take a tour with his young bride during the honeymoon, among his native Highland hills."

The action which brought the above comment in the public journals, had created a great noise and gossip in

Edinburgh, as it involved the future prospects of the defendant, and the innocence of the much injured plaintiff, whose cause the chivalric and honourable Charlie Stuart pleaded so boldly and effectually.

Mr. Melrose, the defendant, who was a promising young man, of respectable parents in Perth, and a fellow student of Charlie's, though two years his senior, was admitted to the Bar at the same time.

His father was on intimate terms with Advocate Forbes, who promised to aid young Melrose, if he proved himself worthy, in his future career at the Bar.

The young man was gifted with many brilliant qualities, and an attractive person, but, unfortunately, given to profligate habits in his private life.

Through Mr. Forbes extending to him his hospitality, as well as his patronage, he became a constant visitor, and frequently met with Catherine, whose warm and affectionate heart showed great kindness to her father's friend, until Charlie made her acquaintance, on whom she placed all her affections, and deprived the disappointed and enraged Melrose of all his fond hopes.

Catherine, never suspecting Melrose's passion towards her, only viewed him in the light of a friend; but, on perceiving Charlie's many amiable and excellent qualities, her heart became at once an unconscious captive, and withdrew the little favour it extended towards the discarded Melrose.

Charlie, who well knew Melrose's profligate habits in private life, and seeing his pretended modesty couched with a pleasing address before the unsuspecting ladies. His own honorable and straightforward principles, propelled by an intense dislike to young men indulging in loose habits, could not suffer such deception on the part of Melrose; we may expect that any degree of harmony could not exist between the newly admitted advocates.

Melrose maintained a deadly revenge against his more favoured rival, whose unblemished character could not, however, give him an opportunity of undermining his reputation in the estimation of Catherine Forbes, until a certain event transpired, on which he thought of building a charge which would be prejudicial to Charlie. Knowing

Catherine's abhorrence of young men possessing the slightest looseness in their habits. One day while holding a confidential conversation with her, they happened to refer to Charlie Stuart, when she, as usual, extolled his unblemished character, and held him forth as a pattern for all young men, both in morality and personal attraction.

This panegyric exasperated the jealous Melrose, who answered her with a malicious smile, which meant that she was ignorant of the young man's private habits, and did she but know as much as he did, she would change her opinion; for instance, he told her that not later than the day before he saw Charlie holding a long conversation with a Highland girl, of very questionable character, in the street. This information at first startled her; but, concluding that Melrose might be mistaken in the character of the girl, she told Charlie, on their meeting, of Melrose's insinuations. Charlie, although long anticipating some antagonism from Melrose, was not ready for such a malicious and unfounded charge; however, on bringing to mind the person with whom he was conversing in the street, a new light flashed through his mind. He therefore told Catherine that the young girl with whom he was conversing was not a doubtful character, but a much-injured creature, whose misfortunes Catherine and the public at large would be soon made acquainted with, although he would refrain from mentioning any more at present concerning her.

The cause of Melrose's unjustifiable remarks can be gathered from the following:—

It transpired about this time that some profligate students, headed by Melrose, had taken a small house in one of the bye-lanes, and placed a sign over the door with the words "Mangling done here"; here the customers, who were mostly servants, were subjected to many insults.

One of these, a girl named Jane Sutherland, being acquainted with Charlie's family, and hearing that Charlie had been admitted to the Bar, called upon him and made him acquainted with the whole of the circumstances of the case, upon which Charlie, accompanied by the girl, called upon Melrose at his chambers, when she instantly recognised him as the man who had insulted her; Charlie immediately served him with notice of action. The case created great excitement. Charlie in this his maiden effort, showed that he was possessed of considerable talent, and in a most eloquent and manly speech pleaded the cause of his client. The defendant considerably damaged his own case by the gross insinuations he cast upon Charlie's character, which brought upon himself the disapprobation of the whole Court. The jury, however, returned an instantaneous and unanimous verdict for the plaintiff, with the full amount of the damages asked. The Lord Chief-Justice, in giving his concurrence to the verdict, told the defendant that he should order his name to be removed from the rolls of that honourable court, no longer allowing him an opportunity of disgracing an honourable profession of which he might have been a great ornament.

After this successful action, in which Charlie acquitted himself so nobly, briefs were entrusted to him from all quarters, and his chambers were constantly being visited by fresh clients. His manly and upright principles had gained for him the esteem and goodwill of all grades of society; but alas! these bright prospects were not destined to be of long duration, for one day he received the mournful intelligence from his servant Donald that his father had been taken seriously ill, and was not likely to recover. The writer went on to state that the letter was written without the sanction of Mr. Stuart, as he still entertained hopes of his recovery, and did not wish to interfere with Charlie's many engagements by sending for him, or even informing him of his illness. Upon receipt of the letter, Charlie made every arrangement for a speedy journey to the Highlands, entrusting the whole of his business to the care of Mr. Forbes.

CHAPTER XI.

A JOYFUL SURPRISE.

Having arrived safely at Kinlochlinn, Charlie, with a heavy heart and anxious mind approached his father's house, when seeing no one about and the blind in his

father's room drawn down, misgivings crept through his
mind; he entered the house and walked quietly up stairs
to his own room, the door of which he found partly open,
and which joined that of his father's.

Entering cautiously for fear of disturbing his father,
a sight met his gaze which compelled him to halt at the
entrance. Before the mirror stood a lady arranging her
hair. Standing spell-bound with the handle of the door
in his hand, he wondered who it could be that had taken
the liberty of using his room; the object of his contem-
plation stood still for an instant, then turned suddenly
round with a half scream, and Bella McKay and Charlie
stood face to face.

Notwithstanding the changes which two years had
made on them, the recognition was instantaneous on
both sides, and the names "Charlie" and "Bella"
escaped unconsciously from their lips at the same
moment. A visible change had taken place in both, but
it was an undeniable improvement. Bella had now
become a tall, handsomely-formed lady; her hair had
taken a darker shade, and a stateliness was perceptible
in all her movements, which struck the young Advocate
with wonder and admiration.

Charlie's looks and manners made a no less favourable
impression on Bella; his former fresh colour had given
place to a slight paleness, his fine high forehead was
stamped by the effects of hard study; this, with a slight
beard, which encircled his chin, gave him a more manly
appearance.

He was somewhat altered in form and stature, and
was dressed in black, which added to his appearance.

After looking at each other for a short time in silence
and confusion, they both adjourned to the sitting-room,
each taking a seat at separate windows. An unpleasant
pause now took place, Charlie finding himself in the
company of his former love, but now, he thought Lady
Lundy; and Bella in the presence of her former love,
but now, as she believed, her cousin's husband.

Bella was the first to break the silence, by asking
whether he was accompanied by Mrs. Stuart, her face
being turned towards the lawn while she spoke, and

her voice being husky and tremulous. Charlie, thinking he had misunderstood the question, replied, "I beg your Ladyship's pardon, I believe I have not heard you correctly, or whether you asked if some Mrs. Stuart accompanied me." Bella turned her streaming eyes upon him, half doubting and half believing her ears, and earnestly enquired whether he was really married to her cousin Catherine. The young Advocate at once satisfied her that he had not yet had that fortune, but in return asked his interrogator whether her noble husband, Lord Lundy, was at the castle. It was now Bella's turn to be surprised, and replied that she never had, or wished to have, the honour of receiving that title.

We will not attempt to describe the happy meeting of the restored lovers, but rather draw a veil over the joyful scene which ensued—the many explanations, the jealousies they suffered, the anxieties of mind, and lastly, the despairing state of their feelings on seeing the articles in the newspapers which extinguished their hopes and crowned their miseries. Solemn vows of constancy were exchanged between them, that no earthly power should in future interrupt the smooth current of their love.

Charlie was, however, sorry for the unintentional impression he had made on the heart of Catherine Forbes, through his partiality to her, on account of her being so like her cousin; and Bella was now made fully confident of her lover's faithfulness by his regard for her cousin, through the resemblance that existed between them. Such was the substance of their joyful union, as they sat side by side on a sofa, Charlie with one arm round Bella's tapering waist, with his other hand imprisoned in her delicate hands, drinking draughts of love from each other's eyes.

Bella related to her lover without reserve, and for the first time, her long and undenying love for him; how her father through the flattery of Lord Lundy, carried her away against her will to London; how his Lordship persecuted her while there with his addresses, particularly when he attained his majority, demanding her as his bride, after gaining her uncle's intercession, which com-

pelled her to leave at once and seek her father's protection, at whose feet she flung herself, entreating his sympathy in her behalf. When her father wished to
know the cause of her objections to Lord Lundy, she
gave as an excuse that she had no inclination to change
her state, at least for some years to come; and through
her tears and supplications he promised his intercession.

On hearing of Mr. Stuart's illness she obtained leave
of her father to visit and attend on him. The day before,
on finding himself getting worse, he consented to send
for his son, and that day she came over earlier than
usual, in order to write the letter, as Mr. Stuart was
unable to do so.

On hearing that Mr. Stuart was asleep, she entered
Charlie's room, laid aside her bonnet and shawl, and
arranged her hair. While doing so, her mind was taken
up with the letter she was to write to her former lover,
but now another's. At that instant the object of her
thoughts appeared before her in the glass, and, not knowing whether it was the influence of her imagination or
his spirit, she gave the scream.

How long the lovers remained in fond communion, or
how the time swept over their heads, they knew not,
until the housekeeper entered with a mournful countenance, intimating that Mr. Stuart had awoke from a
troublesome sleep, and, apparently much weaker, had
inquired whether Bella had arrived.

The lovers' happiness was soon clouded by this mournful intelligence, and Bella instantly sprung up and
entreated Charlie not to enter his father's room until
she had prepared the invalid for the meeting. On entering the chamber, Bella perceived at a glance the truth
of the housekeeper's remarks; a visible change for the
worse had taken place in his looks and voice. On approaching the bedside, he said feebly—"My dear girl, I
fear it is too late now to send for my poor boy; something tells me that my hours are but few in this world,
and that I shall never see him again."

"Have better hopes, dear friend, you will see your
son yet, I hope; what if I were to bring him to you
before night," replied Bella, cheeringly.

"You are indeed my guardian angel, but I fear that that is beyond your power," replied Mr. Stuart, despondingly.

"We will see," added Bella encouragingly; then opened the door, and the impatient son rushed into his father's arms.

The scene which took place between father and son was most affecting, and Bella had to leave the room to hide her tears. The fond and affectionate son was overwhelmed at the ravages the short illness had committed on that once noble form, who could now hardly return the warm embrace of his devoted son.

The invalid, in a feeble and impressive voice, called the young couple to his bedside, then told Charlie of the indefatigable attention that Bella had paid him since her arrival, and now as his last hour was fast approaching, he felt himself in duty bound to reveal certain facts which preyed on his mind, in order to release himself from his share of the obligations which they imposed upon him, and which he always considered sacred and binding on a Christian and man of honour.

He then directed his son to open a private drawer in his escritoire, and to bring from thence some papers which he was to read aloud.

The first of these was a cold and formal notice from Mr. McKay, as Lord Lundy's factor, stating that nobleman's intentions not to renew Mr. Stuart's lease, which would expire on first Martinmas.

After the reading of this document, the young lovers looked at each other in amazement and despair; but the contents of the other two overwhelmed them, one of which was as follows, and was addressed also to Mr. Stuart:—

"I believe a certain rash and inconsiderate agreement was entered into between us at the birth of our children, that when they became of age, and with their own consent, they should be united in marriage. Now, as this was only in conformity with certain absurd and ancient customs, and quite at variance with our modern and more enlightened forms of contracting marriages, I hope you will view it in that light, viz., a piece of romantic folly and invalid, imposing despotic and arbitrary restrictions upon innocent and involuntary young people, especially since my daughter has better prospects in view.   McKAY."

The third, and last document, was a valid contract of

marriage executed, between the neighbours, duly signed
and attested according to the substance of the above
note, that Charlie and Bella should become man and wife
on attaining their majority.

A blush of happiness o'erspread their countenances
for a moment, but this was soon clouded by a sense of
despair, on recollecting the objections to the conditions
by one of the party, Mr. McKay.

Mr. Stuart at once interpreted their thoughts, and
the anguish depicted in their countenances; with a
resigned and affecting tone, he said, that considering
himself in honour bound to express his own feelings
regarding the contract, he would therefore unreservedly
state, that he always concurred with its sentiments, and
never for one moment had he altered his mind regarding
it, provided the young couple themselves were agreeable.
This brought them at once, hand in hand, on their knees
at the bedside, seeking his blessing on their vows of constancy, which they would maintain until death, whatever
obstacles were thrown in their way.

Mr. Stuart was greatly moved at these solemn protestations; then placing his hands on their heads, evoked
the blessing of heaven on their vows, and concluded his
share of the responsibility which the contract imposed
on him, by giving his full consent.

His voice by degrees became inaudible, and the hands
which were placed on their heads became heavy.

Bella at length raised her eyes, and whispered to
Charlie—"He sleeps."

Charlie removed the hand gently from his own head,
which he found cold, when the awful truth at once
flashed upon his mind—his noble soul had taken its flight
to another sphere!

Great was the grief manifested in all parts of the
country at the decease of the generous and amiable
Mr. Stuart. A solemn and large procession followed his
remains to their last resting place.

An incident took place on this mournful occasion which
filled many with admiration and surprise, and which
proved the veneration in which the deceased gentleman
was held by his domestics.

Old Munro, who served all his lifetime in the employ
of the Stuarts as piper, and other useful situations, had
not for some time played except on special occasions, as
his son was now grown up and able to relieve his father
from that task, and was equally proficient, through his
tuition, and the McKay's, the king of pipers.

On this day, however, old Munro struck up his large
pipes to the surprise of all, particularly his own son, and
played as of yore at the head of the procession, beside
his son, keeping pace to the step, and each note of the
mournful wail—"The Lament of the Dead."

The distance to the churchyard was something considerable, and only fit for younger lungs, such as Donald's,
to keep up the strain.   Donald often cast a glance at the
old veteran, expecting every moment to see him drop
under the severe performance, but he was mistaken; the
old piper, as if animated by some spiritual power, with a
firm step, never missed the slightest note, or ceased the
thrilling strain until the remains were placed in their
narrow home.   Then, with heroic animation, he took his
old favourite instrument, which had often swelled the
heart of many a Highlander, and smashed it into atoms
against one of the gravestones, exclaiming in Gaelic—
"*Gu la bhrath cha chlinun mae mather fuuim mo mheur
a'd dheigh.*"   ("Never more shall a mother's son hear
the notes of my fingers after thee.")   This was but too
true, for the faithful old piper had so strained his lungs
that a rapid consumption supervened which carried him
to his grave, and he was shortly afterwards laid near his
old master in Killinn churchyard.

CHAPTER XII.

After the foregoing melancholy occurrence, Charlie
and Bella did not meet, as McKay kept strict watch
upon them.   The term of the lease, or Martinmas, was
drawing nigh, when he would be obliged to give up his
ancestral home, and relinquish for ever his claims to
Kinlochlinn, where he had spent so many happy days,

and first breathed his mountain air. His source of
recreation was now limited to his boat, and visiting the
Islets of Lochlinn to shoot sea-fowl. On one of these
trips, attended by Donald, they sailed close by McKay's
side of the estuary, and to their great joy beheld Bella
McKay and Mary Grant on one of their charitable
excursions, going to visit a lonely woman, who lived in a
small boothie by the sea-side, whose name was Ni Ruari
(or Rodrick's Daughter).

This poor creature had never extended her acquaintance
further than the immediate neighbourhood of Lochlinn,
and was therefore ignorant of many habits, customs, and
other modern subjects; as an illustration of her want
of knowledge, we will give one instance of her pecu-
liarities.

One shooting season, in the absence of the laird, a
Colonel Robertson took up his quarters at the Castle.
Being a Lowlander, and partial to the good things of
this life, he invariably replenished his table with many
delicacies which were procured in those parts at a very
moderate rate, such as fowls, eggs, &c. Ni Ruari,
having heard from a neighbour the excellent market
which presented itself at the Castle for their surplus
fowls and eggs, resolved to benefit by the opportunity,
and started to the Castle with a pair of fowls and a
dozen eggs, with the proceeds of which she intended to
procure some tea, to which she was extremely partial.

On approaching the Castle she was encountered by
an enormous turkey cock, which was the terror of all
females, particularly those wearing any article of red,
and as Ni Ruari had unfortunately enveloped herself in
her long laid-up red tartan cloak, she became an object
for the bird's wrath.

He accordingly arrested her progress by strutting
before her on the path with his bristling plumage, large
scarlet appendages of comb over his beak and breast,
giving utterance to that gobbling sound peculiar to them.
Turkeys being very scarce in those parts, except about
gentlemen's houses, and as Ni Ruari had never in her
life seen or heard of the like, concluded at once it must
be the Corineal (Colonel) of whose person she was as

ignorant as the bird before her, his strange gobbling or language she believed to be broad Scotch.

Making a low curtsey, she exhibited her fowls and eggs, remarking with great humility, in Gaelic, "*Coilleach as ceare ler cead a Choirneil.*" "*Dusan ubh ler cead a Choirneil.*" ("A cock and hen, with your leave, Colonel." "A dozen eggs, with your leave, Colonel.")

A servant, who had observed the attack of the turkey, ran to Ni Ruari's rescue, overheard these amusing remarks, and just as the thankless bird was on the point of making an assault, the maid interposed and explained the mistake. She then conducted Ni Ruari to the real Coirneil, who, as may be expected, greatly enjoyed the affair, paid handsomely for the goods, and treated the old woman to a glass of whisky, and her favourite strong cup of tea.

It may seem strange that although Ni Ruari was so ignorant in most things, she had a wonderful gift for reading people's fortunes in cups, and she had attained such proficiency in that art, that her prophecies, according to accounts, proved, in most instances correct, and frequently shook the incredulity of some of the non-believers in her art.

It was towards Ni Ruari's boothy that Bella McKay was going on her benevolent excursion, her object being to relieve the old woman's wants, and not for the purpose, as some might suppose, of having her fortune told, as she had no faith in such practices. Not so her maid; she hailed with joy the benevolent intentions which led her young mistress to the mysterious habitation, and often wished to have the opportunity of removing the veil which concealed her own futurity.

The young boatmen were no less overjoyed at the unlooked-for prospect of holding an interesting and uninterrupted *tête-a-tête* with their fair ones, steered their light bark towards the beach under Ni Ruari's boothy, then furled their sail, sprung lightly on shore, and were soon in the arms of those they loved.

On the happy couples' entrance under the low roof, its strange occupant hailed the visit of such a rare company with a sort of hospitable greeting which more

resembled a grin than a smile, and which had been a
stranger to the shrivelled physiognomy for many years.
As the reader may be anxious to be introduced to this
strange being, we will endeavour to describe her looks.
It was impossible to ascertain her age, as she had arrived
at that period when it is difficult to judge with any
accuracy, no register being kept of such events at that
time. Indeed it was believed by the majority of her
acquaintances that she lived at the time of the flood, and
would be likely to live until the end of time, as the
oldest among them knew her as Old Ni Ruari. Her skin
was parched and wrinkled, and had become of a yellowish
tint which more resembled vellum than human skin.

Her black locks were (strange to say, without any
symptom of changing its colour) gathered up under a
close cap called *Subag*. Her eyes were small and black,
shaded by a fold of skin in place of brows. Her nose
and chin were sharp, and threatened an immediate colli-
sion whenever she closed her thin colourless lips. Her
voice had a strange unearthly tone whenever she spoke,
owing to the want of teeth and the rolling of her tongue
whenever she articulated any difficult word, which rendered it impossible for anyone to understand except
those who were well acquainted with her. When engaged in cup-reading, it took the tone of the terrible,
and her words conveyed depth of meaning sufficient to
electrify her hearers, and kept them under the spell
which it was impossible to shake of for some time ; nor
dared any of them question or interrupt her while occupied in her great art, however terrible or unpalatable
her prophecies might be to them.

As soon as Mary Grant had unburthened herself of
her mistress's bounties to Ni Ruari, she bustled about the
small apartment to prepare, from her supply of tea, a warm
cup to refresh (as she professed) the mariners, but rather
to gain her own favourite ends.

When the beverage was prepared, each of the company was served with a cup, and Mary finishing her cup
first, handed it to the old woman to read her fortune.

As some may be ignorant of the art, we will follow
Ni Ruari in the performance.

Mary Grant having taken the cup in her left hand, drained off the dregs, turning the cup while doing so against the course of the sun, thus leaving the final leaves scattered promiscuously round the inside of the cup, and then placed it bottom upwards on the table.

At the expiration of about a minute, Ni Ruari took it up in her right hand, drawing the back of her left hand across her eyes and lips, then giving a preliminary grunt, peered into the cup for another minute, and then proceeded to read as follows,—

"Young maid, you are now very happy, and imagine that no obstacle exists between you and the idol of your heart, but he will soon be torn from you, and sent across a great sea! However, you will follow him with good tidings, when you will be restored to each other, and live happily."

After thus breaking the ice (as Mary termed it), Donald Munro followed her example, when the following was read to him:—"Young man, you will suffer great hardships through malicious enemies, and also cross a great sea, towards the south; but your misfortunes will not be of long duration; the bearer of joyful news will seek you out, will make you happy, and you will become the father of many children."

Bella was now entreated to hand her cup in; and, in order to please the company, consented; when the following terrible revelation was made by the prophetess—"Young lady, a bright cloud hangs around you at present, but a terrible dark storm threatens in the distance, which will envelop you for a time in its dark folds, not only in these parts, but in a wild and far distant country! You will be surrounded for a long time with misery and despair, but your true love will dispel them all, and rescue you from the powers of wild men."

Charlie's fortune did not threaten so many calamities, but was rather discouraging, and read thus:—"Young gentleman, you will also meet with reverses, and visit other lands. Your only happiness, and the object of your love will be lost to you for years; however, better days are in store for you; you will get possession of your jewel at great risk, through the assistance of a faithful dog."

A smile of incredulity passed between Charlie and Bella at the termination of these strange and terrible prophecies ; and, although they gave no credence to a single word of it, still a strange idea took possession of their minds caused by the tone and solemn fascination of Ni Ruari's words; but with regard to their servants, each sentence was believed and stored up in their minds, feeling fully confident that all would come to pass.

The cloud which these revelations left on their minds was soon dispelled by a long and confidential chat between the lovers, until the shades of evening warned them to proceed towards their home by their separate routes, promising to meet each other soon at the same rendezvous.

This wish was, however, not granted them ; for on their arrival at home they heard the unpleasant intelligence that Lord Lundy had arrived at the castle, and that he was accompanied by Bella's uncle, who had come to plead his cause, and to prevail on Mr. McKay to bestow the hand of his daughter on his Lordship. Many a highly-born lady in England would have been flattered by his addresses, although none of them as yet were able to banish from his heart the impression left there on first beholding Bella McKay.

Finding her still obdurate and invulnerable to the great prospects, the exalted position, and fascinating accomplishments he offered, he had again to relinquish for a time his proposals. His Lordship, however, prevailed on them to take her once more to London, thinking that time and company would change her resolves, and also to separate her and Charlie Stuart.

Martinmas soon arrived, and Charlie had to part with the extensive farm and stock, and relinquish all other ties which bound him to his native Highland home, without any bright star to cheer him in his future pilgrimage through life. The only prize he valued upon earth was again (and like for ever) snatched from his grasp.

However, he had one consolation this time; if Bella

was to become another's, it would be through coercion, and entirely against her will, after the vows which they made with such solemn obsequies at his father's death-bed.

Having only himself now to provide for, he made up his mind to retire from the bar, never having a great liking for it, and regretting the unintentional mistake he made regarding Catherine Forbes, with whose family he had always been on such intimate terms, fearing they might interpret his partiality to her in the same light as herself. He accordingly gave up all connexion with the legal profession, and took his journey to London with Donald Munro, who would not, on any consideration, have parted with his young master. Charlie's intention was to take passage to some foreign land, or British colony, there to better their circumstances, and to enable Charlie to banish his grief and disappointment among strange scenes and people. But we question whether some other motive did not attract them to London, or whether there was not some one there from whom they wished to have one fond kiss before they parted.

————

CHAPTER XIII.

MEETING AT THE THEATRE.

On arriving in London, Charlie and his faithful servant engaged private lodgings in a quiet part of the city, not wishing to mix with company or visit the great merchant McKay, where the idol of his heart was living. His time was therefore taken up in finding out some ship or expedition going abroad, or some opening for an energetic young man, who intended to push his way through life.

Among other novelties which at this time attracted the attention of the public, and which excited the greatest interest, was the announcement of the young Queen's appearance at the principal theatre one evening. Our hero showed a little of the universal curiosity to

G

have a sight of royalty ; he dressed himself in complete
Highland costume, of Royal Stuart Tartan, and made
his way to the scene of attraction. On entering the
theatre, which was crowded, he managed to obtain a seat
in one of the principal boxes, and being the only person
in the Highland garb, attracted a good deal of attention,
notwithstanding the interest the Royal boxes created.

The Young Queen looked charmingly, accompanied by
the Foreign Prince, whom some knowing ones hinted
would soon stand in a nearer relationship than a cousin
to her. Behind the Royal couple, and in attendance on
the Prince, was Lord Lundy, who was a great favourite
at Court, his noble parent holding one of the most responsible posts under the Crown.

· We will now lead the reader to the Royal box, and
listen to the conversation and remarks made there.

The Royal pair were apparently intently scrutinising
some interesting object in the opposite box, when the
Prince turned suddenly to Lord Lundy, and enquired
whether he knew the young lady so handsomely dressed
in that novel Highland costume?

Lord Lundy coloured deeply, and answered—" Your
Highness, that lady is the daughter of my agent in the
Highlands, and her name is Miss McKay."

The young Queen, who had overheard the conversation, inquired whether the lady was the " Highland
Beauty " of whom she had heard so much? His Lordship answered in the affirmative, when her Majesty inquired whether the young gentleman by her side was her
brother ?

" He is, and an officer in your Majesty's Guards," replied his Lordship.

" I do not mean the officer, but the gentleman on the
other side, dressed in the Highland costume," added her
Majesty.

Lord Lundy turned pale, and, in a contemptuous tone,
replied, " I beg your Majesty's pardon, that young
gentleman was a tenant of mine, but I turned him off
my estate for poaching ; and, being a neighbour of Miss
McKay's, he had the assurance to pretend to her hand,
when she was obliged to leave her home to escape his

addresses, and visit her uncle, who is a rich merchant in this city; and it seems that he has followed her to renew his objectionable addresses."

"It appears she has greatly changed her mind, for she smiles very lovingly on him at this moment," added the Prince, provokingly; to which her Majesty agreed, and said "that it was a great pity that the young gentleman incurred his Lordship's displeasure by his imprudence, for he was the finest specimen of a Highlander she ever saw," and said "a likely match for the young lady, who appeared very much attached to him," and concluded by regretting that she did not know more of that part of her dominions and its interesting inhabitants.

Lord Lundy, during these remarks, was suffering under the most excruciating torments of rage and jealousy, having proof of the truth of her Majesty's remarks, which so fully belied his own account.

Bella McKay justified the remarks of royalty, and shone like a meteor among the brilliant stars of the British capital; she was dressed in her favourite Highland garb of silk McKay tartan, with the costliest and most glittering jewellery which could be obtained from her uncle's bounty, and was accompanied by her brother George.

On taking their seat exactly opposite the Royal Box, Bella recognised Lord Lundy in attendance, with his eyes fixed upon her, and instantly removing her looks towards another part of the theatre, towards which a number of glasses were directed, her quick eye caught the form of Charlie, whom she thought was still among his native hills. With her heart bounding with joy, she pointed him out to George, who immediately beckoned his old play-fellow to their box, although he could not recognise him in the handsome grown-up young man before him, but he depended upon his sister's eyes of love. Charlie, who had observed them, instantly accepted the invitation, and made his way to their box, where a most happy and joyful meeting took place. On taking a seat on the other side of Bella, her brother whispered in her ear—"Oh, you little rogue! I can now see your objection to Lord Lundy's addresses," which words brought the crimson to her face as she bent down, with a feeling of confusion, intermixed with happiness.

The joy which the lovers experienced during that delightful evening, was for years impressed on their memory ; nor was the presence of Royalty, the novelties enacted on the stage, or the powerful strains of the orchestra sufficient to attract their attention, or interrupt the happy current of their thoughts and conversation.

Charlie conducted Bella to the carriage, where he took leave of her and George, promising to meet again on an early opportunity.

Little did Charlie think that evening, while drinking with fond intoxication every word which dropped from the lips of his adorable Bella, that there was another and more dangerous enemy than Lord Lundy within the walls of that theatre, and who watched with demoniacal gaze all his movements ; this other enemy was no other than the profligate Melrose, who, on being disgraced and shunned by all respectable society in Edinburgh (after the exposure of his conduct in the Scottish Court), had made his way to London.

Unable to obtain any respectable situation there, for want of certificates or recommendations as to his previous character, he spent all his money in dissolute habits, and was now on the verge of starvation, unless something occurred by which he could earn subsistence.

Visiting the theatre this evening, and purchasing a ticket with the last silver he was possessed of, he behold his former adversary, Charlie Stuart, entering.

Hearing, through some private source, the rivalry and antagonism that existed between Lord Lundy and Charlie regarding Bella, and watching his Lordship's jealous looks, a diabolical expedient to raise money and satisfy his own revenge seized him at once, which he resolved, next day, to put into execution. He, next morning, went direct to his Lordship's residence, sent in his card, and wished to be admitted at once, on the plea of having business of importance to communicate.

Melrose could not have arrived at a better moment for the purpose of making his base proposition, for Lord Lundy had passed a restless night occasioned by the

dreadful torments of enraged jealousy, through witness-
ing the loving communications of Charlie and Bella on
the previous evening. On looking at the card he thought
he had heard or seen the name coupled with that of his
rival, and told Brown to admit him at once.

On entering, Melrose, with his usual tact and address,
opened his business at once in the following manner:—
" You see, my Lord, that my name is Melrose, and for a
short time a member of the Scottish bar, but who, unfortunately, through the machinations of a villain, and
a fellow member, has been expelled from that position."

" Oh!" interrupted his Lordship eagerly, and be-
thinking himself—" Are you the Melrose whom that
scoun——, I mean that Charlie Stuart brought charges
against in Edinburgh; I read the whole of it in the
papers."

" The same, my Lord, but I hope you are not led by
such partial accounts, which I must declare, were not
favourable to me, but rather one-sided."

" Not at all; I do not mind what the journals state,
as they invariably side with the successful party; but
what has that to do with your business with me? I am
no judge or jury to enter into the matter."

" Pardon me, my Lord, I am aware of that; nor do I
wish to renew the case; but hearing that my accuser
has been reviling your Lordship also, and poisoning the
ears of a certain young lady, and a neighbour of his,
against you, I have therefore come before you with a
proposition which, if you will help me in, will be of
satisfaction to us-both. The proposition I have to
to make, is to supply me with funds to remove from your
path this object of mischief to our common happiness."

" Surely you do not mean to take his life, and impli-
cate me as your accomplice?"

" There are many ways of removing people, for a
time, at least, my Lord, without taking life."

" And how much would satisfy you in that case?"

" To be plain with you, my Lord, I could not under-
take the task for less than a thousand pounds."

" A thousand pounds is a large sum; however, I will
meet your demands in this matter; I will give you five

hundred now, and the remaining five hundred when the lady to whom I am attached becomes my wife."

These terms were satisfactory to both parties, and Melrose left, with demoniacal smile, his Lordship's presence, hugging his ill-gotten bribe. However, instead of having accomplices to prosecute his villainous plan, he plunged once more into his profligate habits, in gambling and other excesses, until his money was again swallowed up.

On finding himself again penniless, and no nearer the object of his revenge, or likely to earn the other five hundred pounds, he purchased a brace of pistols, with the last money in his possession, with the intention either to finish his own life, or take that of his enemy. He debated a long time in his mind which of these atrocious crimes he would attempt, when the love of his own prevailed, and that of taking Charlie's was resolved upon.

Charlie had at length some prospect of going abroad, and had entered upon a speculation by which he hoped to earn a small fortune. This was in joining a partner, named Stevenson, a gentleman of his own acquaintance, who had chartered a vessel to carry articles of trade to New Zealand, for the purpose of exchanging them with the natives of that country for land. This Charlie kept as yet a secret; not even telling Bella, whom he but seldom met, as he never visited her uncle, that gentleman being a great advocate of Lord Lundy's.

Donald Munro was often in attendance upon his master and Mr. Stevenson, visiting places of business, and often noticed a suspicious-looking person, who, in a Spanish cloak and slouched hat, dogged them from place to place. He told his master of the circumstance, but Charlie, not minding it, treated his servant's suspicion as trifling. However, Donald was resolved on watching more closely for the future.

One evening, as the two gentlemen were walking arm in arm through one of the bye-streets, Munro kept on the opposite side, and observed the same suspicious person following them at a short distance. On nearing a cross-lane, where the traffic was less, and badly lighted, the person drew closer to them, and was in the act of drawing something like a pistol from under his cloak, when Donald called out to them, which caused Mr. Stevenson to turn suddenly round, when he received, in his right breast, the bullet which was intended for his companion, upon which he fell into the arms of Charlie Stuart.

Munro pursued the assassin, who flew at full speed through the lane, but the swift-footed Highlander soon overtook him, and, giving him his country's trip, threw him upon his back, and placed his knee upon his chest. The police soon arrived, and took him into custody.

Charlie Stuart, after conducting his wounded partner to the nearest medical man, approached the crowd which had gathered round the prisoner, when, to his astonishment, he recognised in him his former enemy Melrose; then it was that his own providential escape flashed across his mind.

The attempted assassination in the public street created considerable excitement, and great interest was manifested on the day of trial. The prisoner was ably defended by some of the leading counsel of the day, but by whom they were engaged was never known. However, their eloquence on his behalf was of no avail; the case being so clearly proved, the jury, without any hesitation, returned a verdict of guilty. On being asked what he had to say why the sentence of the Court should not be passed upon him, he made a most affecting and touching appeal to the Bench, couched in such brilliant language that he quite surprised all his hearers, and concluded by saying that if he was to suffer the extreme penalty of the law, some person, whose name he would not mention, and who held one of the most noble and exalted positions in society, and who was at that moment listening to him, was the principal instrument in exciting him to commit such a desperate act; and, although he was sorry for shooting or wounding a gentleman with whom he had never quarrelled, he felt greatly disappointed in having missed his intended victim, whom he wished to chastise for former injuries.

Charlie, who was in the court, followed Melrose's eye

while he was speaking, and saw Lord Lundy among the crowd in the gallery, who, on encountering the prisoner's looks, and hearing the insinuations he had given bent his head, and turning his ghastly countenance away, hid himself among the crowd.

A few days after the prisoner was reprieved, his sentence being commuted to transportation for life.

The voyage to New Zealand had been delayed through this unfortunate circumstance, and Mr. Stevenson, whose life was in great danger, entreated Charlie to proceed on the voyage without him, and offered to dispose of his share, and Charlie now became the owner of all the cargo, and was ready for sea.

One evening Charlie again met George and Bella at the theatre, and was holding one more delightful *tête-a-tête* with her, when he related his suspicions concerning Lord Lundy's complicity with Melrose for the destruction of his life. Bella was greatly shocked at hearing this, and, entertaining no doubt upon the matter, she now held Lord Lundy in the most intense horror and disgust.

On their leaving the box, they saw Lord Lundy at the entrance, and, as soon as Bella stepped out, he offered his arm to conduct her to the carriage. The young girl recoiled from him in terror, when Charlie, stepping between them, offered his arm, remarking scornfully, "Miss McKay only accepts the protection of Honourables by action, not by title."

"Dare you insinuate dishonourable actions to me?" replied his Lordship, turning pale with rage, "You shall suffer for your insolence before long."

"At any time and place you choose," replied Charlie with great coolness.

Bella had not heard these last remarks in the confusion of the moment, and the parties separated for the evening.

Next morning, the Hon. Captain Somerville, with a challenge from Lord Lundy, called upon Charlie, who at once referred him to his friend, Lieutenant John M'Donald (John Lom), who had arrived with his regiment in London, being under orders for Indian service.

A meeting took place on the following morning,

when, after exchanging shots, Lord Lundy fell severely wounded.

Charlie was greatly distressed at such an occurrence, and was on the point of giving himself up, when his friend the Lieutenant forced him to leave the place, and impressed upon him the necessity of at once leaving the kingdom.

Having arranged everything for his departure the previous day, and the vessel having cleared the customs in Mr. Stevenson's name, he embarked at once as that gentleman, in order to avoid the punishment of the law. On joining the vessel, without even bidding adieu to Bella, he wrote a long letter to her, giving her a full account of all that had occurred, which would fully account for his abrupt departure, asking her to overlook his transgression should Lord Lundy not survive, and he hoped they would yet meet under better auspices. This letter he sent by Donald, with strict directions to hand it to no one but Bella, and to wait for an answer.

He was not to approach Mr. McKay's until night, lest that should give any clue as to Charlie's whereabouts, and afterwards meet the ship's boat at a given spot and be taken on board.

Donald had followed the first part of these instructions to the letter, and enjoyed a long interview with Mary Grant, who endeavoured to dissuade him from going and remain with her, remarking with tears, that the first part of Ni Ruari's prophecy was already coming true.

Donald at last tore himself from her, and imprinting the last kiss, he left her; but as he was going through the back premises he was rushed upon and seized. The most powerful of his assailants struggled with him, when they both fell and continued their struggle while on the ground. Donald managed to get his antagonist under him, when he heard the well-known voice of John Brown calling out, "Shoot the villain before he gets off." The active Highlander, upon hearing this, rolled over, bringing his antagonist uppermost, just in time to receive the bullet (which was intended for himself) through the back, killing him on the spot.

A crowd had now gathered round the spot, when

Brown and his associate declared that Donald was the person who fired the shot, and notwithstanding his protestations to the contrary, he was arrested on the charge. On being brought next day, to the inquest which was held on the body of the detective, his accusers, Brown and Williams, swore to their previous assertions, the evidence against him being strengthened by the fact that a pistol, with the letters "D. M." upon it, had been found near the spot, and which had been recently used.

Donald acknowledged that the pistol was his property, but said he left it at his lodgings in the hurry of removing. This statement was of course not received, and he was fully committed for trial.

The sessions commenced in a few days, when the same evidence was brought against him. The only witness who could have saved him, was the servant at the house where he had been lodging, who could have proved that the pistol was left there, but she could not be found; he was found guilty of manslaughter, but was strongly recommended to mercy, there being some question as to whether the evidence was thoroughly reliable; upon the verdict being given, the sentence of the Court was passed upon him, which was, that he should be transported for seven years to Botany Bay.

How the innocent but unfortunate piper became a convict, and how it was that his own pistol was found near the scene, and which was the strongest evidence against him, was as follows :—

It will be remembered that John Brown had become a sworn enemy to Donald ever since their visit to the brews, and the ridiculous exposure he had made of him before Mary Grant. Brown had resolved on paying him back, and determined to remove him, as he was the obstacle in the way of his happiness. In order to accomplish this, as soon as he heard that Donald had arrived in London, he bribed the servant at the house in which Charlie had taken lodgings for himself and Donald, made her presents, and also an offer of marriage. He then became leagued to some extent with Melrose, whom he supplied with information which he obtained from the servant; but as Melrose was inclined to take desperate measures, Brown thought it better to steer clear of him altogether and not risk his life. He then associated with another desperado named Williams, who proved to be a housebreaker and highwayman, but who had as yet managed to evade the laws, and whom Brown engaged to forward his plans and those of his master also.

At the sudden and unexpected crisis occasioned by the duel and Lord Lundy's unfortunate fate, Brown set off with his accomplice Williams and a detective, to capture Charlie and Donald at their lodgings. The detective was stationed outside to prevent anyone leaving the house, while Brown and Williams entered to talk with the servant, and obtain all information possible.

Notwithstanding their precipitation, they found to their great mortification, that they had removed, and that Donald on the previous day had taken their luggage in a great hurry, paid the bill and had not returned.

Brown, in order to satisfy himself, asked to be allowed to see the rooms they had occupied, found a pistol, upon which was Donald's initials, hung upon a nail, and which had been overlooked by the lodger while removing the goods; he took possession of it with the determination of soon turning it to some account. On leaving the lodgings, Brown proposed that they should watch Mr. McKay's house, urging that Charlie would never leave without bidding farewell to Bella, and at dusk the three took their station and watched; they did not remain long before they saw Donald approaching, having entered by the back gate. Brown pointed him out, and declared him to be Charlie Stuart; they then waited for his return, and as he was leaving, rushed upon him. Brown well knew who it was that had been seized, and to satisfy his long cherished revenge, gave Williams the pistol he had taken from the room they had inspected, and ordered him to fire.

Upon seeing that the wrong man had received the bullet, they instantly made up their minds to heap the guilt upon Donald, which was successfully carried out, and proved extremely disastrous to the innocent victim of their machinations.

In order to accomplish their wickedness effectually,

and remove any trace of evidence favourable to the prisoner, Brown had prevailed upon the servant to leave her situation, under the pretence of marrying her.

Donald's unfortunate conviction proved distressing in several respects, and caused great anxiety to Charlie.

The poor fellow had the presence of mind to throw Bella's letter over the wall while engaged in the scuffle, which was picked up the next morning by Mary Grant, who gave it to her mistress, thus entirely preventing any clue being given to his whereabouts.

But the greatest sufferer of all was Mary, whose appearance gave evidence of her wretchedness of mind, refusing any consolation at the unhappy fate of her lover, whose innocence she never doubted.

CHAPTER XIV.

THE SHIPWRECK.

Charlie, after waiting beyond the time appointed for Donald's return, came to the conclusion that Mary Grant had prevailed upon him to remain, and that he had given up the idea of emigrating to New Zealand; he was, therefore, reluctantly compelled, on account of his own safety, to order the captain to sail.

The voyage contributed but little consolation to his gloomy thoughts, leaving behind him all he valued upon earth, not even knowing whether Bella had forgiven his late unfortunate act. The weather proved propitious during the voyage, until nearing their destination, when a strong gale set in, driving the vessel at a fearful rate, when at length, about midnight, the terrible reality was made known to them by the man at the look-out, calling —" Breakers ahead! " and before they had time to alter her course, she was carried, on the crest of an enormous wave, on to the reef, where she was left, stuck fast in a slit of the rock. In this dreadful uncertainty they passed the remainder of the night, expecting every wave to seal their doom, but fortunately the tide lowered, but the breakers sent the spray completely over her.

The wished for morning at length arrived, which revealed their fearful position, and confirmed their opinion that the vessel was wedged into a slit or crack in the reef, where she was as firm and solid as in a dock, and apparently without having sustained any injury to her hull. Within a short distance was a barren rock, which hid them from the main land.

Their hope of safety was dispelled on considering that the tide, now at its lowest ebb, would soon return, and in all probability the ship would be broken up, and they found that the only chance they had of reaching the land, was the boat, only one being left. It was accordingly lowered, and some provisions and clothing put in, when all hands abandoned the ship. The sea was running fearfully high, and a sail was set to steady the small craft, but on entering a narrow strait, a sudden squall caught and capsized her. On coming to the surface, Charlie, who had divested himself of all heavy clothing and boots, in case of an accident, beheld to his horror, the boat, keel uppermost, without a creature near. He resolved to gain the boat, as the strength of the current would not allow him to reach the shore by swimming. He immediately struck out with all his strength, and succeeded in reaching the slippery support, which considerably relieved him, and which he trusted would bring him to land.

The boat was fortunately driven into a back current, which set in towards the land; this, with a lull in the gale which had taken place, greatly revived his drooping spirits and strength.

The eastern sun now rose in all its splendour, casting its golden rays on the shipwrecked mariner, as if to cheer him while clinging to the boat. His early practice in the art of swimming, and his native hardy constitution, stood him in good need, amidst the raging billows which had proved so fatal to his companions.

The boat was by degrees driven towards the land, but the castaway was brought almost to the last stage of exhaustion; when it had nearly reached the shore, he beheld nothing but frowning cliffs, which threatened him with instant destruction. A fearful death was, however, averted by the boat being driven through a gap in the cliffs into a small basin, which terminated in a little sandy beach, on which he could distinguish, although his sight was failing, three human forms.

Finding that his strength was quickly leaving him, he resolved upon making an effort to attract their attention; he immediately held up one hand, and gave a feeble cry for aid, but the other hand not having sufficient strength to hold him up, lost its hold, and in a moment the sea closed over him.

He soon, however, felt something grasp him by the hair, which brought him to the surface. His listless form was then carried swiftly through the water, when his consciousness entirely forsook him. How long he remained in this state he knew not, but, on his awakening, he found himself stretched on a couch covered with matting of peculiar workmanship.

On glancing around the apartment, he found it to be a small cave, at the other end of which was a fire, and around it were seated three females. One of these, apparently the youngest, was dressed in a kind of matting, but far superior in workmanship to that worn by the other two, and also wearing several ornaments, which plainly showed her superiority. The three were conversing in whispers, and the youngest, who was far handsomer than the other two, with beautiful large black eyes; holding up her hand, as if to command silence, she listened for a moment, then rose cautiously, and approached the couch with quiet and slow steps.

Pretending sleepiness still, he closed his eyes again, when she knelt by his side, and removing his wet hair from his brow, she murmured some unintelligible words, while her warm breath fanned his face; then, with a deeply drawn sigh, rose from her recumbent position.

Charlie now opened his eyes, and met her's, when she wrapped her robe carefully round her, and a shade of confusion passed over her face.

Seeing him attempting to rise, she instantly changed her looks into that of admiration; kneeling again by his side, and wrapped his covering more closely around him. This he found was necessary, for he felt giddiness and faintness coming over his whole frame, on making the slightest attempt to rise.

The young girl now sent away one of the maids, who, after some time, returned with some refreshments, of which he was pressed to partake. On tasting it, he found it revive him greatly; he was then allowed by his careful nurse to rise from his couch.

A long communication by signs was then held by them, the purport of which was that he was to remain for a time a prisoner in the cave, where he would be supplied with food, but, should he attempt to go beyond its precincts, he would be disposed of in a manner not very agreeable; he was, therefore, compelled to submit to the will of his young protectress, and remained passive in her hands.

Two days had passed in this manner, and the girl, with her maids, came punctually each morning with necessaries, and one of them always, in turn, kept him company during the day (the young one more so), and instructed him in their language, by which he was able to understand several things of consequence to him.

On the third day, being quite recovered, his young nurse came alone, punctual as usual with his morning meal. She then sat by his side, catechising his vocabulary in her own language, and also inspecting his white hands and features with admiration, as if he were an infant; her interesting occupation was suddenly interrupted by the entrance of one of her maids in a state of alarm and terror. On communicating some dire calamity (which Charlie was unable to understand) to her young mistress, the latter sprang quickly to her feet, made him lie down on the couch, and covered him with mats. Not knowing her intentions, or wishing to disobey her commands, he suffered himself to be thus placed, when, to his consternation, four savages rushed into the cave.

The first of these was a middle-aged warrior, who appeared by his many scars and other marks to be a chief, and after him entered two young men carrying enormous bludgeons, and painted over the body in warlike fashion.

· The fourth was also young, and a powerful-looking man, but much fairer, who wore several articles of European clothing, and carried a musket.

These formidable characters stood in the cave facing the maid, who sternly maintained her station before the couch, when, after a few threatening imprecations, the old chief advanced, and, pushing her on one side, she gave a loud scream, flung herself on her charge, giving vent to supplicating exclamations, which arrested the old warrior, and seemed to affect him for a while.

On seeing this the warrior with the musket put in some demonstrations apparently unfavorable to Charlie, and seeming to incite the chief in his first intentions, when the young girl sprung up and retaliated upon the last speaker in words which evidently carried force and argument, and which turned affairs somewhat in her favor.

Charlie now stood up by the side of his protectress, and, with supplications for mercy in his defenceless state, evoked their clemency by many signs and words, impressing upon them his late shipwreck, and being saved from drowning by the brave girl at his side.

A visible change took place in the looks of the spectators at this appeal; the old chief and the two young warriors were evidently favorable to Charlie and his protectress, but the half-civilised savage was unquestionably antagonistic in the highest degree; for, on seeing the tables turned, he rushed from the cave muttering threats of future revenge, and which for the moment affected the others with awe and dread. However, after another exhortation from the young girl, their peaceable intention again manifested itself towards the castaway, and, laying down their arms, a long conversation took place between them and the girl, the subject of which seemed to be the "pakeha" or white man. At the conclusion of this deliberation, the young girl, with a countenance beaming with joy, intimated to Charlie that he was now at liberty to leave the cave, and follow them to a place where he would be furnished with better accommodation, and free from annoyance for the future.

CHAPTER XV.

PAMUL THE MAORI GIRL.

The part of New Zealand on which Charlie Stuart had been cast away had seldom been visited by Europeans, the coast being too wild to admit of any vessel approaching it.

The tribe by which it was inhabited were very warlike, and headed by a powerful chief named Tomato, the father of two sons and one daughter (Pamul), who had so bravely rescued the castaway from drowning, and from the patvo-patvo (clubs) of the father and brothers.

Another and more influential chief named Honi Hiki, held great sway over the others, whose lands adjoined Tomato's, and who had intercourse with the whites for a long time, consequently he had become somewhat conversant with civilized customs.

This shrewd and cunning chief, viewed with jealousy the rapid progress of civilization, the footing the Pakehas were gaining among his countrymen, and the valuable lands which they became possessed of in exchange for trifling articles of commerce. He therefore entered into a secret league with many other powerful chiefs, whose minds he endeavoured to corrupt in order to drive the white people into the sea, and thus regain possession of the land.

Being gifted with a good address, coupled with skill and judgment in warlike matters, having also fire arms and ammunition distributed freely among his tribe, he soon gained the co-operation of several neighbouring chiefs.

Tomato had been for some time a rival chief, and was often at war with him, but being anxious to ally himself with such a powerful chief, who would so ably promote his plans, Honi Hiki endeavoured to bring him also in the league, and for this purpose he proposed for the hand of Pamul, the old chief's daughter, who was considered the greatest beauty among his countrywomen.

It was on this account that he was now a visitor at Tomato's, and was the person who appeared so anxious for the death of Charlie at the cave.

On revealing his intentions to Tomato, and laying his plans before him for the extermination of the Pakehas, whom he described as being a race of robbers, Honi Hiki became the accepted of Pamul, although she was adverse to the match, knowing well the wily chief's disposition. However, she knew it was no use objecting, as she would be compelled to submit to parental authority. Being a great favourite of her father's, she obtained permission to .put off the nuptials for a few days, which was some relief to her.

It was on the morning appointed for her marriage that she sought the solitude of her bathing place (which was held sacred) to give vent to her despair for the sacrifice she was on the eve of making, by becoming the bride of the man she hated. In the midst of her lamentations, while praying that some young warrior would come and take her away to some distant isle, her quick eye caught the castaway clinging to the boat, and calling out for aid.

Under the influence of her romantic inspiration, she plunged into the sea, and swam to the rescue. With great expertness she soon arrived at the spot where Charlie sank, and immediately dived and brought him to the surface.

It was now that her judgment and powers of swimming were put to the test, for although the drowning man could breath, he was too much exhausted to assist himself, and it was not until her slaves came to her assistance that she succeeded in saving him.

That evening, on the plea of indisposition, which was not feigned, she craved for three days more, which was granted to her by her father.

The experienced and quick eye of Honi Hiki, however, detected a change in the manner and looks of his intended bride ; and, by bribing the simplest of her maids, he became possessed of the whole secret, notwithstanding the restrictions Pamul enforced on her slaves to the contrary.

The wily chief became greatly alarmed at this revelation, not only for fear of losing Pamul, whom he really loved, but also the consequence which might follow from the alliance of the white man with the powerful chief

Tomato, who, he feared, might be allured by their fascinating promises and gaudy presents. He, therefore, in a subtle and cunning speech, broke the subject to Tomato and his sons, saying that the white man with the cunning and treachery of his race, sneaked like a shark into Pamul's sacred retreat to deceive her, and then gain possession of their land. This statement aroused the rage of Tomato, when they all rushed to the cave for the purpose of dispatching the intruder at once, and thus save their country as well as Pamul. They were not, however, prepared for the affecting devotion which she displayed towards the stranger. She became a bold advocate of the defenceless, whom she declared to be a helpless castaway on their shore, and ridiculed their actions, particularly her father and brothers, for taking a mean advantage of an inoffensive creature, who deserved their hospitality instead of their rage.

When Honi Hiki heard this unexpected and forcible appeal, and saw the effect it had produced on her father and brothers, he became more enraged than ever lest his plans should fail, and sneeringly exclaimed—" Tomato is a woman when he listens to the ravings of his daughter, who foolishly pleads for the life of a Pakeha."

At these words, Pamul sprung up and declared that the white man had never shown the slightest disrespect towards her, and said that if he was a fair specimen of the pakehas, whom the calumniator described as a race of robbers, she believed that that character was more applicable to Honi Hiki than to them ; and sooner than become his (Honi Hiki's) bride, she would suffer the most terrible death to which she could be put. On hearing this, Honi Hiki left the cave vowing vengeance on Tomato and his new allies, the pakehas.

With a heart relieved from apprehension, Charlie followed Tomato and his children, and after ascending the cliffs by an intricate and narrow path, soon gained the native village, which was situated in a romantic spot on the banks of a beautiful lake, from which ran a river navigable by canoes, and which emptied itself into the ocean.

Through the assistance of Pamul, Charlie was able to give a more accurate account of his shipwreck, the valuable cargo on board, and the probability of yet saving some portion of it, as the weather had become quite calm. Tomato immediately ordered all the available canoes to be manned, and started for the scene of the wreck.

Charlie accompanied Tomato and his sons in the principal and leading canoe, and upon rounding the rock great was his joy at seeing the ship dry and unbroken. On going on board they found also that the cargo was uninjured.

He felt that he could now recompense Tomato for the mercy that had been extended towards him, and reward the noble Pamul for her heroic conduct in saving his life at the imminent peril of her own.

All the cargo and every valuable were taken safely to the village. When this was completed, they broke the hull up, and convoyed that also to the village.

The whole of the cargo was carefully stored by orders of Tomato for Charlie, but who was afterwards prevailed upon to take a large piece of land in exchange.

The chief and his tribe considered that they had by far the best of the bargain, as the principal portion of the cargo consisted of fire-arms and ammunition, which they were deficient of, owing to which he had suffered many defeats in engagements with Honi Hiki. Charlie then commenced a course of instruction in the use of the weapons, with which every able-bodied man was supplied; they then enrolled themselves under Charlie's command. Honi Hiki, true to his threat, invaded their district but suffered such a defeat that he never annoyed them after.

A year had passed, during which time the tribe made rapid progress in civilization through the exertions of Charlie, who gave information to them upon any subject which would tend to their happiness. The only sorrow which weighed upon their minds, and in which Charlie shared to a great extent, was the indisposition of Pamul. This great change in her health was noticed by Charlie while holding a conversation with her, which he did at the suggestion of her father. The subject upon which Charlie was speaking to her, was her stern and steady refusal to accept the hand of Honi Hiki; a match which had been approved of by her father, and which promised great advantages to her father and the whole tribe. In reply to Charlie's questions, and having listened attentively to all his remarks, Pamul hung down her head for a while, when Charlie observed large tears coursing down her cheeks; then, as if determined to check them, she wiped them away with her hand, raised her eyes to his, and said:—

" Do the white women always marry those whom their parents recommend?"

" In some cases they do, and they frequently turn out good matches," replied Charlie.

" And would you now, marry a woman you did not like?" she inquired.

"Certainly not," replied her companion unhesitatingly.

" Oh ! then, you consider females an inferior sex, and are to obey you like slaves," she continued.

Charlie, who was not prepared for this, turned his eyes towards the sea, which would now have been rolling over his remains were it not for a female, and that his questioner. A gush of heartfelt thankfulness and generous acknowledgement took possession of him, and seizing her hand with enthusiasm, he said:—

" My brave and noble Pamul, far be it from me to hold your sex in such estimation; were it not for you, yonder billows would now have been rolling over me; such kindness and devotion I could hardly have expected from my own countryman, much less a female—*save one.*"

" Ah! there is one then," cried Pamul, eagerly catching the last words, which were not intended for her ear, and which was uttered in a lower key.

" Yes, there is one," resumed Charlie with more than usual agitation; " but, although that one might have the wish, I doubt whether she would be able to accomplish such a feat, not being a swimmer like you Pamul."

" And she must indeed be faithful to you," replied Pamul, with an anxious and inquisitive expression; "is she a mother or a sister?"

" Neither," replied Charlie; " but far dearer, and we are under a solemn vow to be faithful to each other while we live."

Pamul heaved a deep sigh, turned her face towards

the sea, and said mournfully, "She must, indeed, be beautiful, and possessing all the fine qualities you have so often described to me, with which your country-women are blessed, and which you wished me to imitate; would that I were able to do so to please you." Then, looking at her hands, she continued dispondingly, "But, ah! what a fool I am, she is of a different colour to me."

Charlie, who was greatly affected at this touching remark, replied, encouragingly, "The difference of colour, Pamul, has nothing to do with the nobleness and upright-ness of the mind, and there beats as many good hearts under a dark skin as under a fair one."

"Now, since you think so much of the small favor I have extended towards you," (resumed Pamul, somewhat soothed,) "by preserving your life, I must ask you one favor in return; that is, never to breathe a word on this subject again, as I am resolved to remain single; and, further, I will ask you to use your influence with my father, and beg of him not to force me."

Charlie could not refuse this earnest appeal, which was made with such candour, and promised never to mention the subject again.

A visible change from this time took place in Pamul, and a lingering illness seized her. She resolutely avoided all company and amusement, and even shunned her former instructor, Charlie.

All her friends and relations became greatly alarmed at the change in her; her appearance soon became emaciated by the ravages of disease, which appeared to be decline.

One afternoon Charlie met her. She was then in the dress she had the first day he saw her, and, on his enquiring anxiously as to her health, she feebly answered, with a forced smile, that "she would soon be well," and proposed a walk to their old favourite spot.

Charlie was delighted at the proposition, as this was the first occasion on which she had spoken to him since their last visit to that place.

On their way he felt sorry that he had consented to take such a walk, which appeared too much for her strength, but he could not prevail upon her to return.

They at length arrived at the spot, and having seated

themselves, gazed around on the familiar scenery, and
when she had regained sufficient strength, Pamul, looking earnestly into his face, said, "I am glad to be able
once more to visit this place, as I think it a befit-
ting spot, and free from interruption, having something
weighty on my mind for some time, and which I wish to
communicate to you before I die, for I feel that my time
in this world is very short." During a short pause, for
she appeared too weak to say more, Charlie endeavoured
to cheer her. He told her that her health might
again return, and then they would be enabled
to resume their walks, and spend many happy
days on the same spot. Pamul, however, interrupted
him by giving a mournful motion of the head, and saying, "Never again in this life, whatever happiness may
be store for me in that other world which you have
taught me to look to, there is none in this, for my hours
are numbered. I know that you, as well as my anxious
relatives, have been uneasy and ignorant of the cause of
my complaint. I thought that even you would never
know it, and that the secret would go with me to the
grave. However, my illness has caused me to throw off
such foolish thoughts, as I consider, by confessing it to
you, I may be doing what I can to prevent any unplea-
santness on my decease. You will remember, the last
time we visited this spot, that you confessed your love
to one of your countrywomen. Little did you think
that that admission would be the foundation of an illness and sorrow that would soon carry me to the grave.
Had I known earlier of such a circumstance, I might
have smothered my foolish hopes and grief; but, alas, it
was then too late. I was ignorant that the hopeless
flame which your first appearance struggling feebly in
the water enkindled in my heart, had taken such a deep
root, and which all earthly powers were unable to extin-
guish. Poor simpleton as I then was, I did not think
of the insurmountable barrier which exists between our
races. Your kindness, partiality, and interest in instructing me was stored up in my bosom, and added to
my passion, until the fatal chasm which separates the
white race from the coloured yawned before me."

Charlie was so much moved at this disclosure that he could not restrain his tears, when Pamul again checked him, and added—"Do not be moved; it was no fault of yours; all the attention and interest you took in me, and which led to my hopeless misery, were only the out-pourings of a benevolent mind. The ignorance and bar-barity of our race raised your pity, which was extended with such liberality towards me in return for the ser-vices I had rendered you. Hence the cause of the trouble you have taken in instructing me, and to some extent modelling my mind, and opening that mind as to the realities of a future state, a state to which I am now hastening. And although your generosity would per-haps humble itself to that extent to take me as your wife, I would never consent were I as hale and happy as formerly; for, thanks to you, I now understand the nature of a solemn promise or vow."

Pamul here described Bella's looks with such minute-ness that Charlie was greatly surprised; but she soon explained all by telling him that on the morning she saved him from drowning, and while he was insensible on the beach, she uncovered his bosom to admit the rays of the sun in order to warm him; she saw something which hung by a ribbon around his neck, and upon her opening it she saw it contained the portrait of a female. Not believing then that any living creature could be so beautiful, she thought it was a relic or talisman which would save him from from drowning, until the day on which he told her of his vow, when she detected him drawing it from his bosom and placing it to his lips.

"Yes!" continued Pamul, "the least motion or change in your countenance was observed by me, and your simplest wishes were law to me, and found an echo in my heart; and you may tell your beautiful intended that however great her devotion and love for you, it never did or will exceed that of Pamul, the Maori girl."

She now gave her reason for making this touching confession, for which she could not find courage for a long time—that lest her relations should guess or dis-cover the cause of her disease and seek revenge on Charlie after her death, she advised him to dispose of his land to some of his countrymen who were living a little distance off, for which they would give him a large sum of money, and then to leave New Zealand for ever; and lastly as a favor, she asked him, when she was no more, to bury her remains near the place they were then sitting.

The approaching evening warned them to return home, and on leaving the spot Pamul cast a lingering look around as if bidding a last adieu to scenes where she passed so many hours; then leaning on her companion's arm they retraced their steps slowly.

That night about twelve they were aroused by the mournful intelligence being brought them that the invalid was much worse, and wished to see them all. Her father, brothers, and Charlie, were just in time to receive her final adieu, and the noble Pamul breathed her last amidst the lamentations of her friends and relations.

Charlie was much affected by her loss, and strictly complied with her last wishes by interring her remains in her chosen resting place. The bereavement caused him also to follow her directions in the disposal of his land, which he succeeded in doing; he sold it to some British settlers who were flocking to that colony, and shortly afterwards took his passage in a vessel bound to Sydney, bidding farewell to the land of the Maories for ever.

CHAPTER XVI.

THE CONFESSION.

Bella McKay's uneasiness at the apprehension and conviction of Donald may be imagined, when taking into consideration the state of mind Charlie would be in, leaving under the belief that his hands had been imbued with the blood of a fellow creature, and that her forgiveness was withheld, which would have been cleared up had her letter been delivered, and would have assisted to lighten his sorrow on his long voyage.

Her maid added to her unhappiness by her despair at the fate of Donald.

Lord Lundy, on recovering from his wound, seeing the coast clear, resumed his addresses with redoubled perseverance, and aided by her uncle, forced her to seek once more the protection of her father.

On arriving in the Highlands, she threw herself on her knees before him, claiming his pity, and begging him not to force her to a marriage which she would sooner suffer death than endure.

Her father was greatly moved at the earnestness of her appeal, but could not understand her objection to such a brilliant match. He took his daughter on his knee, and coaxingly asked her to unburthen her bosom, requesting her to tell him whether her heart was otherwise engaged, since she so strenuously opposed such a splendid offer, which would improve her position as well as that of her relations. If her heart was really bestowed upon another, by her making him her confidant, he promised her all the protection in his power in order to secure her future happiness.

The blushing girl affectionately embraced her father, and hiding her streaming eyes in his bosom, confessed, without reserve, her long and ardent love for Charlie Stuart.

Mr. McKay started with astonishment and anger at the announcement, pushing her from him, and told her in a stern voice that he was surprised to hear her acknowledging affection for one who would at one time have received his sanction, but one who had on two occasions insulted her, and had forfeited all sympathy and claim to her hand.

It was now Bella's turn to be surprised; she gazed with a vacant look into her father's frowning countenance for an explanation, when he told her all he had heard from Lord Lundy.

To describe Mr. McKay's feelings on learning the real facts of the case, as described by his daughter, would be impossible.

The disappointments and sacrifices they had suffered through the malicious calumnies of Lord Lundy, the

scene at Mr. Stuart's death bed, and his Lordship's un-
doubted complicity with the assassin Melrose, all came
to his mind, and increased his agony.

Bella now endeavoured to soothe her father's despairing and self-accusing mind, in being an unfortunate
dupe and passive instrument in his Lordship's hands,
by which an old and estimable neighbour came to an
untimely grave, and a noble and honourable young man
had become deprived of his home and bride. She impressed upon him the necessity of never mentioning it
to George, lest it might cause a meeting between him
and Lord Lundy, which might terminate fatally; and
further, never to let Lord Lundy know that his villany
was discovered. These propositions were approved of
by Mr. McKay, and he resolved not to act for, or
receive any favors from Lord Lundy for the future. He
accordingly wrote to his Lordship, resigning the factorship on the ground of ill health, and recommended his
son as his successor, as he wished him to leave the army,
that he might be near him in case of his death. He also
wrote to George on the same subject, pleading indisposition and unwillingness to attend any longer to business,
as an illness had set in which soon reduced his strong,
robust form.

This change was more apparent after receiving the
following sad intelligence from London:—"You will, I
am sure, be sorry to hear, that the vessel in which your
young neighbour Mr. Charles Stuart embarked, never
reached her distination, and that her total loss, with all
on board, is beyond a doubt. A coasting vessel picked
up a boat's stern with the name of the vessel upon it."

This calamity weighed so heavily on Bella's mind that
she shunned all company, and refused all consolation,
passing her spare time in solitary rambles among haunts
which reminded her of happier days. But the greater
portion of her time was occupied in visiting the poor,
and attending to her invalid father, who, on seeing the
great change in his usually lively daughter whose misfortunes preyed so much on his mind, that he soon
succumbed under his afflictions, and was laid in Killinn,
by the side of his neighbour Mr. Stuart.

Soon after this George and Bella received an invitation from their uncle in London to visit him, as he intended to sail for Australia, with the idea of establishing a branch house of business there, where he intended to remain.

Thinking this might revive his sister's spirits, George accepted the invitation, and both set out on their journey.

On their arrival, an occurrence took place which promised future happiness to Mary Grant, and which gave great satisfaction to others. This was that the housemaid, whom Brown had sent out of the way at the time of Donald's trial, was now in the service of Mr. McKay. On her and Mary becoming acquainted, the latter, among the confidential gossip, related her misfortune in losing her lover through the villany of Brown and his accomplices, and how the valet persecuted her with his addresses afterwards.

The girl was ignorant of Donald's conviction through the evidence of the pistol, and now understood Brown's motives for getting Donald out of the way, and told Mary the whole truth. Another circumstance which established this statement, as well as Donald's innocence, was the conviction of Williams for highway robbery, and who had confessed his complicity with Brown in giving false evidence against Donald; the reason of Williams's confession being, that he always extorted money from Brown for keeping the secret, but the valet getting tired of these incessant demands upon his purse, had left Williams to his fate, without engaging counsel for him at his trial as he had promised, being glad to get the troublesome highwayman out of the way. He was, however, forced to abscond, on hearing of Williams's confession, in order to evade punishment.

The reader may well imagine Mary Grant's joy on getting possession of Donald's free pardon; and, as she was determined to be the bearer of it, she begged Bella to allow her to embark with Mr. McKay.

Bella, although the bereavement would be great, would not allow herself to stand in the way of her maid's happiness, and immediately gave her consent.

Mr. McKay took his departure, after an affecting

farewell with George and Bella. Mary Grant, with many tears and blessings, left her young mistress, from whom nothing but her lover's happiness could induce her to part. George and Bella then returned to the Highlands, there to await tidings of their arrival, and to pass their time in attending to the comfort of the cotters and tenants of Lochlinn.

In due time the wished-for communication from Mr. McKay arrived; and, on breaking the seals, she read as as follows :—" My Dearest Niece,—I would give half my fortune this moment to have you near me, that I could behold once more your happy smile, which I fear has been a stranger for some time to your face. Now if you promise me to be a good girl, and try not to be over-excited, I will tell you something that will make you as happy as ever. You would never guess who the first person was that boarded our ship on our arrival in this beautiful harbour. I will tell you; it was no other than your former lover and neighbour, Charlie Stuart." Bella could read no more, she gave a faint scream, and would have fallen, if George, who had been reading the same joyful news, had not caught her in his arms. After soothing her agitated mind, and congratulating her on the happiness which was yet in store for her, she was at length able to resume her letter, which went on to say, " the surprise they had in meeting with the lost one, his ample fortune, through a successful speculation in New Zealand, his manly and improved looks, and, lastly, his constancy and devotion to Bella." The letter also went on to say that Mr. McKay had entered into partnership with him in a pastoral enterprize, which was considered to be the best paying occupation in the colony, that Charlie would manage the station, and Mr. McKay would attend to his business in Sydney. It concluded with an invitation to Bella to come out by the first favourable opportunity, and gave several reasons for such a proposition.

The first of these was, that Mr. McKay had been suffering a great deal and was not likely to recover, and having no family, he would leave his fortune to her, provided she did as he wished. But the last and most

powerful argument was, that Charlie did not intend to
return to his native land, at least for some time, and that
he also advocated Mr. McKay's suggestion, that their
solemn vows might be fulfilled.

Bella at once came to the determination to accept the
invitation, which as quickly gave way to the consideration of her brother's happiness, whom she did not like
to leave, as she was the only relation left him; nor
could she think of entertaining the prospect of her own
happiness at the sacrifice of his.

While debating on this point, she raised her eyes to
her brother's, he folded her in his arms, and spoke as
follows :—" My dear and only sister, I can easily divine
your thoughts. Far be it from me to harbour for one
moment the idea of throwing the slightest obstacle in
your way, but I hail with joy the prospect of your joining your lover in that far distant land, as a just reward
for the days of sorrow and suffering you have passed for
the last two years. My present situation and circumstances will not allow me to accompany you, yet I hope
the time is not far distant when I shall be able to follow
you, and when, I trust, we shall be all united in that
happiness which has been· denied us in our native land
of late years."

This affecting address brought tears of gratitude to
his sister's eyes, when she kissed her brother affectionately.

A letter was shortly after sent to their uncle, telling
him that she intended taking a passage in a ship commanded by a Captain Hector McLean, who was then on
a visit to his native land, and who had lately married a
friend of Bella's.

A more favourable opportunity than this could not
have presented itself. The Captain, who was a brave
and excellent seaman, was now on the eve of returning
to Australia, and the passage was therefore secured.

CHAPTER XVII.

THE FREE PARDON.

We left Charlie just as he was proceeding on his voyage from New Zealand to Sydney in better circumstances; but although his purse was in a most flourishing state, his mind was far from being happy at the sad and mournful death of Pamul. The unfortunate cause of her early death preyed on his mind, and a feeling of self-accusation disturbed his rest when thinking of her.

His brave and noble protectress, whose quick and fertile mind he had taken so much pains to cultivate, had been ruthlessly torn away in the bloom of youth. He almost wished that he had been lost with his companions, rather than be the unconscious cause of her untimely end. These were the thoughts which harrassed his mind during the voyage to Sydney, until the vessel entered that magnificent harbour.

A ship, apparently from England, was entering at the same time, and Charlie, on looking through his glass, observed among the females on board one who, if not her, was the very image of Mary Grant. His mind was instantly besieged by a crowd of hopes that it might be really her, and that Bella and her father were on board as well. He now levelled his glass, and took a view of the male passengers, but could not discover his faithful servant among them, which strengthened his hope that Bella was there.

As soon as the anchors of both vessels were dropped, he hired a boat to take him on board the ship. Reaching the ship, he climbed her side, and sprang eagerly on deck. On approaching the group of females, who seemed glad to see the first visitor to the ship after their long voyage, he saw he had not been mistaken, for there stood Mary Grant, who however, did not recognise him in his full-grown beard and moustache. But, as soon as she heard his voice mentioning her name, she started in astonishment, and then embraced him.

The impatient Charlie could not get nearer the object of his mission during the outburst of her surprise, but, on recollecting herself, she said, " Won't Mr. McKay be glad ? I'll go and tell him." Suiting the action to the word, she ran into the cabin, leaving Charlie in the same uncertainty, but more confirmed in his hopes. However, the illusion was soon dispelled, on his seeing emerge from the cabin, not his neighbour, but Mr. McKay, of London, who appeared delighted on meeting with Charlie.

A shade of disappointment passed over Charlie's countenance on seeing Mr. McKay, but this was instantly banished by the warm and hearty reception he received. Mr. McKay then told him of Lord Lundy's villany, and how his malicious inventions were found out, which had been the primary cause of the death of Bella's father. He then related the account of Charlie's supposed loss, of Bella's suffering, and of her determination to be faithful to his memory.

Mary Grant filled up any little intervals, and increased Charlie's happiness by the account she gave of Bella's constancy; but her own misfortunes, which she fully related, occupied the principal place in her mind. She then gave Charlie, Donald's free pardon, he thought that he would be more likely to find him out.

Charlie was greatly grieved at the fate of Donald, and congratulated Mary on being the bearer of his emancipation.

On entering into partnership with Mr. McKay, Charlie resolved upon taking up some grazing land, and for the purpose of stocking it, he entered into an engagement with a wealthy old colonist—a Mr. Wilson, (whose private residence was near Sydney, but who had an extensive estate about 100 miles distant), for the purchase of a herd of cattle, as he owned the best breed in the colony.

Having arrived at Mr. Wilson's estate, which was managed by that gentleman's brother, the cattle he was about to purchase were ordered to be collected, as they were at a place named Muroo, about ten miles distant, where Charlie first saw an Australian cattle muster. The first signal of the approaching mob, while he and Mr. Wilson were waiting at the stockyard, was the loud

cracking of the stockwhips, then the shouting of the
stockriders, intermixed with the rumbling noise of the,
galloping herd tearing through the forest. Shortly after
this clouds of dust which enveloped the leading herd,·
were seen; they soon entered the stockyard, the men,
being busily engaged in running in the stragglers.
Among these was one of an inferior breed of bulls, called
by stockmen *Scrubbers* or *Rushians*, which for a long
time had evaded the death-warrant that hung over him, for
whenever he approached the yard he managed to effect his
escape. At this time, after baffling all his pursuers
(except one) by charging them and then rushing off, he
began to show signs of distress and control to his solitary pursuer, who with his stockwhip had inflicted a
severe punishment upon him.

Mr. Wilson asked the stockman who it was that was
following the bull, when he was told that it was Highland Donald. "Ah," replied Mr. Wilson exultingly;
"now there is a chance of getting hold of that brute,"
and turning to Charlie added, "Yonder is a countryman
of yours, and although not two years after stock, there is
not his equal on the run, and I would sooner trust him
than many of the free men."

"Poor fellow," replied Charlie, "he is a prisoner then
—a rare thing among Highlanders."

"He is," added Mr. Wilson, "but I cannot help believing that he is quiet innocent of the crime he was
charged with."

The conversation was interrupted by the approach of
the humbled bull, who entered the yard submissively,
and his pursuer on coming up proved to be Donald
Munro, the piper.

At this moment an individual (who could not boast of
his good looks) and who, by his bearing and talk, Charlie
took to be the head stockman, strutted up to Mr. Wilson.

"Well, Griffin," exclaimed Mr. Wilson, "everything
right and ready?"

"All right, Sir, except that Highland Donald ruining
his hoss for the sake of that scrubber. I've a mind to
pull him before Paddy Plunkett first coort day. Fifty
lashes are too little for him."

" More charges, Griffin? surely getting hold of that
bull is of far more value than the price of a horse. If
that is the only charge you have to bring against the
best stockman on the place, I shall take no further notice
of it."

Griffin seemed quite crest-fallen at this rebuke, and
replied maliciously :—" But you must remember, sir,
that he is always giving me impudent answers, and is
constantly disobeying my orders."

Charlie, who was listening to these trifling charges,
could no longer bear to hear his old servant abused,
replied provokingly :—" It appears to me, Mr. Griffin,
that you have already a good supply of impudence
without *giving* you any more." This well-timed and
merited cut sent Mr. Wilson into a fit of laughter on
looking at Griffin's abashed countenance, as he mut-
tered some unintelligible curses at the *swell* whom he
had no doubt was a J.P.

Donald, who did not recognise Charlie, was ordered by
Mr. Wilson to lead the two horses to a small yard a
short distance off. Charlie, thinking this a good opportunity to make himself known without the spectators'
cognizance, followed Donald on the plea of getting a
parcel off the saddle.

The happiness which the innocent convict experienced
on meeting with Charlie, and the fact of his having his
free pardon, was great.

Charlie then told Donald of the charges Griffin had
brought against him, when he exultingly exclaimed—
" Ah ! the villian, won't I serve *him* out now."

It was agreed between them to return to the yard at
once, and for the present to keep the recognition and the
free pardon a secret.

On their return Griffin was ineffectually endeavouring
to draft the cattle, which proceeding was constantly interrupted by the attacks of the bull before-mentioned,
which sent him in hot haste up the rails at every charge.
On seeing Donald, Griffin roared out with his usual oath
commanding the former to jump in and help to draft,
which was done with a smile.

After once more compelling Griffin to seek refuge on

the side rails, the beast faced Donald, who, with the greatest unconcern. awaited the attack, and as the enraged animal lowered his head to toss him, he struck him a heavy blow on his head with a stout drafting stick which felled him.

This feat brought a cheer of admiration from the spectators, when the animal was instantly dispatched and dragged out of the yard. The troublesome beast having been got rid of, Griffin advanced boldly to prosecute the work, when Donald stepped up to him with a provoking smile and said—" Mr. Punch, you had better hand me that stick, or the drafting will never be finished."

On hearing himself addressed by his nickname, Griffin drew up the stick with all his might to strike the speaker, who nimbly leaped on one side, and thus evaded a blow which would, in all probability have killed him, and the force of which brought the assailant on his face on the ground. Munro instantly sprung upon him, and seizing him by the collar and belt, carried him to the side of the yard, and with one heave, pitched him into an adjoining yard, which was used as a deposit for filth and refuse.

The spectators, who were mostly prisoners or ticket-of-leave holders, stood amazed at the idea of a prisoner committing such an assault on an overseer, although they all thoroughly enjoyed the well-deserved humiliation which Griffin had met with, as he had been for a long time an object of their hatred through his tyrannical behaviour, while Donald was always held in great respect by them. The sorrow they felt was great, for they knew that a severe punishment was always inflicted in such cases.

As soon as the half-smothered Griffin had cleared himself of the mud, he burst forth in a torrent of rage, demanding at once the apprehension of the offender, who was to be given in charge, and brought before the magistrates the first court-day. This just and undisputed demand Mr. Wilson could not with propriety refuse, which, if allowed to pass, would prove a dangerous precedent. .

He therefore ordered the ticket-of-leave men present

to seize Donald, and hand him over to the constable at the homestead.

Munro threatened to serve the first person who would lay a hand on him in the same manner he had served Griffin, when knowing his strength, not one of them dared approach him, which aggravated the case against him and obliged Mr. Wilson to command all present to secure the culprit.

On this peremptory order being given, Donald was instantly surrounded, when Charlie Stuart, with evident authority stepped up exclaiming in a stern voice:—"Lay not a hand on that man; Donald Munro is a free man!" These words acted like an electric shock on the spectators who sprung back from their intended prisoner, when Charlie, to prove his assertion, produced the free pardon, and the *Colonial Gazette*, containing a copy of the same.

Munro was now surrounded by eager and smiling faces, and many were the congratulations he received on his emancipation.

The only person who appeared disappointed at the announcement was Griffin, who at once lost caste among them; Mr. Wilson told him he should not require his services in future, and offered the situation to Donald, with an increased salary. Donald thanked Mr. Wilson, but respectfully declined, saying that he would never serve another man so long as Charlie could find employment for him.

CHAPTER XVIII.

CHASING THE BUSHRANGERS.

Charlie Stuart took up a large block of fine land, which he stocked and formed into a station, after which he went back to Sydney, accompanied by Donald, in the expectation of meeting with Bella, whom Mr. McKay informed him by letter was on her way out and was daily expected. On his arrival he was greatly disappointed and alarmed, the vessel not having arrived although considerably overdue.

In the interval, Donald and Mary were married, and as Charlie could not wait any longer, he was compelled to return to his station, taking with him Donald as overseer, and Mary as housekeeper. Mr. McKay promised to send word by special messenger as soon as the ship arrived, but that happy event never occurred; for years passed away without any news concerning the missing vessel, which filled all parties with intense sorrow. Charlie was thus once more plunged into grief, and this time apparently without the least hope of enjoying the slightest happiness. He blamed himself for encouraging Mr. McKay to send for his niece, and the uncle took all the blame upon his own shoulders, which prayed upon his mind and ultimately brought him to his grave.

Mary (now Mrs. Munro) shared in the universal grief at the loss of her young mistress, and named her first born after her.

On one of his trips to Sydney, Charlie became acquainted with a very respectable and worthy family, named Forbes, the head of which was a brother to the Advocate in Edinburgh, and one of the earliest and wealthiest squatters in the colony. The eldest of the family, a young lady possessing many attractions, was engaged to a gentleman by the name of Melville, who had lately arrived; he was possessed of considerable wealth and was searching for stations, and on his return the marriage was to be celebrated.

This Mr. Melville (whom Charlie had not as yet seen) was also an acquaintance of the Forbes' in Edinburgh, but Charlie could not recollect that name among the visitors at the Advocate's house, he therefore supposed that the acquaintanceship was formed after he left.

About this time, some of the inland districts were infested with a band of bushrangers, under the leadership of a fearful desperado, known as Captain Melrose, whose depredations outrivalled those of any gang in the annals of colonial history. Not a week, or hardly a day, passed without bringing some fresh intelligence of outrages committed by them.

A large reward was offered by government for their

apprehension, but without effect, and the audacity and coolness with which their leader carried on his practices completely eclipsed all previous acts of bushranging.

Naturally of a captivating manner, and possessed of great personal attractions, he invariably succeeded in ingratiating himself in the estimation of unsuspecting and respectable society, representing himself as a man of fortune in search of stations.

In this disguise he became possessed of information regarding parties carrying cash and other valuables, and in some instances where valuable property had been deposited for security, which was soon pounced upon, as he had his followers always on the alert.

The mails were constantly robbed, banks and stores ransacked, prisoners were liberated, in fact, society seemed completely paralysed by the accounts which day after day appeared.

Charlie, with his overseer Donald, had been upon business to Sydney, and on their return journey passed through a township which had the previous night been visited by the notorious Captain Melrose and his band, under the following circumstances :—

The day before was the annual race day in that town, when all the people in the surrounding country met. Among others there was a strange gentleman, who put up at the principal hotel ; he visited the race-course, and by his engaging manner and apparently affluent circumstances, had attracted the notice of many, among whom were the stewards, who gave him a most cordial invitation to the ball, which took place the evening following.

According to custom the *elité* of the district attended the ball, and the stranger, who gained the confidence of all present by his gentlemanly behaviour, became a great favourite.

The night being warm and the room rather close, Captain Melrose sought the cool air about one o'clock in the morning. After being absent for a short time, he returned, to the consternation of all present, and was followed by a band of armed men ; he then commanded everyone present to *bail up* on one side of the room, his

men presenting their arms at the time at them. He then
addressed them, saying :—" Ladies and gentlemen, I am
truly sorry to interrupt your amusement for a short
time in such a manner, and also for treating your kindness towards me in such an ungallant way, but you must
think that *Captain Melrose* could not withstand such a
display of jewellery and other valuables while he and his
brave band were in need; I have therefore respectfully
to command that each and every individual present will
at once hand over his or her valuables to my lieutenant,
Mr. Williams, and to do so without any hesitation or
murmur, or I shall be compelled to adopt more unpleasant measures."

The very name, " Captain Melrose," filled the audience
with terror. Ladies unhesitatingly handed over their
ornaments, and gentlemen gave up their wealth. Having obtained possession of all that was valuable to them,
the party then helped themselves to the refreshments on
the side table, and then took their leave, the leader
taking a polite farewell of the assembly, and wishing that
they might continue their enjoyment as no more interruption would take place from him or his party.

It was on this morning of excitement that Charlie and
his overseer arrived at the scene of the outrage, and
heard with indignation the unequalled effrontery and
unfeeling conduct of the notorious Melrose and his
gang. Many of the ladies were still suffering from the
fright they received. A local paper gave a full account
of the robbery, and a list and description of the articles
stolen, with rewards offered for each ; messengers were
dispatched to the various police stations, and a number
of volunteers enrolled themselves for the pursuit of the
gang.

Charlie and Donald resolved upon searching carefully
on their way for the perpetrators. After leaving the
township they obtained some clue as to where the band
separated, evidently to baffle pursuers ; they found that
two of the party had taken the very road that Charlie
and Donald had to go, and a rapid pursuit was instantly
commenced. After riding for a considerable distance on
the tracks of the bushrangers, they arrived at cross

roads, when they heard cries of distress proceeding from
the bush. Riding rapidly in the direction of the cries,
they found a lady and gentleman tied to separate trees.
The unfortunate victims were a squatter named Ramsey
and his wife, who had been riding in their carriage, when
they were met by two well-mounted bushrangers, who
robbed them of their money, tied them as described, and
drove off in their carriage.

On being liberated, Mr. Ramsey begged of his
liberators to follow them at once, while he and his wife
would walk to the nearest police station, and lodge the
information.

This advice was instantly adopted, Charlie and Munro
renewing the pursuit, but this time with more ease and
rapidity, as the wheel tracks were quite visible despite
the tactics employed by the driver in keeping the hardest
part of the road in order to leave no traces behind.
However, nothing could baffle the eager pursuers, who
traced them to a small village, where the traffic obliterated the impression of the wheels. On enquiring at
different places, the only carriage that had been seen
was one which conveyed the clergyman to Mr. Forbes'
station on some pressing business. This somewhat
puzzled Charlie, as he did not think a poor clergyman
was a likely subject for a bushranger. While considering what course he should pursue, Donald came in
hurriedly, telling him that he had discovered the tracks,
and which evidently led to Mr. Forbes'.

As Charlie intended calling on Mr. Forbes, they started
forthwith, and on their arrival they saw a carridge in
front of the house.

Donald led the horses to the stable, while Charlie
entered the house, where Mr. Forbes met him very
cheerfully, and introduced him to the clergyman, being
the only person in the room besides themselves. Mr.
Forbes then said—" I am extremely glad to see you,
Mr. Stuart, and you have arrived just in time to share
our happiness. You are already aware that my eldest
daughter has been for some time engaged to Mr. Melville, whom, I believe, you have not seen, as he has been
travelling in quest of stations. He has arrived, but did

not succeed in finding anything to suit' him, and is resolved upon proceeding at once to Port Phillip. He has
sent on a large number of sheep and cattle, and came a
few minutes ago, accompanied by our own worthy
pastor, for the purpose of celebrating the marriage at
once, and will start off immediately after with his bride.
Indeed, the proposition at first took us all by surprise,
and I did not like the idea of parting with my daughter
at so short a notice, but, as the young couple were un-
willing to delay, I was forced to yield. I may also add
that Mr. Melville proves himself worthy of my
daughter, and a very eligible match in every respect, if
we may judge by the valuable presents he has made to
every member of my family. You may hear the
applause and noise in the next room, which is caused
solely by his bounty."

The last remark was correct, for each member of the
family came rushing into the room, exhibiting his or her
rich and glittering treasure.

The dinner was now ready, after which the ceremony
was to take place, and every one took their seat at the
table. The last that entered the room was the bridegroom, leading his intended bride.

Mr. Forbes instantly stepped forward, and introduced
his future son-in-law to Mr. Stuart, but great surprise
was experienced by the whole family at the two gentlemen as they approached each other suddenly stopping,
when both turned deadly pale, were unable to give
utterance to a single syllable, and stared sternly in each
other's face.

The bridegroom was the first to recover himself;
then, bowing stiffly, he took his seat beside Miss Forbes
at the table. Charlie took his place immediately opposite, when all the spectators, particularly the host, concluded that Charlie Stuart, by his singular conduct, had,
at one time, been a rival of Mr. Melville.

During dinner Mr. Forbes, in the course of conversation, inquired of Charlie as to what was the principal
news down the country, when the latter gave some
account of the daring outrages of the bushrangers,
handing a copy of the newspaper containing an account

of tho sticking-up caso at the Raco Ball. Tho host road aloud the article in question, which contained a full account of Captain Melroso's atrocitics. The brido, who naturally folt for the unfeeling conduct, turned her face towards her lover, and oxclaimed, " Did you over hear of such an unfeeling monster ?"

Melroso, who sat with his head bent forward, made no reply, but turned palo, and scowled with unnatural ferocity not peculiar to him, which sent a thrill of terror through her frame.   Mr. Forbes now camo to that portion which contained a description of tho articlos stolen, when the description of ono remarkablo and costly pair of bracelets attracted the brido's attention ; sho unconsciously dropped her eyes on thoso she was wearing, and which had been presented to her by her lover only a short timo before, and which exactly corrosponded with tho description her father road.

A strango feeling seized her, and upon raising her eyes to Charlio, she saw him staring with eyes full of indignation and distrust at her scowling lover ; springing to her feet sho made an attempt to approach tho open French window, but in passing round hor fathor's chair, sho fell with a scream insensible on the floor.

Charlio who was tho quickest flow to hor assistanco, raised her, and, in entrusting her to tho caro and attention of her father, said, " Tako your much-injured daughter ; your would-bo son-in-law is no other than Captain Mclroso the Bushrangor," then rushed from the apartment after him, ho having made his oscape amid tho confusion.

On coming out of tho house, Charlio mot Munro with tho horses ready, who, on seeing his master, understood tho cause of his hasto, and exclaimed, " Thero they go," pointing at tho samo timo to tho two horsemen in full gallop making towards tho forest.   Lot us mount and after thom replied Charlie, when both vaulted into their saddles, and driving their spurs into their horses' sides, flow after tho fugitives.

CHAPTER XIX.

THE CAPTURE.

It often occurred to Charlie, as well as Donald, that Captain Melrose of bushranging notoriety, was identical with Melrose of Edinburgh and London repute, but it never occurred to them that Williams his lieutenant,. was Donald's accuser, and who was the cause of his. transportation.

Donald's recognition of him was instantaneous, not- withstanding Williams's altered appearance; for, on going to the stable with the horses, he heard Williams convers- ing with the groom, and saw the haste he was in in pre- paring the horses for a start as soon as the marriage ceremony was over ; he therefore concluded that all was. not right, and without making himself known, watched. Williams's movements, and on the same plea of hurry to- start,.had his horses ready also.

Williams, who was on the alert, evidently expecting the pursuit, never went within doors, but watched every direction, leading the horses about, while the carriage was being got ready. On Donald leading his horses. from the stable ready saddled, he saw Melrose rush from the house ; on coming up to Williams, he said, " Mount and be off, we are sold," when both started off at full speed; but their former bush tactics were of no avail to them this time, for notwithstanding their- twisting and turning, clearing logs and creeks, they could not shake off their intrepid pursuers. The chase now became exciting in the extreme, each horseman was employing all his skill, and was straining his. horse to its utmost speed, but it soon became evi- dent that the bushrangers were overmatched, as their- pursuers were gaining upon them every moment, when coming upon some open ground, Melrose wheeled round, exclaiming with a fearful oath—" We'll fight them,. Williams, there are only two against two ;" he then fired at Charlie, who was nearest to him, the ball pene- trating Charlie's hat.

Before he had time to draw his second pistol, Charlie

shot his horse through the heart, wishing to take Melrose alive, who, on coming to earth with his horse, got
entrapped, having one leg fast under the carcase.

Charlie sprung from his saddle to disarm him, but on
approaching him, received the other charge in his left
side, which made him stagger, but the ball fortunately
glanced off his powder flask, which he carried in the
breast pocket of his coat. "Shoot me, you villain, you
have a charmed life," roared the disappointed bushranger; but his captor refused the demand, and secured
him on the spot.

The combat between the other two did not last so
long, for on exchanging shots, Williams fell wounded,
and became an easy captive to his active antagonist.

A party of troopers who were scouring the neighbourhood, through the information of Mr. Ramsey, were
attracted by the firing, and made for the spot, when the
bushrangers were handed over to their charge.

On Charlie's return to Mr. Forbes', a scene presented
itself which was heartrending to behold. Miss Forbes,
who a short time before was in the height of happiness,
was now the picture of despair as she lay upon her
couch. The family, who had been congratulating her so
recently, were now bewailing her approaching end in
the noontide of her youth and beauty, and heaping execrations on the head of the destroyer of their peace.
The clergyman, who had come to solemnise her marriage,
was now engaged in administering to her dying moments.

On seeing Charlie return, she feebly beckoned to him;
when he approached her, she whispered in his ear, "you
have not taken his life?" Charlie told her that he had
not, but that he had secured him. She then replied—
"Thanks, I shall now die happy. I feared that you,
above all others, should stain your hands with his blood,
since you were the saviour of our family from disgrace;
but alas! you are unable to save my life, which is as well,
I hope. Farewell, may your life be longer and happier
than mine." She then called around her the weeping
family, and after an affecting adieu, breathed her last.

The excitement manifested on the apprehension and
trial of the bushrangers had never been equalled in the

colony. Crowds of spectators flocked from all parts to
cheer and congratulate the brave captors and their
deliverers from such a scourge, while execrations were
heaped on the heads of the merciless malefactors.

The court was crowded to suffocation, while a large
number who could not obtain admission, awaited with
great anxiety the issue of the trial. A number of witnesses
from all parts appeared to identify the prisoners, and to
connect them with the several robberies committed by the
band; but the extraordinary skill exhibited by Melrose in
cross-examining the witnesses threatened to defeat the
ends of justice, were it not for Charlie Stuart's knowledge of his previous character. The appeal which
Melrose made to the jury in defending his own case,
had never been equalled for forensic eloquence in a
colonial court of justice. The effect of this was, that
many who had hailed his approaching doom were now
moved to pity him.

The judge, however, partly dispelled the effects of
this extraordinary oration, by telling the jury that their
duty was simple justice, and that they were not to be
influenced by the talent displayed by the prisoner,
which, instead of improving his case, would only aggra-
vate it, if they considered that the charges brought
against him were proved. The jury at once found both
guilty, and sentence of death was passed upon them, on
hearing which, Melrose exclaimed—"The gallows is not
erected, neither is the rope manufactured, which will
hang me."

This was, indeed, true, for the next morning he was
found dead in his cell, having strangled himself with his
necktie.

The following was found, written upon the wall of the
cell :—" Charlie Stuart, nor any other person, shall have
the satisfaction of seeing me swing. They will find me
with a smile of contempt upon my lips. The fates have
been against me, being twice crossed in love by my con-
queror. After being deprived of one, I never thought
that he would present himself and prove a stumbling-
block in my way of gaining the second, whom I truly
loved, but who is now, through me, no more."

CHAPTER XX.

CHARLIE DISCOVERS NEW COUNTRY.

The affecting and trying incidents which had followed each other, in such rapid succession during the last few years, were sufficient to overwhelm even a stronger mind than Charlie's, and they had such an influence on him that the monotonous bush-life he now followed was insufficient to eradicate its effects.

The first of these reverses was the unavoidable desertion of his country, leaving all that was near and dear to him behind; then came his shipwreck, and the singular manner in which he was saved; then followed the loss of the noble-hearted Pamul, with the mournful cause of her death; then Melrose's strange and terrible fate, added to his troubled mind, and kept open the wounds which the loss of Bella had caused. This last terrible blow came, too, at the very moment when his whole mind was filled with joy at the hope of every moment expecting to hear of her arrival, when his happiness would be complete.

In order to bear up under these hopeless reminiscences, and to banish them entirely from his mind, he resolved upon putting into execution a project which had for some time occupied his attention. This long-cherished idea was no less than to attempt to explore some parts of the yet unknown interior of Australia. The discovery of Australia Felix, and the many exploits of Sir Thomas Mitchell, had enkindled within him this idea.

Appointing a manager for his station, he, attended only by Donald, started to the most inland station, which was at the foot of the Australian Alps, resolving, if possible, to cross that hitherto impenetrable barrier, being under the impression that some good country lay between them and the coast. On arriving at the station he heard from the aborigines that some fine plains and rivers were beyond the mountains, stretching out towards the ocean; but as no great reliance could be placed on the accounts given by natives, no one as yet had undertaken the journey. Charlie could find but one among the whole tribe in whom he could trust for guidance across. This was a strong and intelligent fellow named Quandak, and who, according to his own report, had once been on a warlike expedition against the Warrigal tribe, as he called the natives of that district.

As the mountains which they had to cross were inaccessible for a heavily equipped party, Charlie resolved upon proceeding, accompanied only by Donald and Quandak, taking pack-horses to carry a supply of provisions.

After a great deal of fatigue and hardship, the passage across was successfully accomplished.

On crossing the last of the eminences, a sight burst upon their view which repaid them for all the difficulty they had endured. Underneath them, and stretching out towards the sea as far as the eye, aided by the glass, could reach, lay beautiful plains fringed with strips of forest, intersected by rivers rising in the Alps and discharging themselves into the lakes near the sea.

The charming scene reminded them of their native land, and filled them with such pleasant thoughts as they had not experienced since they left home.

The remainder of the journey was passed with lightheartedness and speed, as they travelled over extensive meadows never before seen by Europeans. In their rambles they suddenly came upon a small encampment of natives, who manifested great surprise at their appearance. A number of them gathered round Charlie, feeling him and his horse; but on seeing them dismount they rushed off in great terror, leaving all their effects behind them.

The small supply of provisions they had taken would not allow them to remain long; they therefore made a hasty return to the settled districts, highly gratified with their explorations.

On his return Charlie disposed of his station and started off again to the new country, taking with him Mary, several other servants, and all requisites to form a settlement. He led the expedition himself, leaving Donald to follow with the stock. Being the middle of summer the cattle were taken safely across the mountains, and the party took possession of the best part of the plains and watercourses.

Unable to procure bark for covering in the buildings until the wet season set in, they erected a building, which, although unroofed, would serve as a stockade or protection from the attacks of the natives, should they show any hostile disposition.

One evening, after coming home, and while hobbling their horses, a doctor, who accompanied the expedition, strolled a little distance from the stockade. Being unarmed, the natives who were in the vicinity, took advantage of his unprotected state and endeavoured to seize him. He fortunately, however, perceived them in time, and testing his legs to the utmost of their power, arrived at the stockade and reported the case. The party, on seeing the intended attack of the natives, took shelter within the building, barring the entrance, and then discovered that the affrighted medicus had ensconsed himself underneath a pile of bed clothes.

The disappointed besiegers, who now surrounded the place in force, were at a loss to know how to attack it, seeing no aperture through which they could drive their spears. However, their leader soon devised a plan which threatened destruction to all within the place, as they could not fire upon their antagonists. The plan which the besiegers adopted was to throw their spears in the air; this they did with such exactness that they fell inside the building, and but for the activity of the besieged, their destruction would have been complete.

Charlie, annoyed at not being able to retaliate, after a careful search found a small aperture between two slabs, in which he managed to place the muzzle of his rifle, and on taking aim, beheld the very object he wanted. This was the leader of the party, who was encouraging his men with a joyful countenance. Aware that the fall of their leader would disperse the enemy Charlie fired, and, as he expected, brought him to earth, which produced the desired effect.

An amusing incident took place on Charlie and his party leaving the stockade. An Hibernian, who filled the office of cook, and who was known

by the name of "Doughboy," seemed more curious
in his examination of the dead body, exclaimed in true
Irish brogue:—"By the hole in my coat masther, but
its a mighty polite or deeateful rifle that of yours, instead of sending the ball bouldly in the face of the
black, be dad it sent it round his head, and popped in at
his pole."

This remark, the party found on examination to have
some foundation, for the only wound to be found
was in his pole, although they knew the savage was
facing them when shot. This mystery was soon solved,
for they found the ball had entered his mouth.

Nothing of any importance happened to Donald while
travelling up with the stock save one, and which we will
here relate, as it gave an opportunity for him to gratify
his propensity of playing tricks.

One evening, just as the party had completed arrangements for their encampment, they saw something which
was a novelty in the bush; it was a rider dressed in
black, with a regular English hat (a bell-topper) on,
mounted on a black horse, and making towards the
encampment. On drawing near, Donald at once
identified him as the man who officiated as clergyman on
the stations, and was well known by the name of
Parson Croaker, but who had been expelled from holy
orders on account of his eccentric and unchristian pecu-
liarities, and who was now on his way to Port Phillip in
order to improve his circumstances. Donald who had
already played some tricks upon the ex-minister, was not
recognised, nor did he wish it, hospitably received
the traveller, giving him shelter and accommodation, as
no station or place of refuge was near.

At the time of retiring for the night, a difficulty presented itself to the parson which had been overlooked
until the last moment. This was how to secure his
horse, being naturally of a restless disposition and apt
to break away, especially as there were horses belonging
to the party feeding about, he was afraid that they
might entice him away and leave his master in the bush.

This was however got over by a proposition made by
Donald, and to which the parson agreed, which was

K

to the following effect:—that on lying down for the
night before the fire according to bush custom, the
parson was to fasten the end of his horse's tether round
his own leg, then, should the animal possess any inclination to stray, his owner would have full and ample
warning.   In conformity with this suggestion, the parson and Donald stretched themselves on the earth,
placing their saddles under their heads, having their feet
towards the large fire, which was constantly replenished
by the man on watch.   The ex-minister fastened his
horse's tether to his leg, and considering that all was
perfectly secure, was soon fast asleep.

His long and weary ride, together with this being the
first time he had slept on such a hard bed, caused him
to have fearful dreams.

Donald, who expected to have some amusement from
his invention, never closed his eyes, when at last the horses,
belonging to them came round; on seeing them the
stranger's horse made one bound towards them, dragging
the unfortunate parson through the fire.

Donald was somewhat alarmed at the scene, and was
unable for a short time to arrest the animal or liberate
his visitor, who, after all, got off with merely having his
clothes and hair singed.   The parson took some little time
to be convinced that he was still in the land of the living.

The task of forming the new station, and of holding
possession against the attacks of savages, now devolved
upon Charlie, and many skirmishes took place between
his men and the aborigines, who appeared determined to
drive the white-fellows from their hunting ground.
Every day fresh tracts of splendid country were discovered, and many places he took great pleasure in
naming after favourite spots in his own country.

Many settlers followed in his track, and took possession of the vast plains and pastures, which soon formed
a strong party to resist the savages.

Charlie had by this time built a pleasure-boat, in which
he made many excursions among the lakes, accompanied
by some of the neighbouring settlers and Donald.   The
first of these took place one beautifully calm day, when
Donald, having his bagpipes with him, was desired by his

master to play the old favourite pibroch, an air which he
had abstained from playing ever since the loss of Bella,
lest it might awaken sad thoughts in the mind of Charlie.

As the rowers measured their time with the thrilling
strain, and as the boat glided leisurely round one of the
picturesque islets, Charlie, who was seated at the helm,
became overwhelmed with mournful thoughts, which
were awakened by the favourite pibroch, and the surrounding scenery, which forcibly reminded him of happier days.

In order to hide his grief from his companions, he
turned round and directed his gaze towards the islet
they were slowly passing.

While his eyes were fixed on the islet, his thoughts
carried him back to the scene at the Bridge of Linn,
when he heard his lost Bella's endearing appeal on that
memorable morning, calling to him—when, hark! the
identical sound—"Charlie, dear, save me," struck his
ears above the strains of the music. With one bound
he sprung up, and rushing to the bows, pulled the
chanter from Donald's lips, and with looks of strange
wildness, exclaimed—"Did you not hear her?"

The bewildered company, who concluded that he was
under a delusion, asked for an explanation, when he
replied—"I am certain it was her voice." One of the
party now informed them that he saw a black-fellow
carrying a female in his arms into the scrub on the
island opposite, and that she seemed to resist him by
screaming out, which was probably what Charlie had
heard, and, mixed with the sound of the music, took it
for the voice of some acquaintance.

The rest of the company coincided in this supposition,
adding that if he had been thinking of some one at the
time, the force of imagination would construe the voice
of the Warrigal female into what he fancied he heard.
This argument tranquilised his mind a little, still the
sound and the words, with the never-to-be-forgotten
voice was too real to be erased from his memory or mistaken, and nothing but the improbability of Bella being
alive could allay or satisfy his mind, nor could he shake
off the strange impression caused by the occurrence.

Another strange circumstance happened at this time, which enveloped him still deeper in the mystery by which he was surrounded.

One evening while sitting in his room after the labours of the day, Donald, who had been on his usual rounds among the shepherds, entered breathless, with a countenance which bespoke terror and hesitation, when his master addressed him as follows :—

"Well, Donald, everything all right among the shepherds? No more attacks of the Warrigals, I hope? Why you look as though you had seen a ghost."

"To tell the truth, sir," said Donald, "If it was not a ghost I saw, I certainly saw something approaching it. But before I proceed any further, I wish to ask a question, which I trust you will answer."

"Certainly Donald, out with it," said Charlie.

"Well then," continued Donald, "I wish to know whether you are (as I have heard) a descendant of the Meoble family."

"Undoubtedly I am, Donald, I hope you have not seen the *Cu Glas*," replied Charlie.

"I'm sorry to say that I think I have," said Donald; "as I was riding across the plain, just now, my horse began to prick up his ears, and look behind him; it struck me first that the blacks were after me, but, on looking round, I saw a dog following me. Thinking it was a dingo, I slackened my pace and drew my pistol to have a shot at him. He then came up to me, when I beheld in the place of a wild dog, a large grey staghound, the very picture of poor Bran you left at home, stood before me. Being positive that no such animal was to be found in this colony, and according to the description of the *Cu Glas*, I instantly bethought myself that you were a relation of the Meoble family, and that he had followed you to Australia. After sniffing at me for a few seconds, he gave a whine, and left me."

"A rather long journey he must have had Donald. I thought you had left all your superstition on the other side of the line," replied Charlie, smiling at his servant's tenacity to Highland superstition.

As some of my readers may be ignorant of the meaning of the *Cu Glas*, Mheobail or Mcoble's grey dog, I would just say that an ancient impression existed among the Highlanders that a sort of follower, or *tuhich*, was connected with every old family, which, on certain special occasions, made itself visible—such as before a death, or any important event taking place, or occurring to a member or descendant of the family. Each family had its own *tuhich*, in the shape of an animal; hence the Mcoble had its *Cu Glas*, or large grey staghound.

Although Charlie did make light of Donald's *Cu Glas* at the time, he had in a few days, proofs of its existence.

A party of settlers had formed themselves for the purpose of driving from the neighbourhood a tribe of troublesome natives, who were slaughtering the cattle, and harassing the shepherds. After scouring the surrounding woods without falling in with the Warrigals, they, on their return came upon a herd of kangaroos, among which was a white one—a great rarity in the colony—after which the whole party with their dogs gave chase.

The animal flew at a tremendous speed towards a steep-banked creek that intersected the plains, near which stood a clump of scrub; but, on his approaching it, a large grey staghound' sprung out, causing the kangaroo to face the creek, which he cleared at a bound. The strange dog followed his example, and, in a short time overtook his prey, which was despatched on the spot; the dog then trotted off towards the forest on the opposite side of the plains.

The astonished equestrians and their outmatched dogs, on coming to the creek, were obliged to pull up, not being able to clear it.

Charlie Stuart, who was among the leading horsemen, gazed with astonishment at the dog, which none of the party knew, when Donald drew up to his master's side, and whispered in his ear, "I suppose you will believe your own eyes, and me now." Charlie turned sharply round, and replied, "If Bran exists, that is him."

"No! no!" added Donald, dubiously, "the *Cu glas*, and no other."

CHAPTER XXI.

A JOYFUL DISCOVERY.

Many efforts were made by the settlers to decoy or capture some of the Warrigal tribe, in order to civilize them, or bring them to amicable terms, but they were quite unsuccessful. The natives perseveringly held aloof, and annoyed the whites on every possible occasion, thus widening the breach that existed between them. On one occasion, while Charlie, in company with some of the settlers were exploring round the border of the lakes, they suddenly came upon a small encampment of natives among the tea tree, but owing to the thickness of the scrub they were unable to capture any. However, on a closer search among the scrub, Charlie found a little urchin hidden. On capturing him, he screamed out, "Lindigo! Lindigo!" with all his might. Charlie and his friends naturally thought that he was calling for his parents. After a good deal of coaxing and patting, Charlie was enabled to carry the little Warrigal before him on the saddle, and, on arriving at the station, he clothed and fed him, treating him with great kindness, by which means Takawarrant (for that was his name) soon became quite satisfied with his new home.

Charlie took a great deal of interest in his foundling, who manifested far more intelligence than his appearance indicated. He exhibited a great deal of curiosity and surprise at the various things he was shown. Among other things, Charlie showed him the miniature of Bella, which he wore round his neck. On seeing it, Takawarrant's surprise was far beyond that exhibited on previous occasions. Taking the likeness in his hands, he stared at it for a few moments, when he commenced to dance about, still looking at it, and exclaimed, " Pigininni Lindigo! Pigininni Lindigo!"

Charlie, seeing his excitement, endeavoured by many signs to find out the meaning of the word Lindigo, and told him that the likeness was intended for a white woman, while Lindigo (whom he imagined to be Takawarrant's mother) was black. His arguments, however, had no effect on Takawarrant, who still persisted in his former conduct, muttering some unintelligible sentences in his own language, in which the name Lindigo was most conspicuous. The substance of Takawarrant's explanations, although a mystery to his protector, was yet quite sufficient to set him speculating in his mind, and added greatly to the strange impressions with which he had been lately haunted.

About this time his faithful guide and tracker, Quandak, met with a sad loss at the hands of the Warrigals, which greatly oppressed him, and annoyed his master. This was their carrying off, by force Maria, Quandak's wife. The faithful fellow was greatly distressed, and vowed that he would never rest until he had recovered his lost bride, by tracking the Warrigals, and rescuing her at night. To pacify poor Quandak, and encourage him with some hopes, Charlie proposed a plan which might give Quandak an opportunity of regaining his wife, at the same time clear up certain doubts which had taken possession of his own mind, and also gratify his ambition for the further exploration of the Australian Alps.

It was accordingly arranged that both should start on foot as they would have to travel through wild country inaccessible to horsemen, taking with them only a scanty supply of provisions which they carried in knapsacks, as Quandak would always be able to procure game which would sustain them during the journey.

This arrangement met with the hearty approval of Quandak, who knew that the Warrigals visited the mountains at this season of the year, where he fully expected to meet with them, and as he would be free from the trouble of having a horse to look after, he would be able to prosecute his searches with greater security, and by sneaking into their camp, obtain the object of his search.

Everything for this perilous journey was prepared privately. Charlie, on communicating his intentions to Donald, besought him to keep the affair a profound secret, giving him at the same time two sealed packages, one of which Donald was to break open at the expiration of four weeks. This contained all necessary instructions for Donald's action; the other package was addressed to Mr. McKay, in Sydney, and which was to be forwarded to him by Donald at the expiration of the four weeks, did Charlie not return in that time.

Donald was very much against his master's strange and perilous undertaking, and strenuously endeavoured to dissuade him from taking such a course, arguing that sufficient country had already been explored, and although he might possibly extend his discoveries, the fruits of his toil would only fall into other people's hands, who would not even thank him for his philanthropy.

These arguments, although stamped with truth, did not alter Charlie's determination, and Donald was obliged to relinquish his task, muttering to himself, on taking leave of his master:—"I know the *Cu Glas* had some particular business in coming to Australia."

Charlie and Quandak, after great fatigue and hardship in penetrating steep gullies and ranges, came upon some good grazing country fit for a settlement, and having satisfied themselves with its extent and capabilities, they commenced their homeward journey.

Quandak was greatly disappointed at not meeting with or perceiving any traces of the Warrigals, with whom Maria was a captive.

One evening, however, they came to an old encampment among the ranges, where they intended to pass the night, when, just as they were about to light the fire, the quick ear of Quandak heard some indications of an approaching tribe, who by the sound were evidently on their way to the Alps. His countenance at once brightened up; he told his master that they must at once look out for a place of concealment, from which they could with safety reconnoitre.

The judgment with which Quandak conducted any case of emergency, and his indisputable experience in the habits of his own countrymen, led his master to be guided by his counsel; but the only cover or place of refuge within a short distance of the encampment (where Quandak said the tribe would stop for the night) was a

large tree whose foliage promised perfect security. A
difficulty now presented itself, and which they had overlooked until the last moment, which was, that although
Quandak could easily climb the tree, Charlie would be
unable to accomplish such a feat.

A second search was accordingly made, when they
found a hollow stump standing near the encampment,
into which Charlie was obliged to lower himself from the
top and crouch down. Quandak had barely time to gain
the position allotted to him, when the foremost of the
tribe made their appearance, and, fortunately for the
explorers, they were too tired and hungry to notice any
tracks or indications of the presence of any foe. The
darkness of the evening, which was now closing in,
favoured Charlie and his companion greatly.

The clamour and noise made by the natives in erecting
gunyahs, together with the preparation of their evening
meal, struck strangely on Charlie's ear within his narrow
prison, and he expected every moment that some of
them would set fire to his refuge. This was not done,
and he was left unmolested to commune with his own
thoughts, and meditate on his peculiar and unsafe situation.

As the darkness advanced, and the glare of the fires
became more visible, Charlie observed that a small crack
in the shell admitted a little light from the opposite fire,
and through which he peered, in order to obtain a view
of those immediately before him ; when, to his surprise,
he saw Maria, Quandak's wife, in her old calico dress, in
close conversavion with another female in a fur dress,
but whose face was turned from him.

There being no other person at the same fire, he kept
his eyes fixed on them, as he was anxious to see the face
of the woman talking with Maria, and whose dress appeared to be made in a more civilised manner than those
worn by aboriginal women.

Maria now replenished the fire, which sent up a bright
blaze, and, at the same time, her companion turned her
face full upon it. Was it a vision Charlie now beheld?
his face felt cold, his limbs trembled ! He gasped for
breath, and, wiping his eyes, for he doubted them, he

stared wildly. Nay! It was no vision! There sat before
him the never-to-be-forgotten beautiful form and face of
his long lost Bella McKay !

His late hopes and presentiments were indeed true; it
was her well-known voice that he heard above the sound
of the bagpipes, while on the pleasure-trip among the
lakes. She was the Lindigo that little Takawarrant
called on, the day he was captured, and afterwards recognised her by her portrait ! What was he now to do ?
Would he at once go forth and claim her, thereby risking
her's, as well as his own, life ?

While thus debating in his mind, he heard the snuffing
of a dog round the tree, and on coming to the crack,
behold another old and faithful friend, his stag hound
Bran. This was Donald's *Cu Glas* ! But how came
he here, or was all a dream? His old familiar *Bran
bochd* escaped unconsciously from him. A fatal recognition, which threatened destruction to all! for, on hearing
the well-known voice and words, the hound flew at the
thin partition which separated them, with such manifes-
tations of joy, that his whining and tearing attracted the
attention of some of the savages.

Charlie now saw one powerful fellow approaching his
refuge apparently with the intention of ascertaining what
game was hidden there, and which the dog was so
anxious to unearth; for, on coming up, he walked
leisurely round the stump, repeatedly tapping it with a
stone tomahawk.

At this moment a long and shrill whistle sounded
through the valley, which, with its peculiar note, arrested
the attention of the savage, and he stood listening as if
expecting its repetition.

Charlie was looking through the crack at this time
watching the females at the fire, when he observed
Maria, who had heard the whistle, start unconsciously,
but, as if checking herself, she stared cautiously around
her, then whispered in her companion's ear, but instantly placed her hand on her arm, as if commanding
silence.

The savage, whose curiosity was attracted by the restlessness of the dog, walked towards the fire where the

females sat, and, as if speaking of the game the dog had found, took up one of the fire sticks, with the apparent intention of smoking it out. On seeing this, Maria whispered in her companion's ear, when the latter sprung up instantly, and approached the shell, which the dog was still tearing at.

This was the opportunity for the pent-up prisoner to make his presence known, as the native was now returning with the fire-brand; placing his lips to the crack, he had only time to whisper, " Bella, dear, if that be you, save Charlie Stuart, or we both shall be lost." With wonderful self-possession and presence of mind, she turned round, and in a tone which bespoke gentleness and persuasion, arrested the savage in his intention. The meaning of the petition Charlie could not understand, but the voice was unmistakably that of Bella, and whatever was the purport of her supplication, it had sufficient influence over the savage, as he instantly yielded possession of the weapon, which she carried back to the fire, at the same time calling Bran to her side, and also coaxing the savage to follow the example. On returning to the fire, she invited him to seat himself between her and Maria, when both females engaged his attention, thus warding off the terrible fate which threatened Charlie in his cell. But, alas! these hopes were but of short duration, for he had hardly time to feel thankful for his deliverance, when another of the tribe, who had evidently been an eye-witness to the scene, thought he might perhaps secure the game in a quieter manner, by climbing up to the top of the stump, and harpoon it with his spear. Just as he gained the top, the mysterious whistle rang a second time through the air, with a strange and piercing shrillness, and which for a few seconds arrested the savage's attention. During this interval Charlie had time to raise his rifle to his shoulder, and when the savage was in the act of setting his feet on each side of the stump, so that he could properly use his spear, he fired.

The unexpected and loud explosion from within the shell, and the death-yell of the savage, as he fell backwards on the ground, made an awful and unearthly

noise through the valley, and which produced such a
panic among the tribe that they made a precipitate
retreat under cover of the darkness, shrieking and yell-
ing as they went along.

When quietness again reigned in the valley, Charlie
and Quandak seeing the coast clear, emerged from their
hiding places, but alas! their prizes were nowhere to be
found.   In vain did Quandak send his shrill whistle
through the valley, but no response was returned by
Maria, who, with her companion, was still in the power
of the savages.

The darkness of the night and their ignorance of the
route the fugitives had taken, prevented them from
prosecuting the pursuit until daylight would enable
them to follow the tracks.   This misfortune filled Charlie
with alarm, on being informed by Quandak that the
Warrigal tribe invariably put their captives to death
when pursued, sooner then surrender them, and which
generally took place at their first encampment.   However, as they were unable to proceed at present, they
anxiously awaited the breaking of day.

CHAPTER XXII.

THE WHITE CAPTIVE.

While Charlie and Quandak are eagerly looking for
the dawn, we will carry the reader back several years to
an account of events which had taken place, and which
were closely connected with one of the principal characters of this tale.

The scene was on board ship, and the time sunrise.
The sea was perfectly smooth, and the air calm; not
a breath to fill the listless sails, and the vessel stood
still; flocks of mutton birds flew past, proceeding in
thousands to their fishing grounds.

A lady passenger, of uncommon beauty, attired in a
tastful but simple dress, stepped lightly upon the quarter-
deck.   A cheerfulness spread over the countenances of
the weather-beaten sailors as they washed down the

decks, and the mute obeisance of the officer on watch testified to the high estimation in which she was held on board.

Advancing towards a large dog-kennel, she applied a key, and instantly a large grey stag-hound sprung out, manifested his joy at being released by dancing around her. After having gone through these joyful evolutions, his mistress called him towards her, and patting his head, said fondly :—" *Bran bochd*, you will soon obtain your liberty I hope, and may be find your master again, for being such a good fellow on the passage." The last words of this address were uttered in a low key, and although only intended for a dumb animal, they brought a blush to the countenance of the speaker, which was partly hidden in the shaggy coat of the hound.

The reader can easily recognise in the passenger, our heroine, Bella McKay, who, ever since the departure of Charlie, had taken under especial care his favourite hound.

On receiving the joyful intelligence of his safety, and accepting the invitation of her uncle, she resolved upon taking the dog with her, not only on account of his usefulness, but also to prove to Charlie her constancy and unaltered love. The generous and obliging Captain appreciated her devotion, and made all necessary arrangements for the accommodation of the dog as well as his mistress.

Another person now appeared on deck, who, after surveying the four quarters of the heavens with the experienced eye of a thorough seaman, approached Bella with an outstretched hand, and wished her a hearty good morning. Captain Hector McLean was a fine specimen of the British sailor. His strong and well-formed person above the middle height, with an elastic and firm step, proved at once an active, as well as a brave sailor. His fine intelligent eyes, under finely arched black brows, contrasted admirably with his ruddy countenance. Born of a respectable family, in one of the western isles of Scotland, he was, as an early age, brought to follow the seafaring life. The whole of the family emigrated to Australia in a vessel of their own, where they took possession of some fine land, which, by good management, raised them to affluence; this, with the uprightness of their character, gained for them the good wishes of all classes.

After exchanging the greetings of the morning, Bella teasingly said:—"How is it, Captain, that sailors always look more serious and concerned in beautiful weather when so near land, and within a short distance of port. I really believe you would prefer being in the middle of the ocean, with a gale of wind. I hope Mrs. McLean is no worse, since we have such delightful weather; why do you look·so anxious?"

"I am happy to see you look so cheerful, Miss McKay, but at the same time I must confess that you have partly guessed the cause of my seriousness, Mrs. McLean is indeed not so well; she is much more restless and feverish than I have seen her during the voyage, and although the distance to port is not great, I doubt whether she will live to see it."

"Nonsense, Captain, you will soon see her on deck with me to enjoy this delightful scene."

"You are, indeed, very attentive, but I fear your benevolence and kind attentions will fail this time; but, did you ever believe in dreams, Miss McKay?"

"Surely, Captain, you have long ago forgotten our Highland superstitions, and are not influenced by such nonsense now."

"You may smile my dear friend, and I assure you I always placed as little faith in dreams as anyone; but last night's has made such an impression on my mind that I cannot shake it off—everything appearing so real."

"And pray, Captain, what was the substance of your dream, may I ask?"

"Well, as I see you are a non-believer, I will relate it. I thought that a fearful hurricane overtook us, which drove the vessel ashore, and as soon as we escaped the waves we became the victims of savages, who destroyed all but you. Now, ridiculous as you may think this, I hope you will not mention it to my wife, as I have not told her a word of it for fear of increasing her restless-ness. But, bye-the-bye, Miss McKay, don't these white rocks remind you of some of the ruined castles in the Highlands?"

" The very thought which occupied my mind when you
came upon deck. See, yonder stands *Castle Tioram in
Moidart;* and there frowns Barra Castle, where St. Clair
was exiled ; and those two are your chief"s castles, opposite *Duart* as *Donalla Muchoineamh a chiele* (Duart and
Dunolly *vis-à-vis*). But this comparing will not do ; I
must be away to my patient and bring her up, for it
would be selfishness on our part to enjoy such scenery
without her sharing it." As soon as she had said this,
off the lively girl tripped on her benevolent mission.
The Captain watched her until she had disappeared down
the steps, then drawing a sigh, the word " angel " escaped his lips.

" Rouse, yourself, my dear Mrs. M'Lean, and accompany me on deck, where you will see some most delightful scenery, which will banish all the sufferings you have
experienced during the passage." Such was Bella's
morning salutation to her invalid friend on entering the
cabin. She soon saw that the Captain's account of his
young wife's state of health was quite true ; a change for
the worse was evident ; her looks and voice bespoke
restlessness and feverishness which was not observable
the night before. She acknowledged the kind inquiries
and encouraging propositions of her friend with a mournful move of the head, adding—" You have indeed been
very kind ever since we came on board, but I doubt
whether you will be able to get me out of bed alive ;
some fearful despondency weighs upon my mind, and
many terrible presentiments that I shall never see the
end of the voyage."

" Nonsense, my dear, that all comes from lowness of
spirits, caused by your being obliged to keep your cabin ;
but it will all disappear when you get on deck and feast
your eyes on scenery which will rival your Highland
home."

" I doubt it, Bella; and to add to my former indisposition, I was visited last night with such a frightful dream,
the effects of which I am unable to drive from my mind,
for every circumstance appeared so real ; and although I
know you will ridicule my superstition, I cannot help
relating it, for I could not find sufficient courage to

mention it to the Captain, as I know he would only laugh at my silliness."

"And pray, my little prophetess, what was the substance of this terrible dream," replied Bella, with a feigned indifference, for something struck her that it was very remarkable both husband and wife should be visited in the same night by such dreams.

"You may smile my dear, I have always been an unbeliever in dreams as well as you, but that of last night had such terrors connected with it: I imagined that a storm came on, which drove us on land, where a number of wild savages seized upon us, the fright awoke me with a start, and I am unable to banish it from my mind."

"Is that all," replied Bella, provokingly, at the same time forcing a smile. "Have you never heard that dreams go by contraries? Now I shall take upon myself, for the first time, to be a reader of dreams, and yours of last night indicates, according to this rule, that this fine weather will take us safely to Sydney, where we shall be received by our friends with open arms."

Bella McKay, with her usual cheerfulness and encouragement, succeeded in coaxing the invalid to dress herself, and accompany her on deck, when the beautiful prospect soon dispelled part of the gloom and anxiety which had taken possession of her mind.

During the whole forenoon the same calmness continued, but Bella noticed that the Captain constantly watched the weather-glass and sky with more attention than usual. At length, beckoning her to the other side of the quarter-deck, apparently unperceived by his wife, and on her approaching him, he spoke as follows:—" My dear Miss McKay, you have always acted the part of a kind friend to my wife during her illness and the voyage, and I shall be obliged if you would take her below, as I expect a strong gale of wind soon (or, as we call them in Sydney, a brickfielder) from yonder black cloud. These sudden gales are very prevalent in these latitudes, and are generally preceded by such calms and stillness as we have had to day. You need not be alarmed, for if we are hard pressed, we can find shelter in some small

covo on tho coast until it blows over, although I would
rather bo caught in tho wido ocean, than in theso straits
and currents."

Bella now looked at tho cloud, which appeared liko a
black spock in tho heavens, but which every minuto increased in sizo. Without betraying any concern, sho
conducted Mrs. McLean to her cabin, which they had
hardly gained, when tho loud and clear voico of tho
Captain was heard calling out, "All hands ready, tako
in sail!"

Tho astonished seamen could hardly believe their
ears, and stared in each other's faces, when the captain
again called out:—"make all ready for a galo of wind."

This well-known command mado them spring up tho
rigging, and it was well that they had exercised such
rapidity, for no sooner was tho vessel mado snug, than a
sudden blast struck her aloft and would have sent her
on her beam ends, had not tho few sails set given way.

Tho galo now set in with fearful violence, driving tho
ship under baro poles before it, until darkness closed
around them, which rendered their situation moro
perilous. Tho experienced commander well knew that
if the galo lasted long, they would bo forced upon a leo
shore before morning; ho therefore endeavoured to
bring her head up and lie to, but tho forco of tho hurri-
cano mado this a difficult and hard task.

Tho night was passed by all on board in tho utmost
anxiety, which was greatly increased on tho first appearance of daylight, for the wind and current had driven
them far beyond tho captain's anticipated distance, and
in sight of tho ninety-mile beach, which extended as far
as tho eye could reach on their leo and which offered no
shelter to them. Each moment they approached nearer
and nearer to their inevitable doom; tho bravo captain at
length mado known his intention to beach tho ship,
which was tho only chance of saving themselves.

This terrible expedient, which would bo attended by
so many dangers, was determined on, and everything prepared accordingly. Tho captain took tho wheel himself
in order to run her with as much case as possible towards her foaming berth, while each seaman stood with

L

his axe in his hand ready to cut away spars and rigging when she touched.

The moment was an awful one, each man stood ready at his post with a pale and resolute countenance, and as the ship rode furiously on the crest of the surf which carried her to her doom, the implements came down at one swoop at the word "cut away my lads!" when the tall masts with the entangled rigging fell over the side with one fearful crash, which sounded above the roaring of the billows. When the wreck was cleared away, the longboat was launched and all on board were got safely into it at great risk; she was then cut adrift, when a furious billow, which washed over the hull, struck her amidship, capsized her, and sent all on board into the raging surf.

Bella's first recollection was to find herself swept with fearful velocity on to the sandy shore, and when on the eve of being drawn back by the receding surge, she felt that something held her tightly by her clothes, which saved her from being drowned. The succeeding wave carried her still higher up, and in retreating the same firm grasp held her, but this time it dragged her out of the reach of further danger.

Bella then lay for some time quite exhausted, and unable to move, or even see, as her dripping hair covered her face, when some fierce growls struck her ear. Terrified at this second danger, and expecting that the growl proceeded from some native animal, she was afraid to open her eyes.

The warm rays of the morning sun soon revived her, and infused strength into her saturated form. The growling of the animal became more fierce, which was at length accompanied with the snapping of a dog, as if keeping some animal at bay. She now removed her dripping hair from her eyes, when a sight which filled her with awe and terror presented itself, and sent a thrill through her frame which almost deprived her of life. Within a few yards of her were ranged a number of natives, with dark skins, and painted with white stripes over the body, which gave them a horrible appearance. Each of them was armed with several war-

like implements, and whenever they attempted to
approach her, her brave guardian, Bran (from whom the
growling proceeded) made a spring at them, which sent
them back in affright.

Captain McLean and his wife's dreams recurred to
her at the moment, and she now guessed that her
faithful dog was her preserver, when near death by
drowning; and now the faithful brute stood by her in
another, and perhaps more trying time, protecting her
against the savages.

On seeing the terror the noble dog kept the natives
in, and gaining courage by the hopes that he might be
the means of protecting that life which had been so
wonderfully preserved, she considered it her bounden
duty to exert herself in fulfilling her share of the
responsibility.

Raising herself from the wet sand, which had almost
benumbed her, her first act was to look round for her
companions; but, alas, no sign or vestige of them could
be seen, and the admired Bella McKay, the idol of the
Western Highlands, was now a solitary exile and wanderer in a wild and unknown land, with not a creature
save her faithful dog, to protect her, or administer to
her wants.

How vain now all the attention and homage which
had been paid her by the noblest gallants in the British
Kingdom. Alas! the condition of the poorest and
simplest mendicant in her fatherland would now be
hailed by her as an inestimable blessing in her present
forlorn state, her very existence being threatened
to become a sacrifice to those most terrible-looking
savages.

These thoughts were soon interrupted by the
approach of a tall and powerful-looking savage, who,
by his manner and looks, appeared to be their chief.

With a significant gesture and word of command, he
sent the whole party up the beach, but they returned in
a short time unarmed, each holding up a green branch.
This she understood to mean peace, having heard and
read of similar practices among savage nations, which
greatly alleviated her fears, and which, with the sus-

picious and terrified looks they cast on Bran, filled her
with some hope of security.

The chief, meanwhile, displayed many signs of sympathy for her pitiful and uncomfortable condition, pointing to her dripping garments, and then pointing to some
smoke that appeared to issue from a fire above the
beach among the bushes, by which she understood that
he invited her to warm herself.

Seeing opposition unavailing, being entirely in their
power, and having the protection of Bran, who appeared
to hold some mysterious influence over the savages,
(which had they possessed sufficient courage, they could
easily have despatched with their spears,) she consented
to follow them.

On arriving at the fires, round which some small sheds
were constructed of sticks and bark, the chief brought
from the largest of them a rug made of skins of animals,
and apparently the best change of clothes in his wardrobe. This she folded round her, which, with the heat
of the fire, soon warmed her.

Great care and attention was paid to her and to her
comfort by the chief and the whole tribe, which she had
no idea was in their nature. The most delicate portions
of fish and game were prepared and offered to her as her
food, with some berries and other native fruit.

A more commodious and secure shed was constructed
for her accommodation, and which was kept strictly
private for her and Bran, who kept watch over her day
and night.

CHAPTER XXIII.

MATOKA, THE WARRIGAL YOUTH.

The feelings which overwhelmed Bella in her captivity,
and the many hardships and sufferings she had to endure,
would have crushed many a stout heart. The fate of
her companions she could not learn, but the fatal evidence of seeing the clothing and other articles distributed
among the tribe, left no room for conjecture; but, how

came she to be saved? it was beyond her comprehension. Many articles of value to her and her captors were saved from the wreck. Everything portable was removed to the main encampment, which was situated on one of the lake islands a short distance inland, where all the women and children of the tribe were at the time. Among the latter Bella, or Lindigo, as she was named, became a great favourite through her kind attentions to their wants, particularly those suffering from illness. A medicine chest belonging to the ship was among the articles saved, by which she was able to cure several cases among them.

On becoming acquainted with part of their language, after a great amount of trouble on her part as well as her instructors, she understood the reason why herself and Bran were so much venerated among the tribe.

It appeared that the chief, Bungilina's father, had the year before been fishing at the very spot where the vessel was wrecked, when an enormous shark carried him off. On the tribe seeing the ship cast on shore, and the people struggling in the waves, Bungilina's attention was attracted by Bran saving the body of Bella, and never having seen an animal of that sort, he thought that it was his father, who had taken upon himself the form of a large dog (a general belief among the aborigines) in order to save Lindigo, who, like a spiritual being was sent to their tribe to confer many benefits upon them. Bungilina was so impressed with this idea that he gave positive orders that Lindigo and Bran were not to be interfered with, neither was any insult to be offered to either.

Lindigo, as we shall now call Bella, derived a great deal of instruction from a youth of the tribe named Matoka, who was apparently about seventeen years of age, possessed great intelligence and activity, and was remarkable for his appearance, being far above the rest of the tribe. He considered Lindigo as a spiritual being, and was guided by her instructions in the improvement of his mind and habits. His instructress had gained his confidence to such an extent that all the intentions and secrets of the tribe were communicated to her by him. Her least wants and comforts were attended to with the most scrupulous nicety. Her *gunyah* was constructed with a greater regard to neatness and comfort than any of the rest, and was tastefully decorated with many curious ornaments. Her clothes were made of the finest skins of the *Tuon* (a small squirrel), and her food consisted of the most delicate game, such as the Wonga Wonga, Quail, &c., so that her captivity became more endurable every day, as she became more reconciled to her fate.

Her dog also gained a more exalted position in their estimation, and fully confirmed their first opinion that he was Bungilina's father, being equally as good a hunter as their lost chief. A plentiful supply of kangaroo and emu were run down, so that they had more food than they could consume, and their former enemies, a neighbouring tribe were entirely subdued, all owing to the advent of Lindigo and her dingo among them.

Years passed away without bringing succour to the forlorn captive, but her hopes never deserted her.

The tribe shifted their haunt occasionally between the lake islets and the plains, where game was procured in abundance, through the services of Bran. While they were on the plains, they were all surprised one evening at the sudden return of the men who had gone on a hunting expedition, and who were not expected back for a few days, plainly telling by their looks and manners that some extraordinary event had taken place which sent them back so precipitately.

Bungilina and Matoka, not being of the party, met the hunters before they entered the camp, to ascertain the cause of their unexpected return, the females being seldom admitted into their conferences or secrets. A long consultation took place among them, which judging from the excitement manifested by all parties, was of great importance, and Lindigo observed that several suspicious and stolen glances were directed by them towards her during the deliberation, filling her with dread and insecurity.

She missed from among them the leader of the band, who acted on such occasions as Bungilina's substitute

when the latter remained at home, and the grief and
lamentation of some of the woman who had gathered in,
left no doubt in Lindigo's mind that the missing man
had been killed in a fray with some other tribe, and of
which she was evidently to be kept in ignorance, as she
could not by any means ascertain the facts. Matoka,
her former friend and confidant, kept aloof on this occasion, and held down his head with apparent distrust and
sorrow whenever she caught his eye; this added considerably to her alarm. During the night preparations were
made for a speedy removal to the lakes, and at the break
of day they commenced their journey, and arrived safely
at their island home.

Many unsuccessful attempts were made by Lindigo to
induce Matoka to divulge the secret, but the fear of
punishment, and the strict discipline of his brother
Bungilina, kept him silent, knowing well that any
breach of the laws would be attended by fatal consequences.

Since their arrival at their island encampment, which
was situated in the middle of a clump of tea tree,
Lindigo sought the shade of a favourite cherry-tree near
the margin of the lake, where she had often passed a
quiet hour, reflecting on bygone days and happy hours,
which were apparently never to return.

On this day, which was beautifully calm, her thoughts
and meditations took a more affecting and mournful turn
than usual, occasioned by her having lost some of the
confidence of those in whose power she was, and particularly that of her kind friend Matoka, who had become
daily more reserved. Her own sad fate appeared more
awful to her mind, and her early happiness among those
she loved, contrasted with her present situation sadly
oppressed her mind.

The still and glassy lake before her carried her
thoughts back to Kinnlochlinn, on whose waters she
had so often gazed while waiting for Donald's pibroch,
telegraphing his young master's love to her ears.

How well she remembered each note, after so many
years! and how plain they sounded through her ears
and imagination at that moment! Strange! her imagi-

nation never before betrayed her into such a delicious
trance, or charmed her ears with such enchanting strains
of music!   Yes; every note of the never forgotten
pibroch became more and more distinct, and instead of
dying away on the air, and leaving her far more forlorn
than ever, it increased in power, and became more real!
Could it be a dream, or a prognostication of some
calamity?   She moved herself to ascertain whether she
was really awake, and turned her eyes towards the part
she imagined the sound came from, when! Did her
eyes deceive her?   Or was it a vision?   There, truly,
was the model of Charlie Stuart's boat gliding round the
point of the islet! and Donald Munro, as of yore, in the
bows, playing the well-known pibroch! Yes, it was him,
for she could not mistake his playing, for many a
delightful evening she had listened to it.   But, who was
that sitting at the tiller, and turning his eyes towards
the shore? It is he! It is Charlie Stuart! How
piercing are the eyes of love!   She could not be
deceived! She gasped for breath while in the act of
calling on his name! Her limbs trembled under her
when she attempted to rise!

A harsh voice now whispered in her ear the well
known words, "Wynn bah" (not yet), and a powerful
arm seized her.   "Charlie dear, save me!" were the
only words she could utter, when she fell insensible in
her captor's arms, and was carried back to the camp by
Bungilina.

On recovering from her swoon, Lindigo found herself
stretched on a couch, with Matoka bathing her temples,
and Bungilina bandaging his arm, it having been seriously
injured by the teeth of Bran, who was growling at her
side.

When the chief was removed out of hearing, and
Lindigo was able to converse, her kind friend Matoka
told her that Bungilina, having been fishing on the
opposite side of the island, heard the strange music
from the whitefellows' canoe; he then ran home, under
the belief that they were coming to rescue Lindigo.
Not finding her at the camp, he made for her favourite
haunt the cherry-tree, from which he carried her to the

camp insensible. When Bran saw her in Bungilina's arms he sprang upon him, and would have torn him to pieces, had not the chief instantly laid her down.

The weakened state of Lindigo, and the tears she shed at her disappointment in not being seen and liberated by Charlie and his companions, moved the young savage to pity her.

He now told her the purport of the secret which had been kept from her; how it was that the hunting party had so suddenly met with the loss of their leader.

This was that they discovered a number of white men, with many strange animals and other things belonging to them, had taken possession of their hunting grounds; that when they attempted to drive them away, and surrounded them in their building, fire and thunder was sent upon them, which killed their leader at once. Hence their precipitate retreat to the island, lest they should all share the same fate if Lindigo was found in their possession. He also told her that strict commands on pain of death were given by Bungilina, that she was to be kept ignorant of the discovery lest she might make her escape.

Lindigo finding Matoka so communicative, and softened to such a degree towards her, thought this a favourable opportunity to gain his pity and assistance in making her escape from where she might remain a captive all her lifetime, and at the same time so near the only person she loved on earth. She worded her petition in the following manner, according to the custom of the tribe:—

"The brave Matoka knows well that a poor woman who was never used to living in the thick forest, or swim the deep water, or paddle the canoe like his own native women, is unable to make her escape without the help of a warrior! and who could she seek help from in an undertaking which would bring to her the greatest happiness she could desire, but her kind, generous, and brave Matoka; who had always attended to her comforts, and whose quick eye and swift foot hunted down the fastest kangaroo which furnished her with food and covering, whose skillful hand constructed her bowers and adorned them with the tails of the Wallna Wallna (Lyre Bird), whose sharp spear brought down from the tallest tree the nimble Tuon for her furs, and from the densest scrub the shy Wonga Wonga for her food!"

This appeal to the savage caused an apparent struggle in his mind, and he seemed to waver awhile between sympathy for the pleader and the stern commands and duty he owed to his brother the chief. But, alas! the latter predominated. The terrible punishment and over-lasting disgrace (should his loyalty to his tribe fail) determined his mind, and he answered—"It must not be. What would the Warrigals say if I were to assist you in your escape? They would say—'There goes the traitor Matoka, who betrayed his brother and tribe! He has opened the track for the white men to make thunder and spit fire upon us! Our wives will become widows; they shall wear clay on their hair, and our children will be orphans! Who will then hunt the kangaroo and emu? Our enemies shall hunt our game, which will make way for the white fellows' big animals! The cor-roboree will be held no longer, and the coocy and war shout will be silenced by the white man's thunder, and the loud crack of his snake (stockwhip)!' When you are gone there will be no smiling face to cheer Matoka when he returns from hunting his game and fighting his enemies. Who then will say a kind word to him, or teach him how the white man does his wonderful work? Lindigo will then become the wife of the white man, who will take her to his gunyah, where she will forget all about Matoka."

"Bravo and noble Matoka," replied Lindigo, "you are greatly mistaken; never will Lindigo forget her kind and generous Warrigal friend. If you help me you need no longer fear your tribe or their laws; the white man will be your friend, and that of your tribe, if you will but restore to them their long-lost Lindigo. They will give you their spitfire (gun), and teach you how to use it, when you will be able to chastise your enemies and kill your game. You will have no need to tire your limbs in your hunting, for a *Yarraman* (horse) shall carry you after it. Every one will then say—'There goes the

brave Matoka, who brought back our long-lost Lindigo !
Wo will make him a great chief over all the tribes ! We
will clothe him like ourselves, and give him back all his
hunting-ground.' "

It was enough ; the right chord was struck ; Matoka
surrendered to the musical voice of the pleader. He
could no longer withstand her look, and the touching
appeal of the white woman. His eyes brightened; he
grasped his nulla-nulla more tightly, then looking at his
half-naked limbs and inferior war implements, he whispered cautiously "Malae," (I surrender); "to-night, when
all are asleep." "Wah!" exclaimed Bungilina, who thought
the time given to Matoka had been exceeded, when the
young man sprung out of the gunyah, afraid that his last
words had been heard by his brother.

· With great anxiety and hope Lindigo watched for the
coming darkness, the time went wearily until the last of
the tribe had laid down for the night. Her dog kept
close by her side within the gunyah, and sat up as if
watching something. At length he gave a slight growl,
which was instantly interrupted by the hand of his
mistress being placed on his mouth, when the crouching
figure of the faithful Matoka was seen at the entrance.
Without a word he took her by the hand, leading her in
the same recumbent position, while her dog instinctively
sneaked behind her, and followed in a slow and measured
step.

· In passing close by Bungilina's gunyah they heard, to
their terror, that either his lacerated arm or suspicion
kept him still awake ; they had, therefore, to crawl
more cautiously, dreading every moment that he might
spring up and seize them. However, they cleared the
camp safely, and penetrated the narrow strip of tea-tree,
which separated the encampment from the border of the
lake where the canoes lay. Matoka pushed his canoe a
little further 'out, when Lindigo and her dog seated
themselves in the bottom. But, horror ! the faithful
guide had hardly taken his place when the alarm was
heard in the camp, and, instantly a rush was made to the
canoes. Matoka made the best use he could of the start
by shooting out into the lake, and, with his usual skill,

plied his paddles with great quickness; but, alas! his
pursuers were equally expert in that art. The yells
and screams of the pursuers, which pierced the still
night air, nearly frightened poor Lindigo to death.
However, by the encouraging words of her guide, she
endeavoured to keep her spirits up.

One canoe, which shot ahead of the rest, closed upon
them at every stroke, when Matoka uttered the word
Bungilina, which sent a thrill of horror through Lindigo's heart, knowing the chief's superiority in pro-
pelling his canoe. The chase now became exciting and
alarming to the fugitives, for the chief's canoe was
almost abreast of them, apparently Bungilina had the
intention of heading them.

The brothers now strained every nerve, when the
chief's wounded arm began to bleed, which greatly
weakened him, and was thus unable to gain an inch.

Seeing himself likely to be defeated, he seized his
boomerang, and hurled it violently at the fugitives, but
fortunately missed them, striking, however, the side of
their canoe, which, being nearly cut in two, sunk instantly under them. As Lindigo was sinking, her
faithful dog, for the second time, saved her life by holding her up, when the chief once more had her in his
power, and she again became his captive. The faithful
Matoka was picked up, greatly exhausted, by one of the
canoes, and brought back a prisoner to the camp.

Next day the sentence was passed on Matoka for
attempting to carry off the white captive, thus violating
the strict laws of his brother the chief, and the whole
tribe, who had prophesied their own extirpation should
Lindigo be restored to her own race, having no doubt
but that she would reveal their sacrificing her shipwrecked companions.

The sentence passed on warriors holding such a high
position as Matoka did, was generally to have a certain
number of spears thrown at him, according to the
nature and extent of his offence, and should he be skilful
and active enough to ward them off with his narrow
shield, he would be forgiven and raised to a higher rank.
But on the other hand, should he be unfortunate enough

MATOKA, THE WARRIGAL YOUTH.

to receive a wound, or be killed, his executioner would
step into his position. Matoka having therefore committed such a heinous offence, and being the rightful
successor to the chieftainship, his punishment was to be
more severe, which was that fifty spears should be
thrown at him by picked men.

The idea of escaping was almost hopeless, as the
tempting reward was sufficient to bring out the executioner's skill. The victim was accordingly brought
forth, and placed on the spot chosen in the presence of
the whole tribe. The chosen warriors were ranged
before him with their terrible spears, each eager to be
the fortunate victor.

Lindigo, in a flood of tears, endeavoured to arrest
them in their intentions, but it was of no avail. The
brave youth took his stand with a cool and determined
air, without the slightest manifestation of fear in his
manly and open countenance. His bold and confident
attitude was the admiration of all, and not a little aggravated his executioners' thirst for his life.

Lindigo wrung her hands in despair, blaming herself
for being the cause of the noble youth's untimely fate,
and she prayed that he might be spared.

Divesting himself of all covering except a fur kilt,
Matoka awaited the coming storm. Looking all round,
as if taking a last farewell of all, and giving one affectionate glance at Lindigo, who returned it encouragingly, he placed his right foot before him, and raised
his shield.

It would be superfluous to detail each aim, and the
determination exhibited to accomplish the object by the
executioners, or the extraordinary agility and expertness
with which their intended victim evaded and parried
each spear as it was darted with precision at his heart.
Not being at liberty to shift his position, which was
prescribed by a small circle, just sufficient to stand in,
nevertheless when a spear threatened his head, he
ducked down, and when one threatened his lower extremities, he sprung up, so that the spears, one after the
other, fell harmless in his rear, and stuck in the ground.

Those spears, however, which threatened his heart,

were more terrible; and required more skill to parry them off with his small shield, but they also shared the same fate, being met with wonderful steadiness, amidst the acclamations of the tribe, until the whole had been thrown, when Matoka was led forth in triumph for his unparalleled victory.

CHAP. XXIV.

A WELCOME STRANGER.

The attempted escape of the white captive led Bungilina to set a strict guard over her day and night, and her heroic companion, Matoka, was forbidden holding any conversation with her, merely supplying and attending her, with necessaries for her subsistence and comfort. This added greatly to her unhappy and forlorn state.

The loss of Matoka's company and confidence was, however, partly replaced by a little orphan boy, whose father had been, as already stated, shot by the white men, when besieged in their stockade, and his mother having died of grief at the loss of her husband.

Lindigo took pity on the boy, and as an atonement for the unfortunate and unavoidable act of her own race, she adopted him and became his protectress. Takawarrant fully acknowledged the kindness and attention thus bestowed upon him, which exceeded that of his mother, and, consequently, he became more attached to the generous Lindigo than to his late parents, whose loss he soon forgot.

His insignificance and youth admitted him to the meetings; he thus became aware of the secrets and intentions of the tribe, through which Lindigo was made fully acquainted with their transactions since Matoka's estrangement. But, alas! since the fates had apparently set their faces against her, this last source of happiness was soon snatched from her; for one day, as some of the tribe were visiting the mainland, and had encamped in the scrub, near the lake, an alarm was raised by the man on watch, when she was forced by Bungilina through the dense tea-tree, along with the rest. Under the impression that the unknown enemy were a hostile tribe, she willingly submitted, and sought cover until the tribe had mustered again, when she found that the only one missing was her poor adopted Takawarrant. His loss not being thought of any consequence to the chief of the tribe, she knew it was vain to apply for his rescue from his captors, so that she had to submit.

The time had now arrived when, in accordance with the custom of the tribe, and Matoka having attained age and importance among the Warrigals, it became incumbent upon him that he should take to himself a wife, who was to be stolen from some rival tribe; and in order to sustain that dignity which by his bravery he held, he chose to carry off his bride from among his most hostile enemies, the more risk and danger he ran in such an undertaking the more exalted would be his position in the estimation of the tribe. One moon was the allotted time for accomplishing his undertaking.

True to the confidence placed in him, Matoka returned before the specified time with a female stranger, and to Lindigo a very welcome one, on seeing her wear a European calico dress, and above all her being able to converse in broken English, a language she had not heard for many days.

The joy experienced by Lindigo was great on listening to Maria, as she called herself, and which name she said was given to her by "Massa Duart," her own and her husband Quandak's white master. She then told how she had been ruthlessly taken away while Quandak was from home, how kind Massa Duart was to them, and so beloved by all his servants and acquaintances, how she had been nursing Mrs. Munro's little boy and girl "Charlie and Bella," how Mrs. Munro kept house for her master, and her husband Donald acted as overseer, how little Takawarrant became quite happy in his new home, and lastly how Quandak on his return would institute a search for her.

These were the acceptable and joyful details furnished by the communicative Maria to her eager listener, who drank in every word of the narrative, although couched in many distorted and ill-used English words, but never-theless the intelligence was sweet to her ear. Fresh hopes now filled her mind that her rescue would be soon effected through Maria's loss, and that he would be sure to tell of her being with the Warrigals.

Maria's company was now a source of happiness which she little anticipated, and Matoka, who as yet had made but little impression on his forced bride, patiently waited until the impenetrable heart of Maria yielded to him, made no objection to the intimacy which had sprung up between her and Lindigo. He accordingly begged the latter to plead his cause with Maria, and endeavour to reconcile her to her fate, but she remained faithful to Quandak, from whom she was so ruthlessly stolen.

Matoka had now earned for himself a great name for penetrating the territory of the white man, and forcing from thence a bride of the natives attached to them.

In acknowledgment of these honours he resolved on making amends for his former disloyalty (in attempting to restore Lindigo to the white men) by keeping strict guard over her and Maria lest they should make their escape; so that any hopes of him being serviceable to them in obtaining their liberty entirely vanished.

The summer season was now advanced, and the time of visiting the Alps (on the disappearance of the snow) according to their annual custom had arrived. This, with a dread of a search being made, or the knowledge of the captive being in their power, made them move towards the mountains for greater security from their white neighbours. Such a proposition and resolve extinguished the last hope which Lindigo entertained, but Maria never despaired, and always encouraged her by saying— "Neber bear; Quandak berry good tracker, bye-an-bye come up with white fellows; plenty shoot him Warrigal."

These were but poor consolations for the white cap-tive, who knew better the character of their captors, their determination, and the motives which governed them to keep possession of their captives; and she also knew that should a forcible attempt be made for their rescue, their own sacrifice would be the consequence sooner than the Warrigals would give up possession of them.

Under these harassing thoughts, Lindigo, with her swarthy companion, was obliged to commence their weary pilgrimage towards the Alps, and leave behind the level plains, where Charlie was stationed quite ignorant of her sad fate.

Many a languishing and sad look she cast behind on gaining each eminence from which she could view the property of him who would sacrifice all for her sake; and she, the poor exile, suffering so many hardships and sorrows, which even the most wretched black on his station would view with horror. Another source of terror presented itself on the fatal journey, and the near approach of her being entirely out of reach. This was a strenuous appeal made by Matoka to plead his cause with Maria, otherwise he should be under the necessity of compelling her to enter his gunyah, although Lindigo had as yet dissuaded him from taking such a course. But another threat made by him filled Lindigo with more terror than anything she had experienced for many years, and which she would sooner suffer death than endure. This was that Bungilina intended to put in force the same condition respecting herself. At this announcement she almost fainted, but still having some slight hope, she told Matoka that he might entertain some hopes of gaining Maria without having to resort to such extremities.

That evening on arriving at an old encampment among the mountains after a fatiguing day's journey, while Lindigo was communicating the threats to Maria at the fire, a strange whistle pierced the air, the latter suddenly started, and quietly said:—" Ah! Quandak?" then checking herself, she whispered in her fair companion's ear, that she was positive it was his signal whistle, and that they might make their escape before morning.

While thus indulging between fear and hope, Matoka approached the fire, expressing a wish to know what Bran was besieging with such eagerness at the stump, and on his searching for a fire-stick, with the intention of smoking the game out, Lindigo sprung up in terror, lest the hidden game should be connected in any way with the signal whistle. It was under this impression

M

that she approached the hollow tree where Charlie was in ambush, and on hearing his well-known voice, she turned quickly round to arrest Matoka in his intention. Being fully prepared for any emergency, she with un-common self-possession and with an insinuating voice, took the fire-brand out of his hand on the plea of horror at seeing a poor animal suffocated. She then wished him to follow her to the fire where Maria was sitting, with the hope that some favourable agreement might take place between him and the latter.

Flushed with these hopes, Matoka willingly surren-dered his fire-brand, and Lindigo calling Bran to her side, warded off the fatal blow which threatened her lover.

Placing him between her and Maria, giving a signifi-cant glance at the latter, she adroitly engaged his atten-tion by encouraging words as to the change in Maria's disposition towards him, when the same mysterious whistle again sounded through the air. "Wah!" exclaimed Matoka, impressed with a superstitious awe on hearing so strange a sound, being conscious of never having heard it before that night, and certain that it was not made by any night animal or bird, he said:— "Have you heard that? I am certain that such a strage sound forebodes fatality to some of the tribe."

While Matoka was under the influence of the dreaded whistle, Maria whispered in Lindigo's ear, "Look out again." The latter sprung to her feet a second time, and hearing some of the savages gathering round the shell, she approached it, when she espied one of them in the act of drawing his spear to strike her lover, at the same instant the explosion, with the death yell of the savage so impressed her, that she fell insensible on the spot.

How long she remained in this state she did not know, but on recovering her consciousness, she found herself carried in the powerful arms of Bungilina, through wild and rough country in the dark, and the whole tribe seemingly on the move around her.

CHAPTER XXV.

THE RESCUE.

It was a night of anxiety for Charlie and his faithful guide, and with great joy they hailed the first streaks of day-light, when they set out on their perilous journey in the track of the Warrigals. Quandak's vision and judgment were never before put to such a test, and bravely he encountered every obstacle which the fugitives left behind in order to obliterate their trail. The bush was set fire to in several places, and all traces were adroitly confounded, but to no purpose, the experienced tracker surmounted them all, and like a blood hound, was gaining quickly upon them.

The course taken by the fugitives led along the summit of the range, parallel with a wild mountain stream, until arriving at a certain point where some tracks diverged from the main, down towards the river.

Quandak was at a loss which of these to follow, as the Warragals had apparently separated, in order, no doubt, to baffle pursuit. He, however, followed the most legible which the largest body of the tribe had taken.

After travelling for a little distance with great care, he came to a dead halt, exclaiming, with a doubtful shake of the head, " Baal come up· this way," and instantly retraced his steps to where the tracks separated.

He then followed those leading towards the cliffs, when he suddenly picked up something off the ground, and with delight exclaimed, " Ah Baal! stupid Maria," at the same time exhibiting a bit of that female's calico dress, evidently dropped by her in order to lead her husband on the right track.

This signal infused fresh vigour into the trackers, who prosecuted their task with indefatigable energy. They now scrambled down precipitous cliffs and other obstacles towards the river, Quandak picking-up several pieces of calico.

On arriving at the last ledge of rocks overhanging the river, a sight burst upon their view which filled them

with a mixture of fear and hope. Immediately opposite
on a small point of level ground, and on the same side
of the river where it had taken a sudden bend, were encamped a number of natives, elaborately painted and
armed (a sign of hostility), which plainly denoted that
the pursuers were not a moment too soon, as there was
a visible commotion, indicating that some extraordinary
act was about to take place.

They had formed themselves into a semi-circle, within
which Charlie and Quandak beheld the two females they
were searching for tied with their backs to two trees, and
with their arms bound. Quandak told Charlie that this
was the manner in which these savages put their captives to death when hard pressed, which fact Charlie had
the most positive proof of on seeing two of the savages
step forth with their spears poised, and each placing
himself in front of his intended victim.

Charlie, whose blood curdled in his veins, proposed to
charge the savages at once, but Quandak held him back,
saying, that before they could get round the bend of the
river, the work of death would be complete, and proposed
instead that as their rifles would kill at that distance,
and as no time was to be lost, that each should take a
true aim at his adversary both firing at the same time,
when they saw the executioners shake their spears in
the air.

In conformity with this proposition, the riflemen
elevated their rifles, and with a steadiness and truer aim
than ever they practised before, at the expected signal
both fired.

The sharp ring of the rifles, the death shriek of the
savages as they rolled on the ground, while the spears
which were intended for their victims stuck quivering
in the trees above their heads, caused such a panic
among the savages that some plunged into the river,
others ran for shelter among the scrub, and all deserting the scene and their victims, whom they intended to
sacrifice.

With bounding steps the fortunate marksmen flew
round the bend of the stream, cut the currijong which
bound the captives, who fell into their arms.

What a moment of joy was that for the long-separated lovers, and now resored to each other under such strange circumstances. When the first effusion of love was over, Bella was the first to find speech, and whispered in her lover's ear, "Charlie dear, I have been true to you."

What a load of anguish these words removed from his mind. Folding her still more closely in his embrace, he exclaimed, raising his eyes to Heaven, "I believe you, Bella. Providence has been bountiful to us, both."

Quandak, leading his faithful Maria, interrupted this happy re-union, by reminding them that their safety was not yet complete, and entreated them to make a speedy retreat from such dangerous quarters, remarking that when the effect of the sudden fright was over, the Warrigals would take courage, and attack them from the cliffs. Bella seconded this proposition, well knowing the disposition and determination of the Warrigals, especially Bungilina and his brother, whom she felt certain would face death sooner than surrender herself and Maria. A speedy retreat was accordingly commenced, but the steep ascent and intricate path made it a hard task, especially for Bella, and delayed them considerably.

On surmounting the last obstacle, and considering themselves comparatively safe, what was their alarm on seeing two powerful savages, with heavy bludgeons, advancing to contest the passage. "Save yourselves," exclaimed Bella, in terror, when Charlie and Quandak presented their rifles; but, alas! misfortune still clung to them, for they found that their sudden happiness had driven from their minds the duty necessary for their safety, namely, the re-loading of their rifles.

They had no room for consideration or time to repair the deficiency, for the savages attacked them at once, and their only means of defence was to take their rifles by the barrels, and ward off the blows, which were aimed at their heads, but the stocks flew to pieces at the first blow.

It was now that the small sword exercise, which

Charlie had practised with his friend J
him in good need. Bungilina, who at
plied his weapon with great skill and s
much disappointed that his white adver
skilful in parrying the blows intended f

The contest now became hot and to
and Bungilina, who was exhausting his
rage with which he forced back his a
the cliff, when, unfortunately, Charli
caused an opening in his guard, whic
seized, the savage bringing his bludge
head, felling him instantly.

Bungilina stood over him with a mali
ing with one hand his matted hair fr
order to deal the finishing blow with
That moment Bran, who had been imp
in a small cave, broke loose, and miss
followed on her trail, and arrived at this
One look, and one command from her i
air" (Seize him)—was sufficient; th
sprung at Bungilina's bare throat, fast
him, and brought him to earth. The sa
a terrible superstition, caught the how
when both rolled over and over in their
until they disappeared over the cliff.

Bella now ran to her lover's assist
head in her lap, and bathed his pallid fa
The blow, which was partially broken,
him, and after a short while he revived.

The contest between Matoka and Qu
severe, for both were well matched and
the use of their arms; however, a slight
the side of Matoka, whose implement wa
the struggle, and Quandak, like his m
on the defensive, while his antagonist
very hard. But, fortunately for the f
friend was near who watched over him
quietly behind him, snatched his tomak
and concealing it among her clothes, c
behind the excited Matoka, then with
aim she buried the blade in his skull.

Charlie, who had recovered at the time, perceived the act, while Bella covered her eyes with her hands in horror; but as Charlie justified the act she became calm.

It was now that she satisfied her lover as to the cause of his escape from a violent death and who had been the agent, when both approached the edge of the cliff in order to ascertain the fate of the chief savage and the faithful hound, when a frightful spectacle presented itself.

The body of Bungilina lay apparently lifeless among the loose rocks, while the poor hound, whose spine had been dislocated, was struggling to raise himself. Their sorrow at the fate of the poor dog made them descend to the spot, hoping still to save him, but, alas, it was in vain, the poor animal whined and licked their hands without being able to rise, which made them shed tears for him. Their lamentations were soon disturbed by the cooey of the approaching savages who were coming to ascertain the fate of their leaders, when the necessity of saving their own lives compelled them to bid the last adieu to the faithful Bran who had sacrificed his life to save theirs. On seeing them depart, he made one more effort to rise, but with a mournful and heart-rending howl, he fell lifeless on the body of Bungilina.

A precipitate move was now made from the scene of such a frightful tragedy, but they were not long gone when the yells and lamentations of the savages over their fallen leaders caught their ears.

Quandak halted for a while, and exultingly exclaimed —" Ah, big one frightened Warrigal now. That one too much coward, come up when chief tumble down." This proved correct, for no more annoyance was offered to the party who continued their homeward journey without any molestation on the part of the natives.

The four weeks which Charlie allotted as the time when Donald was to break open the package containing his instructions, were now expired. On the last evening Donald and his wife, with their two little ones, Bella and Charlie, after removing the tea things, sat down with great anxiety to puruse the contents, Donald, with little Charlie on his knee, and Mary with Bella in her lap.

The letter stated that, although the writer had made up his mind to extend his explorations towards another part of the Alps, he was also actuated by other motives; the strange impressions he felt, and the proofs which had come to his knowledge that a white captive was among the Warrigals, caused a great amount of anxiety to him, believing as he did that the captive was his long lost Bella McKay.

The faithful overseer could read no longer, and his fond wife burst into tears, embracing her little one, she exclaimed—"It must be true, Donald! I thought as much! Do'nt you remember Ni Ruari's prophecy? Takawarrant told me this very day that there was a white woman like me among the Warrigals! Alas, they are both lost now." Donald, who concurred in these opinions, gave expression to his grief in the same manner, fondling his little boy in his arms. The faithful servants having now no doubt but that their master and mistress had fallen victims to the savages, were rocking themselves in their chairs, with their moistened eyes buried in their children's curly locks.

How long this outburst of sorrow would continue it is hard to conjecture, but it was interrupted by Mary feeling two soft hands laid on her shoulders, when, suddenly raising her head, she beheld two dark eyes gazing affectionately in her own. "It is her! It's her own beautiful eyes! I would swear to them!" And rising up, the affectionate and overjoyed Mary was locked in the fond embrace of her long lost mistress.

The scene which ensued is impossible to describe. Mary Munro was seized with her old fit of delight. She danced round the room, giving utterance to her joy, exclaiming, "She is as beautiful as ever! The sun has made her more charming than ever, only for that frightful fur dress."

After the last remark, Mary conducted Bella to her own room, and brought from her wardrobe the largest and best dress she had, which she offered to her as a substitute for her squirrel-skin robe, which, when cast off, caused no little amusement to them. Nor did Bella's change of dress lessen their merriment, it being far too short for her.

On returning to the room, Mary laid a comfortable meal before the famished and almost worn-out travellers, after which Quandak, Maria, and Takawarrant were called in.

The joy which the latter manifested on seeing his generous and beloved Lindigo was most affecting, and all the company felt more gratitude and happiness than they had known for years.

A solemn and binding agreement was entered into by all, which was that the whole should be kept a secret from the public, until they had left the country, which was decided upon. Several reasons induced them to form this resolution, one of which was that Bella could not fancy herself secure while in the vicinity of the tribe, and amid scenes where she had endured so much suffering.

CHAPTER XXVI.

THE MAJOR HARD PRESSED.

On the first favourable opportunity, Charlie, accompanied by his incognito Bella, proceeded to Sydney, where they found Mr. McKay dangerously ill. The meeting which took place between him and his long-lamented niece was most affecting. An alteration in her favour was instantly made in his will, by which she was left all his wealth. A clergyman was sent for, and the marriage of Charlie and Bella was solemnized at once.

The ceremony took place near the death-bed of the worthy man, giving the whole an unusually solemn appearance. The clergyman, immediately after the marriage, administered the last rites to the invalid, who after breathing a blessing on the young couple, passed away without a struggle.

After consigning Mr. McKay's remains to the tomb, Charlie returned to the new country for a short time to give delivery of his station to the new proprietor, having disposed of the whole when in Sydney. Having settled all his business, he again started for Sydney, taking with him Donald and Mary, with their family, as well as

Quandak, Maria, and Takawarrant, who were anxious to go with him. He then sold Mr. McKay's interest in the business in Sydney (which now belonged to Bella), and after having arranged all his business in Australia, he took passages in the first ship sailing for England, bidding farewell for ever to the sunny shores of the south.

The class of vessels which were now trading between Great Britain and the colonies, were more expeditious and comfortable than those used at the time they came out.

On arriving in London, they took private lodgings, neither Charlie or his wife wishing to mix in society. Bella noticed one morning at breakfast-time, that her husband, on reading that day's *Times*, became greatly interested in some article which had arrested his attention, but when Bella asked him what it was, he did not give her a direct answer, but told her he would surprise her one day, and having cut something out of the paper, he took up his hat, saying he should not return until evening. Bella contented herself for the present, remarking that whatever secret was kept from her, she knew was perfectly satisfactory, as Charlie appeared in good spirits, although he absented himself for a portion of several days, at the end of which he expressed his intention of visiting Scotland.

After a speedy journey by rail, they arrived in Edinburgh, where they found Advocate Forbes and his family in the enjoyment of good health; the daughters still unmarried, but all of them engaged, and on the eve wedded life, both the eldest to their old lovers, Captain Campbell, and *John Lom*, now Major Campbell, and Captain McDonnell, who had lately returned from India with honours, having distinguished themselves in the Affghan war. Catherine was engaged to her cousin, George McKay, who was still agent for Lord Lundy on the Lochlinn estate. The last-mentioned, according to accounts, turned out to be one of the most unprincipled profligates in the United Kingdom, and was fast running through the only property he had left, as his father had disinherited him on account of his fearful character.

The spendthrift, Lord Lundy, lived mostly in the Highlands, and the Forbes' were in great fear, lest his example and company would have any influence upon George McKay. In this apprehension Charlie and Bella joined, and in order to avert such consequences, they proposed a visit to the Highlands at once, or as soon as the marriages of the two elder Miss Forbes' had taken place.

We may imagine the joy experienced by the officers when Charlie paid his first visit to the castle, meeting once more on the old spot after years of trouble and hardship. Great interest was manifested as each recounted his exploits, and the major was in ecstacies at Charlie's New Zealand and Australian life; remarking with delight to his friend the captain:—"It beats Affghan hollow." But on hearing that Charlie had brought with him several implements of war and other curiosities, particularly the aboriginal couple and boy, his delight knew no bounds, and he proposed to call at Mr. Forbes' next day and see them.

The day after, Charlie, Bella, Miss Forbes, and Catherine enjoyed themselves by taking a walk in the forenoon, while Matilda remained at home. On their return, expecting a visit from the officers, the party, on approaching the house heard strange sounds proceeding from the sitting-room, and the well-known voice of Major Campbell roaring out: — "Hold you black scoundrels! I'll cut you down, you cannibals! Oh! my side," &c.

The door of the room being open, the party, on entering the passage, beheld a most extraordinary and amusing scene. Major Campbell with a drawn sword, was bailed up in a corner foaming and cursing, while parrying off thrusts made at his corpulent person by a black couple, robed in true Australian fashion, and armed with long spears, when one spear thrust was warded off on one side another attacked him from the other. On seeing the party at the door, he roared out:—"By Jove, Charlie, if you don't withdraw your black forces, I'll sabre them."

The attacking party turned suddenly round, and the females rushed into a side room with a merry laugh which betrayed the person of the mischevious Matilda, her companion in arms being no other than John Lom, as of old, playing off his tricks on the Major.

The following is an account of how the imposition was carried out. The Captain seeing the great anxiety manifested by the Major to see the Australian natives, resolved upon amusing himself at his friend's expense. He therefore forestalled the Major in his visit to the Forbes', and finding only Matilda at home, a plan was immediately arranged, that both should disguise themselves and represent Quandak and Maria. Having secured the assistance of Quandak, Maria, and Donald, they were duly painted and robed, the Captain in a large opossum skin cloak, and Matilda in Bella's squirrel skin dress, each being armed with a long spear.

Being fully prepared, the Major, as anticipated, made his appearance, and not finding anyone at home, he begged the servant (who was put on the alert by the captain) to send in the Australian blacks, in order to amuse himself before the party returned from their walk. The servant having communicated this to the captain and his partner, they immediately entered into the room where the Major was waiting, who, upon seeing the swarthy couple, was highly amused. Patting the female's head, the Major gallantly remarked—"Pity you are so black, with such handsome features," when the imagined husband seemingly jealous at such freedom towards his wife, drew his spear, which compelled the startled Major to seek refuge in a corner ; he then drew his sword to defend himself. This action induced the female to join her husband, when both attacked the luckless officer, who, on parrying one blow, received a thrust in his side from the other. It was in this plight the party found him, streaming with perspiration from exercise and fear, anathematising his cruel tormentors, who, on seeing the returned party desisted, to the great relief of the Major, who was greatly annoyed when he discovered the trick.

A few days after this the marriages took place, and the party proposed a trip to the Highlands, to visit George at Kinlochlinn. Charlie and Bella prevailed on

Mr. Forbes to allow Catherine to accompany them, that the nuptials between her and George (which had been delayed for some time) should take place, and which would save the latter being carried away by the profligate habits of Lord Lundy.

Hiring a small steamer from the Clyde, the whole party arrived at the entrance of Lochlinn on a beautiful summer's afternoon. ·

With feelings of joy and happiness, Charlie and his wife viewed all the endearing and well-remembered scenes of their happy childhood. Each spot which recalled many incidents connected with their first love was pointed out by Bella as she rested on her husband's arm, standing on the quarter-deck of the steamer, which glided swiftly through the smooth waters of Lochlinn. But on coming abreast of the rocks which had nearly proved fatal to her on the morning the pony ran away with her, a cold shiver came over her. This feeling soon vanished on coming in sight of the ruins of Ni Ruari's boothy, the delapidated appearance of which told plainly that its mysterious tenant had gone to her long home. The strange revelations made to them by her flew to their memory for the first time since that memorable day, and the remarkable truthfulness of the prophecy now forcibly struck them.

"You are perfectly right, she would tell a person's fortune to a T," exclaimed Mary, who, with her husband, was indulging in the same reminiscences.

CHAPTER XXVII.

On landing at Kinlochlinn the party proposed to take George by surprise, and therefore did not send him notice of their arrival, they accordingly walked direct from the place of landing to his house. On their going through the copse-wood, game of all descriptions started before them and Donald, who was carrying a fowling-piece, longed to have a shot at them. Walking up to his master, he said "What a pity that people have not the same license here as they have in Australia." Charlie, understanding Donald's impatience, replied "I know, Donald, your finger is itching to pull that trigger; I will be responsible for you this evening, at least, so you may fire away." Munro needed no more encouragement, for the reports from his double-barrel told that the work of destruction had commenced.

On the party approaching Mr. McKay's house, a noise, as of revelry met their ears as it issued from the dining-room, which drowned the sound produced at their entrance. When they had gained the dining-room, the door of which was open, a scene presented itself which exceeded any Australian bushman's spree they ever saw.

Around a large table, on which were scattered a number of half-emptied decanters and glasses, a large party of dissipated sportsmen, evidently affected by drink, were seated. At the opposite end sat the host, George McKay, who, although taking part in the scene, was not overcome by imbibing, neither did he seem altogether at ease with the dissipation around him. At the nearest end, and with his back towards them, sat the profligate Lord Lundy, apparently the ringleader of the riot.

On seeing the strangers George rose in confusion, and some of the guests, whose eyes were less clouded by their deep potations, endeavoured to follow his example, but in attempting it they fell over their chairs, rendering the confusion still greater. Lord Lundy, who was ignorant of the cause of the commotion, roared out, "What are you all about," accompanying it with a fearful oath.

George McKay now advanced towards the strangers, and instantly recognized his cousins, who introduced the officers, but taxed his own memory with the recognition of the other couple, Charlie and Bella. The latter, who was veiled, stood aloof, but Charlie, advancing towards his brother-in-law, said, "You do not appear to recognize me, George." The voice was sufficient, the two friends were instantly locked in each other's embrace, and for the first time for many a year, George McKay dropped a tear on his friend's shoulders, whispering, with a tremulous voice, "All would be well now, if she were here." Charlie, who understood the remark, exclaimed triumphantly (at the same time stepping over to his wife, and removing her veil), "Behold her George! I have brought her back again! She was not drowned, as was supposed, but was for years a captive in the power of savages, from whom I rescued her, and for which she has rewarded me with her hand, and you now see Charlie Stuart and Bella McKay man and wife."

The latter portion of this sentence fell with a heavy shock on the ears of the half-stupified Lord Lundy. His former hatred and animosity towards his now successful rival returned with tenfold force, but which was arrested by the affectionate meeting of George and his long-lost sister. Not an eye in that room was free from tears, even the callous debauchees were obliged to turn their heads, and hide their emotion.

Lord Lundy could not bear to hear the glowing terms in which Bella eulogized her husband's bravery when rescuing her, and see the sweet looks with which she acknowledged Charlie's devotion. The enraged spendthrift picked up his hat, exclaiming in a rage, "I thought Charlie Stuart knew his place better than to place a foot on an estate from which he had been so ignominiously expelled, and from which he would be horsewhipped, were it not for the connexion he has so surreptitiously formed."

On hearing this Charlie, in a delightfully cool and defiant manner, walked across to where Lord Lundy stood, when, standing erect, and fixing his eye firmly upon him, said, "I beg your pardon, my Lord, but I will just inform you that, so far from the proprietor of this estate inflicting any such punishment upon me, *he* would rather apply it to your Lordship." At this moment he handed a sealed packet to Lord Lundy, and added, "In place of your horsewhipping me off *your* estate, I have now to request that you will quit *my* estate at your earliest convenience."

At these words his Lordship turned pale, broke the seal of the package, when the first lines that met his

eyes were terrible proofs of Charlie's remarks, that the
Lochlinn estate was now the property of his rival
Charlie Stuart, who added, " I am sorry to be the bearer
of your downfall, my Lord, and also having to present it
on the present occasion, for it never was my disposition
to triumph over the misfortunes of a rival; however,
you must blame yourself, and I hope the lesson will be
of benefit to you hereafter. You are young, and by at
once seeking and following the paths of truth and recti-
tude, may yet regain that position which you have so
foolishly sacrificed."

The company's attention was now drawn to some
fresh commotion on the stairs, which sounded like forcible pushing and dragging, accompanied by the following expressions :—" Come up here my beauty. I'll
soon show you manners for poaching on a nobleman's
estate. His Lordship and Mr. McKay will put you
through your facings, my fine gentleman."

The cause of all this bouncing and scuffling turned
out to be our old acquaintance, John Brown, Lord
Lundy's valet, who had met with his former rival and
adversary, Donald, shooting. Being this day at the
Post-office, and having to call at Mr. McKay's as he
returned to leave the letters, he met with Donald. Not
recognising him, Brown demanded his license for
shooting on the estate. Munro, not wishing to make
himself known as yet, admitted that he had no license,
when, after giving other unsatisfactory answers, Brown
marched him off to the factor's house, where he would
be dealt with by his Lordship and Mr. McKay. In
order to make himself more officious, he used several
unnecessary epithets, and pushing Donald into the
presence of his judges, laid the charge in the following words :—" My Lord, I have just popped on this
here man, shooting, as if he had full liberty from you to
do so. I hope you will make an example of him."
Lord Lundy, whose mind was occupied with his own
misfortunes, only asked Brown if he had any letters for
him,—on receiving which, his Lordship was more confirmed in his downfall, and immediately took his
departure.

Charlie now told Donald of his fortune, and the turn affairs had taken; on hearing which Brown attempted to follow his master, but Donald was too quick for him, and held him firmly by the collar, threatening to give him up to justice for perjury at the trial.

It was amusing to see the terror-stricken valet; his knees shook under him, and his looks were fearful, seeming almost as if it would be his death; Charlie here told Donald to let him escape a little longer, as his conscience would be a source of punishment to him.

Another person now appeared on the scene, Mary Munro, leading her two children; hearing that her husband had been accused, and brought before Lord Lundy, had entered to plead his cause, but she was delighted on seeing him not as the accused, but the accuser. The guilty conscience of the valet quailed under the gaze of the faithful mother on recollecting his own diabolical charges against the father.

Donald agreed to his master's lenient mode of dealing with him, and allowed him to follow his disgraced master.

On the departure of the revellers, and order being restored, Charlie's friends flocked around him, congratulating him on his fortune in becoming the possessor of the Lochlinn estate, and his happy wife teazed him a little for his closeness in keeping the secret, when he reminded her that he promised her a surprise some day when they were in London. It then occurred to her that the article which he cut out of the paper had a reference to the estate, which was the case, for, on running his eyes over the list of estates for sale, he saw the following:—"For sale, by order of the trustees, the Lochlinn Estate, the seat of Lord Lundy, in the Highlands, apply," &c., &c. Charlie cut the advertisement out, applied to the agents, and a bargain was immediately made.

It appeared that through Lord Lundy's extravagance and his being disinherited by his father, he had been obliged to mortgage his estate heavily. As the trustees could see no prospect of reform in the young spendthrift's habits, or hopes of the estate being released, its sale became necessary.

N

What were the feelings of the profligate as he left the house where an hour before he was leading the revelry, cannot be described. He now saw himself to be what he really was, an outcast, without a friend on the face of the earth. Even his associates of the last hour deserted him on learning his downfall, leaving him a solitary wanderer to commune with his own harassing thoughts. He cursed the first morning that he saw the Bridge of Linn, and he believed himself bewitched on that occasion by its romantic scenery, and above all, by the fascinations of Bella, whom he now blamed for all his misfortunes.

But why had she appeared before him again to open afresh the wounds she had caused? And how had she come? Why, as the bride of another, and that one his rival! What a triumph! He who was turned off the estate as the stumbling-block to his Lordship's happiness, now returning to retaliate, not only as being the possessor of the prize, but also the owner of the estate, driving him as an outcast from the last possession he had. And they so happy; how lovingly they gazed on each other! How happy would he be were the least of those smiles bestowed upon him. He would have gladly endured all Charlie had done, if he were to be rewarded with but one single glance of kindness from her.

These and such were the thoughts which harassed his troubled mind as he wended his steps towards that castle which was now no longer his, and which he would be compelled to leave without a soul near him, with the exception of the perjured Brown.

The thoughts which tormented the latter were no less excruciating than his master's. The vengeance which awaited his previous conduct began to loom over his guilty conscience. What a pitiful contrast his harrowing thoughts and situation presented before his innocent, manly, and happy rival and former victim Donald Munro; the fond, matronly wife Mary, and the beautiful children.

CHAPTER XXVIII.

CORROBOREE IN THE HIGHLANDS.

Great were the rejoicings among the tenantry and all others in the district on hearing of the arrival of its present proprietor, Charlie Stuart and his wife, for whom they had mourned for years.

A bonfire on an extensive scale was given by the proprietor in commemoration of the happy event, which every person on the estate attended. Games and sports of all descriptions, calculated to enliven the guests, were introduced. After the banquet dancing was commenced, which was kept up with great spirit. About one o'clock Charlie led his lovely wife to seek the refreshing air on the balcony, when they halted on the very spot where ten years before they had exchanged the sighs of ardent love. Ten years! and through what vicissitudes they had passed during that period! So awful that they were now almost afraid to think of them! Would it were in reality a dream! "Yes! ten years!" whispered Charlie, "and you are as lovely as ever."

A great rustling of silk and shuffling of feet could now be heard by them, and the whole company came out to inhale the fresh air.

It was now proposed that a procession should be formed, when each gentleman leading his partner, was to proceed to the side of the lake, and see what was going on there; they accordingly started, the whole being led by Charlie and his wife. Immense cheering, and throwing of hats and bonnets, met the new proprietor and his wife, as they walked among the tenantry, and many blessings were heaped upon them.

Around one of the fires was seen a crowd of curious spectators, apparently enjoying something which was quite novel in the Highlands, judging by the strange sounds issuing from the group and the additional spectators it was constantly receiving. Charlie and the party now directed their steps towards it, when they beheld, to their astonishment, a representation of an Australian corroboree,

The author of this novelty was John Lom, who had engaged the services of Donald, Quandak, Takawarrant, his old servant and our old acquaintance Popgun. They were blackened and decorated according to Quandak's instructions, and being armed with long spears, they went through their wild dance to the tune of Maria, who was beating time as she sung the trango air in her native tongue.

The impression which this produced among the superstitious Highlanders was most striking. The dark spectres, whose wild and curious attitudes were increased by the glare of the fire, reminded the spectators of descriptions they had heard of the inhabitants of the lower regions.

When the leader of the dance perceived, by the looks and gestures of the spectators, that their superstition was raised to its highest pitch, he gave a pre-arranged signal, when they all shook their spears in the air, gave one simultaneous yell, and darted towards the thickest part of the crowd, as if charging them.

This produced great alarm, a passage was made for them through the dense and terror-stricken crowd. Men and women screeched and yelled, some were sprawling on the ground, and some clung frantically to each other, while their supposed enemies made their escape to the castle.

Charlie and his friends succeeded, after some time, in pacifying the people, and convinced them that their imagined spectres were really human, and meant to do them no harm. When order was at length restored, they found that the casualties were only a few bruises scratches, &c. The dancing was then resumed, and kept up for some time, until the advancing morning warned them that it was time to return to their homes, when the corroboree became the staple of their future evening fireside tales.

The marriage of George and Catherine was another joyful event, which succeeded the bonfire, and added one more to the links of happiness and friendship, which Charlie and his wife had brought about among the people.

CHAPTER XXIX.

A GENERAL MUSTER.

Our tale is now drawing to a close, but before we drop the curtain, we will give the reader another peep at the different characters.

It will, therefore, be necessary to mention that, after Charlie Stuart's departure from Australia, vague rumours of the captivity of a white woman being among the Warrigal tribe, daily increased. These surmises first gained ground from some hints dropped by Takawarrant, when Charles and Quandak were away on their expedition, and also from a few Warrigals, who were mixing with the civilized natives. Consequently an expedition was set on foot by some philanthrophic and chivalric colonists for her rescue.

After a great deal of fatigue and expense, this was abandoned, little expecting that she was settled comfortably at home with her husband. The band of natives who witnessed the rescue of Lindigo, and the death of their leaders, became so alarmed that a similar fate awaited them, that they sought the security of the snowy mountains, never afterwards holding intercourse with other tribes. They sometimes visited the 90-mile beach, but always kept aloof from civilized society.

Our last budget from the Highlands contained the gratifying intelligence that the Lochlinn estate is progressing favourably, under the able management of Charlie, assisted by George, who occupies both farms, the latter's wife declares that she has quite weaned her husband from taking a spree, ever since the day he was caught.

Major Campbell and his friend, Captain John McDonnell (John Lom) have both succeeded to their parents' estates after having distinguished themselves in the Crimea. They, with their families, annually visit the Lochlinn estate. On these occasions the Major indulges freely in his whiskey toddy, while John Lom, who has not forgotten his tricks, never fails to gratify his propensity, and frequently favours the company with the "Battle of Inverlochy."

The real "Fighting Jack" has passed away at an advanced age, leaving his wealth to John Lom for having so successfully personated him at the Forbes'.

All our friends are united in their endeavours to bring up their children that they may prove not only a pleasure to their parents and friends, but also ornaments to society, and may their endeavours be crowned with the most complete success.

Donald and his wife are surrounded by a numerous family, who are uncommonly destructive to the corn-ricks, by pulling out straws for whistles. Donald plays at the castle on special occasions, and always gives great pleasure by his skilful execution.

Quandak and Maria are not quite so satisfied, and would have no objection to return to Australia, and resume the opossum cloak.

Takawarrant has become an accomplished sportsman, and is a great enemy to all kinds of game. He is also an excellent horseman, and is quite delighted with the life.

But the last, and most interesting part of our communication, was to the effect that Bella had presented her husband with twin girls, and that they had been named Pamul and Lindigo.

THE END.

WALKER, MAY AND CO., PRINTERS, 99 BOURKE STREET WEST, MELBOURNE.

www.ingramcontent.com/pod-product-compliance
Lightning Source LLC
Chambersburg PA
CBHW030546040726
47497CB00008B/2601